C2000004355405

D1150253

Douglas Lindsay was born in Scotland in 1964. He is the writer of the cult Barney Thomson crime series, which began publication in 1999. He currently lives in eastern Europe with his wife and two children.

Also by Douglas Lindsay,
available from Long Midnight Publishing:

The Long Midnight of Barney Thomson

The Cutting Edge of Barney Thomson

A Prayer For Barney Thomson

Barney Thomson & The Face of Death

The King Was In His Counting House

The Last Fish Supper

The Haunting of Barney Thomson

Lost In Juarez

Douglas Lindsay

Long Midnight Publishing

This edition published in Great Britain in 2008 by
Long Midnight Publishing, Suite 433, 24 Station Square,
Inverness IV1 1LD
e-mail: longmidnight@douglaslindsay.com

www.douglaslindsay.com

*A catalogue record for this book is available
from the British Library*

ISBN 978 0 9541 387 7 6

Cop

Printed in [illegible] TD

for Kathryn and
Jessica & Hamish

The house stood on the side of a hill looking down over the glen, across the Ullapool road, out over Ben Wyvis. A modern house, built for the location, huge panoramic windows front and back. Wonderful views, the estate agents had asserted. The buyer of the house had often had cause to remark that the wonderful views were usually hidden behind the grey drizzle of Highland rain. Or, as on this day in late January, a rare blizzard, a thick, all-encompassing snowfall seemingly dragged in from years earlier.

Up the hill and around the house there was the silence of a snowstorm. Large flakes fell, the air was consumed by snow and mist, visibility was no more than a few yards. In the driveway of the house two cars were parked. A police Land Rover and a white van with the markings of the BBC. The front door of the house lay open.

The snow fell, birds huddled in trees.

The silence was obliterated. A figure in a dark green jacket. Three quick steps, arms up to protect his face, and Lake Weston smashed through the window on the first floor, fell sharply in amongst flying glass and landed feet first with an ugly bump on the roof of the television van. He grunted loudly, a grotesque ejaculation of pain, before his momentum carried him awkwardly off the top of the van and onto the ground. Cuts on his hands, blood on the snow.

Weston forced himself to his feet, pain everywhere from the bottom of his back down to his ankles, and looked quickly back up. Two police officers looked down through the shattered window. A glance between them. The senior officer wasn't jumping.

'Crap,' said the constable, then he kicked at the sharp shards of glass at the bottom, knocked away the broken glass at the top. The sergeant turned away from him and started running through the house.

Weston opened the van door. No key in the ignition. He looked up as the police constable came flying down from the first floor. He landed harshly on the roof, a grotesque bark, obviously hurt, and slid forward, losing his balance. Arms flailing, head first.

Lake Weston swung the car door shut and it caught the top of the constable's head. A dead crack, another dull cry of pain. Weston caught his breath, the constable slumped forward.

He could hear footsteps, shouts from the house. He turned and started running. Two yards and his ankle buckled under the pain, sharp shards shooting up his leg. He let out another cry, stumbled, fell forwards. His leg screamed.

The footsteps behind him reached the steps at the front. He didn't turn. Lifted himself to his feet, forced the movement. No option. He ran to the small stretch of garden. A shed, a few tools left propped against it, uncared for. Beyond that, a classical Highland landscape. Heather and grass, a few trees, all of it obscured by the freezing depths of bleak midwinter.

The footsteps closed behind him. Three or four people. Someone slipped, a woman's voice cried out. A man barked *fuck's sake*. Weston could feel the breath at his shoulder, the outstretched hand.

His ankle felt as if it might snap. A last effort. The garden shed loomed out of the snow. He heard the cry of *fucker* at his shoulder.

He reached the shed, grabbed the old spade with his bloody hands, lifted it, swivelled as he ran and swung the spade back in a great looping parabola, all in one movement.

He connected with the side of a head. A police officer he hadn't seen before, one who hadn't been in the room with him. Another officer started to slow as he approached, only a few yards behind, little control in the snow. Weston heaved the spade up and swung massively once more. The officer raised his arms, Weston brought the spade thumping down on his forearm. A muffled crunch through padded jacket, he stumbled and fell. The other fallen policeman grabbed at Weston's legs. He kicked out, a desperate boot. Twice, three times, felt a solid connection. Another loud grunt.

The second officer was swinging at him. He fended him off with the spade, felt the crack of bone as the edge of the spade caught a bare hand. A moment as the guy winced with pain, then Weston brought the spade down on the side of his head. He fell back, Weston followed round with the movement, jabbed the spade down at the guy on the ground.

Shouts through the snow. Weston had a second. Adrenaline flowing, every sense bursting, except the pain. For the moment, in desperation and panic, his body was not acknowledging the pain.

'Fucker,' said a voice from his feet, as one of the officers made a grab at his leg. Weston looked down. A bloody face, a vicious slash across the nose. He kicked out again, a more tired boot, less of an impact, just enough.

He threw the spade down and turned. Shouting behind, more voices in the snow. A woman. Angry shouts. And he ran, ran on his weak ankle, ran on his aching legs. Suddenly full pelt, running with freedom. Visibility only a few yards, snow all around, but he knew the hills, he knew the contours, he knew the small streams.

1

He awoke alone, which wasn't unusual in itself, but he was sure there had been someone else there the night before. The policewoman. Kate. Maybe it had been Kate. Caroline?

The phone was ringing. Muggy, uncomfortable day outside. He lay in bed, looking at the empty pillow next to him. There was a dent. The size of Kate's head. She'd said she wasn't working in the morning. Hadn't they talked about coffee and croissant and the morning papers? Though he'd said he wouldn't have much time because he had to go to the school today. The school. He groaned, pressed Kate's pillow down so that he could see the clock. 0815. Still early.

The phone persisted. No one called him at eight-fifteen.

It would be Penny. He pushed the light duvet away from his legs. Just the thought of her made him feel too warm, ill at ease. He looked at the curtains, the bright edges of sunlight around them. Another hot day out there. Could hear traffic, muffled. Kate had wanted to sleep with the windows closed. He'd thought they'd be eating breakfast.

The phone persisted. Maybe it was Kate explaining why she wasn't where she should be.

He leaned over and looked at the phone, then let his head slump back down onto the pillow. At least it wasn't Penny. He lifted the receiver.

'How did you know I'm home,' he said.

'You mobile phone's switched off,' said Joanne. His editor's PA. 'I didn't have any other numbers to ring.'

He rolled over in bed and stared at the halo around the curtains. Mid-July. He hated London when it was this warm. Just another couple of weeks and he'd be able to get back to the Highlands.

'Why?' he said.

'Calling to remind you about the school engagement.'

'That's not until eleven,' he said sharply. He hated Joanne reminding him about things he was already remembering.

'I presumed you hadn't seen the news,' she said, ignoring his tone.

'What news?'

'The city's in a state. Police chased a couple of men at King's Cross. Opened fire. Killed three passers-by, one of them was a child. King's Cross is shut, the city's just horrible with the knock on.'

He sighed heavily and stared at the ceiling. Immediately thought, maybe the kid was from the school I'm due to read at and it'll be shut for the day.

'The child was an American tourist,' she said quickly, reading his thoughts. 'You'll need to walk to the school, then try to grab a taxi to get to Rocket's for lunch.'

Lunch with his editor. That he had forgotten about.

'Walk to the school?' he said.

'It should take you about an hour,' she replied. 'Call it an hour fifteen and walk slowly. It's hot out there, you don't want to arrive a dripping ball of sweat.'

He smiled, despite himself.

'Anything else?'

'Remember not to swear at the children,' she said sharply.

The phone went dead. Lake Weston closed his eyes.

Weston dripped sweat quietly onto the floor, waiting to be introduced. The children in the small sports hall eyed him nervously. The sun beamed in through high windows. No air-conditioning. He'd fallen asleep, woken in a rush, couldn't get a taxi. He didn't look like he'd had a bucket of water poured over him. He looked like the bucket.

'...and Mr Weston has kindly agreed to come today to talk about Fenton and all the scrapes he gets into. Now, hands up anyone who's ever read a Fenton Bargus book?'

Weston looked around the sea of faces. Virtually all of them. Mr Blunt, the large-nosed and dull head of Key Stage Two, beamed. He turned and smiled at Weston, an embracing look. Weston grimaced in reply.

'Chardonnay,' said Mr Blunt, turning back to the pupils, 'you've never read any Fenton books?'

'Think they're shite,' she said, and a giggle rippled round the room.

'Chardonnay!' snapped Mr Blunt. There was nothing sharp about him. No wit, no trace of authority.

A few more giggles. Weston raised an eyebrow. Chardonnay, he thought, wasn't too far off the mark.

The second of Lake Weston's two ex-wives was called Travis. Mid-40's, did something reasonably senior at the Home Office. He had never been entirely sure what, but put that down to his own lack of interest. They had met while he had still been married to Penny and Travis had been married to a dreadful suit in the FCO. They had seen the best in each other, divorced their partners, married, and then seen the worst in each other. In the end it was Bob Dylan who had driven her out. The two of them had indeed been right for each other, they just couldn't live together. Weston had considered her Low Maintenance, and their life just about as perfect as living with another person could be. She just hadn't liked Bob Dylan. Or the fact that Weston tended to sleep with too many other women.

Penny, on the other hand, had been a clear runaway ten out of ten, Queen of High Maintenance. She had sucked him in with great sex and a few laughs, and then shown her true colours within minutes of the ring. He had never been entirely sure what he'd been thinking, but had had plenty of time and two children to think about it. Bravest thing he'd ever done, he thought, looking her in the eye and telling her he was leaving. Hated leaving the kids, but had taken her punch to the jaw, and had smelled freedom the second he'd walked out of the house. She was still there, of course, ever present in the backfield. They had two kids, he had an unbelievable amount of money, she had never met anyone else. She called him every day. Every day. Even though the kids were now at boarding school and there was little reason to see or speak to each other.

He liked to think he'd never marry again, and sometimes he even believed it.

'When did you write your first book?'

'How much money do you make?'

'How long does it take you to write a book?'

'Is Fenton based on you?'

'Why did you become a writer?'

'What's your favourite book?'

'How many books have you written?'

'When did you write your first book?'

'Do you make more money than my dad?'

'How long does it take to write a book?'

'My mum says I've not to talk to you 'cause you're a womanizing drunk.'

'Why did you become a writer?'

'Is Fenton based on you?'

The questions flowed. The same every time. He had never managed to overcome that slightly awkward moment when he was asked the exact same question which he'd just been asked by another kid three and a half minutes earlier.

Weston stared at the sea of bored faces. The well had ebbed and flowed, had dried up. Time to go. He fingered the iPod in his pocket. Lunch, the chance to have the old discussion about what to do post-Fenton Bargus, if ever he reached a post-Fenton Bargus period. And a good bottle of white wine.

A hand shot up in the crowd. The kid had only just woken up, or was the one who didn't want the thing to end. Either because he was a big fan or else he didn't want to go back and do maths.

'How many books have you written?' asked the kid.

Mr Blunt smiled benevolently at Weston. Weston ignored him.

'Well, the next Fenton book will be the ninth,' he said.

'You said that already,' said a blonde kid in the front row. Weston looked through him. Mr Blunt looked like maybe he wanted to say something, but didn't.

'And I've also written a couple of books that haven't been published yet,' added Weston, annoyed at himself that he'd been goaded into saying more than the last time.

The kids stared at him. Weston waited for the obvious question about why these other books hadn't been published. But to kids, the questions which are obvious are rarely the same. No one had anything else to say. Mr Blunt clapped his hands together in a self-satisfied gesture of finality and smiled at everyone. Weston put his hand into his pocket.

2

Lake Weston hadn't written a couple of other books. He'd written seven others. Four of them when he'd first started out. None of them published. One of them had come close, and had had him checking the post every morning for six months, in the golden days before e-mail. The small publisher in Edinburgh had turned him down in the end. Then one week he'd written a story for children about a boy who has every bad thing happen to him in one day that a kid could have happen, called it *Fenton Bargus Takes On The World*, and popped it in the post to every children's publisher he could find in the *Writer's Handbook*. He'd thought he had no feel for children's books, he hadn't enjoyed writing it, he almost made the decision just to pop it in the bin rather than the post.

He received three offers of publication, and the deal was done. Lake Weston was a children's author. Stamped on his passport, stamped on his life. For life. Lake Weston, children's author.

The three books which he'd written during his children's author period, attempts to break free from the prison, had all been turned down by his publisher. The latest, *They Cried In The Night*, a dramatisation of a single incident of mass slaughter during the Rwandan massacre of 1994, had not kept his editor's attention too long. That it had been a great book was of no significance to him. Lake Weston did not write books about rape and carnage and mass acts of brutal murder. Lake Weston wrote books about a seven year-old boy called Fenton Bargus.

Eldon Strachan looked up from his soup.

'Too much dill,' he said.

Weston looked suspiciously over the top of his second glass of Chablis. He could tell there was something wrong. Strachan only ever fussed about his food when avoiding more difficult subjects.

'You're complaining about your food,' said Weston.
Strachan looked up, then raised an eyebrow and smiled.
'Ok, you've got me,' he said.
Weston started on the thin slivers of his tuna carpaccio.
'Out with it,' he said, a morsel of sliced parmesan on his lips. He dabbed at his mouth with his napkin, took another sip of wine.
'Manchester United have backed out,' said Strachan slowly.
A second, then Weston laid down his knife and fork and sat back.
'What the fuck is that about?' he said. 'I thought they were up for it?'
'So did I. We all did. Someone higher up's pulled the plug.'
'Ferguson?' snapped Weston.
'Don't know. Don't think so. You know, that guy does football not merchandising.'
Weston took another drink, a long one. Half the glass.
'Fucking hell,' he muttered. 'So how far along are we? Has anyone spoken to Arsenal or Chelsea?'
Strachan pushed a couple of pieces of herb to the side of his bowl.
'They're not interested either.'
'Liverpool?' asked Weston, still aghast. Still annoyed.
'Joanne spoke to someone up there and they sounded like they might go for it, but you know...we just can't.'
'Why?' barked Weston. Drained the glass. Started looking around for the waitress, glancing at the bottle in the ice bucket a few feet away.
'*Fenton Bargus Takes On Manchester United*,' said Strachan. 'Perfect. No one's thinking, what the fuck is that all about? Great marketing for us *and* them. Arsenal, Chelsea, they make sense. But *Fenton Bargus Takes On Liverpool*? What are we talking about here? Fenton takes on the entire city? That's what it sounds like. You can't say that. You know what that lot are like. You'll be up there apologising in minutes. So what do we call it? *Fenton Bargus Takes On Liverpool Football Club*? How clumsy is that? It can't be Liverpool.'
Weston shook his head. Looked round at the wine, thought about stretching over and grabbing the bottle. Their waitress hovered outside the door to the kitchen, looking anywhere but straight at him.
'Anyone else?' he asked. He could feel the sweep of depression come over him, that instant kick to the enthusiasm, the instant down. His phone rang. He had it set so that it played the *Emperor's March* from *Star Wars* when Penny called. He reached into his pocket and clicked it off.
'The only Premier League side who are totally sold on the idea are Wigan,' said Strachan.
'Jesus...'

'I know, it's not happening.'
'*Fenton Bargus Takes On Wigan Athletic*,' muttered Weston.
'I know, I know,' said Strachan. Placating the author. Something he was well used to doing with his catalogue of easily-bruised egos.
'So what are you saying?' asked Weston.
'We might get our guy in Madrid to approach Real.'
Weston stared across the table. Played *Fenton Bargus Takes On Real Madrid* in his head. That didn't sound too bad.
'But don't get excited. And you know, if we go to Madrid, you're going to have to do a hell of a lot of rewrites.'
'Oh, come on.'
'Lake, if Fenton goes to Spain, you're going to have to rewrite.'
'Crap.'
Strachan waved his arms and returned to his soup.
'Crap,' repeated Weston.

Weston stepped out into Chapel Place, the rush of heat after air conditioned comfort. Stopped, looked up and down. Strachan had booked a later meeting at the club for another one of his authors. He liked to double-team. Weston hated it, made him feel like the warm-up act, one of many, rather than the guy's main point of interest.
He watched the traffic on Oxford Street, which seemed busier than normal. He remembered the shooting of the tourists that morning. He hadn't watched the news and they hadn't mentioned it at the school. It had seemed the type of place where it wasn't acknowledged that *Bad Shit Happens*. Fumbled in his pocket, brought the earpiece out and quickly plugged it into his head. Touched the iPod. Halfway through *Things Have Changed*. He breathed in the sound.
Wiped his brow. It suddenly occurred to him that the shooting would have been the reason Kate had had to leave early, had had to go into work on her day off. And her name hadn't been Kate, it had been Kelly. Maybe he would hear from her again.
Took his phone from his pocket, switched it on. A guy coming out of the restaurant nearly bumped into him and muttered at his back, walked off, head down. They used to say if you had a road accident or nearly bumped someone's car, everyone would get annoyed, everyone would shout. But bump into someone on the street and it's apologies all round and helping you up with your bags. Not any more, thought Weston, watching the hunched shoulders trudge off. People are now just as likely to shout at you in the street as from their car. Pavement rage.

Four messages rang onto his phone. He looked down the list and read them quickly, unemotionally. Three from Penny. Asking what he was doing. Why he hadn't called. Hadn't he remembered that it was today she'd been scheduled to have her cervical smear. The fact that she'd cancelled it because she'd had a headache notwithstanding, it showed how little he cared about her. And a text from Mr Blunt thanking him for his trouble and saying how much the students had enjoyed his visit.

He looked up and down the road again. What now? Go home and start working on *Fenton Bargus Takes On Real Novosibirsk?*

He looked right. He looked left.

Lake Weston, children's author, was lost.

He turned and started to walk towards Oxford Street. He'd buy the Guardian, sit in a café somewhere and drink coffee for an hour or two. Go to a movie. Fight the feeling of emptiness. Drift.

He didn't have another engagement in the city for four days. Maybe he could just get on a plane, go to the lodge. Highland air, deer on the hills. It'd be cooler and he could dive into the cold black depths of the loch, freeze to the bone. But he had had enough of planes, enough of travelling. He turned onto Oxford Street, glancing into the cars where drivers sat, hot and uncomfortable and annoyed.

Eldon Strachan sat back and rested his head against the framework of the chair, closed his eyes and cursed himself for not having told Weston the main piece of bad news which he had been supposed to deliver. He would have to go through all this again the following week. He would arrange the lunch, Weston would think he was being called in to discuss AC Milan or Juventus, when in fact he was being called in so that Strachan could give him another giant-sized shafting.

It was almost enough to make him feel bad. But not quite.

3

'I know...mmm....yep......I know, I know......no, no, I know....yep...'

And so it went on. Weston's usual end of the conversation with Penny. Penny's never ending complaints. Penny never talked about anyone else, never complained about anyone else. It was as though she never had any contact with anyone other than her ex-husband, and the blame for every single bad thing that ever happened to her could be directly traced to him in some way or another. The fact that she had been chronically depressed when they'd first met had been long since forgotten. Ever since they had first acknowledged some sort of relationship between them, she had been miserable because of him. Quite how he had blundered into it, he had never been able to understand. It couldn't all be explained by sexual attraction. There must have been, he always reasoned, some large element of downright stupidity on his part.

She was complaining about him not having responded to an e-mail she'd written three days earlier. That they had discussed the matter – their younger son's inability to grasp the basic concepts of mathematics – on the phone twice since had seemed at first a reasonable point to Weston. Penny, on the other hand, had been looking for something in writing, as she had initially raised the subject in writing. There was nowhere for the argument to go, so in the end, as invariably happened, Weston had given up and she had continued.

Sitting in a small coffee shop not far from Rocket's, one of his usual haunts when retreating from a bludgeoning from his editor. Three cups of coffee and the Guardian. The waitress hovered beside his table, bored, tired, wondering if it was OK to remove his empty cup. She had answered the advert looking for a Front Of House Café Assistant with eyes wide open. He gestured that he would like another, she smiled weakly. Their eyes stayed locked a little longer than necessary, long enough for her to know he was speaking to a neurotic woman, for him to shrug it off, for her to extend some sympathy. She turned away.

Penny marched on, German tanks across the Polish plains, her talk a never ending tale of insults and aspersions, indignities and defamations.

The coffee came, this time the Front of House Café Assistant was distracted by a request from another table. He had wanted a normal coffee, but she had brought a cappuccino.

Penny finally finished, had to go off somewhere. For all that she acted like she had no life, she clearly had other things to do that didn't involve him and which she obviously didn't feel the need to discuss with him.

He closed the phone and laid it down on the table beside the paper. Felt his usual palpable sense of relief. She rarely called twice in a day, and once the call was out of the way he knew he could relax. He had been naïve to think that leaving her would be the end of their relationship, but a half hour call every day was just about manageable. More than anything else on the planet, he wanted her to meet someone else, someone with whom she would fall in love. Someone who would make her miserable the way she had made him miserable.

He doubted anyone would have her.

◉

He stepped out onto Oxford Street. No traffic, a lot of pedestrians. Low cloud had come, the day was stifling hot, now muggy and close. A thunderstorm coming. He felt the sweat instantly forming on his brow. With the music turned down low, he could hear a police siren in the distance. Stared up at the clouds, looked along the busy street, then reached into his pocket and paused the music. There were cars parked but nothing moving. A guy loitered past reading that morning's *Metro*. Weston had already read the headline at least fifteen times that day. *ID Cards To Hold DNA Info*. No one else was carrying the story, just a single London freesheet.

'What's going on?' said Weston.

The guy noticed the movement, stopped, removed his earphones. Raised his eyebrows in question.

'What's going on?' repeated Weston. 'Why are there no cars?'

They had been talking about it in the café, but Weston had missed the conversations because he'd been listening to Dylan. The guy gestured to the end of the road.

'Like some bomb threat somewhere,' he said, the tone rising at the end of the sentence. 'Not here, but they've, like, closed all sorts of shit.'

Weston thought of the afternoon of 11th September, walking around Inverness, seeing people standing at shop windows watching television, wondering what they were all looking at. He had presumed it was some awful soap or quiz show that he wasn't interested in. Head in the clouds.

'Cheers,' he said.

The guy nodded, inserted the earphones, walked on. Reading the sports pages. England batting collapse. Weston stood at the edge of the pavement, looking up and down Oxford Street. Oxford Street with pedestrians and no traffic. Like some weird Twilight Zone Oxford Street. An Oxford Street before the invention of the wheel.

Everyone was still walking on the pavements, as if they suddenly expected the traffic to start zooming along the road, catching them off guard in the middle of the street.

Weston had nothing to do. The payback for a comfortable life. Generally he was all right in the Highlands. He could walk in the hills all day. Fresh mountain air, sit by a loch, come home at night, eat dinner and drink wine. It was a comfortable life. In contradiction, once he was in the city he felt lost. Too much to do, none of it grabbed him. He would sit in pubs drinking wine, sit in cafés drinking coffee.

Every now and again Dylan played Wembley Arena. Sometimes he would follow him around Britain. Occasionally further afield. Since 1983, he had seen Dylan in concert one hundred and fifty-seven times. He had planned stays in London, meetings with his editor to coincide with Dylan. Same with meetings and press junkets around the globe. Now Dylan hadn't been in over a year, and here he was in London, too blind to go and see anyone else, too bereft of spirit to be moved by art.

He turned and walked back into the café. The Front of House Café Assistant looked up. A peculiar look, then they smiled at each other and he knew. He likely would have something to do this evening after all.

4

They lay in bed, still hot and damp. Her name was Daisy. 'Like the flower,' she'd said. It hadn't turned out so bad, however. She had dragged a second orgasm from him, and as they lay in bed, staring at the ceiling, she had surprised him. She was self-aware.

'Tell me something,' he said. The sound of traffic had returned. They hadn't just closed off Oxford Street, they had closed down the city. And in the end nothing had happened. There had been no bomb, there had been no fleeing terrorists. The city had been brought to a halt for nothing, that was what people thought. The terrorists had won.

The security services said they had foiled a plot, no one believed them. If the bomb didn't go off, then the public didn't believe there was a threat. If the bomb exploded, then people blamed the government and the security services. That was how it worked. Weston just thought that the government won every time, and that the terrorists won every time. A relationship that worked in perfect symbiosis.

'What do you mean?' she asked.

She was smoking. Weston hadn't smoked in years, but he liked that she did, and that she had lit up unapologetically without asking permission.

'I'm a writer,' he said needlessly. Most people in the country knew who Lake Weston was, Daisy was amongst the multitude.

'That means I should tell you something?' she asked, the notion amusing her. 'My first boyfriend? When I lost my virginity?'

He was staring at the ceiling, head resting on his right arm, arm starting to tingle. As soon as sex is over, women like to lie and caress. They don't necessarily need conversation, but they need affection. As soon as sex is over, men start to think about something else. Anything else. More than all after sex, Weston wanted to turn to the CD player. *It Ain't Me Babe*.

Penny, in particular, had been keen to tell him how much women didn't like that. And so, in order to get around the awkwardness of the moment, an instant in time when men and woman are never more polarised, he had developed his routine of throwing any old question into the air. The fact that he barely knew Daisy meant that the question had had to be all the more vague.

'I don't know,' said Weston. 'Something I don't know about you.'

'You don't know anything about me.'

'And yet, we've just engaged in the most intimate act possible between a man and a woman,' said Weston.

'Don't you think,' she said, blowing smoke straight up into the air, 'it's more intimate for two people to kidnap someone and murder them? Bury the body together in a wood and keep the secret. Forever.'

Weston lifted his head, leant on his elbow and looked at her.

'You're dark,' he said.

'Not really,' she replied. 'You just seem disappointingly prosaic.'

Weston stared at the thin face, green grey eyes looking at the ceiling, waiting for the edge of the smile to come to her lips. It didn't. She flicked ash onto the wooden floor. He wondered what she would do with the stub when she was done. He wondered how long she was going to stay in his apartment. He wondered if that last remark gave him *carte blanche* to go and take care of the music.

'You tell me something first,' she said. 'The great author.'

Weston looked away. Spoke the words *fuck's sake* in his head.

'Used to play in a band,' he said quickly. 'Me and Ben Hammond. Played in clubs, pubs. Had a laugh.'

'What did you play?'

'Dylan,' he said. 'Just Dylan. It was Ben who first got me into him.'

'I meant, what instrument?'

'Oh. Guitar. I played guitar, Ben played the mandolin, some guitar.'

'What happened?'

He looked at her. She was staring at the ceiling. He wondered if she was remotely interested.

'The wife. Kids.'

'Ah.' She smiled.

'Your turn,' said Weston. Embarrassed. People didn't call him disappointingly prosaic.

She turned on her side, pinched the end of the cigarette with her fingers, dropped it on the floor. Rested her head on the pillow and stared across the room at nothing. Playing the game with the famous author. She had been waiting tables for eighteen months in London while working slowly through her media studies course. Weston was the fourth customer with whom she had ended up in bed.

They could feel the first flutter of an early-evening breeze, a slight movement of warm air across the room. A hint of the storm that was to come to drain the day of its suffocating heat.

'I used to go fishing with my dad,' she said. Soft voice. Weston closed his eyes. Heat and traffic, lying in bed with a strange woman, a woman he had placed in the psychiatrist's chair. The warm sound of her voice enveloped him like the heat of the day.

'He'd fish, I'd play on the riverbank. He tried to teach me, but it just bored me. I was six...seven... Too young.'

'What was your mother doing?' said Weston, his voice sounding harsh and out of place.

'Painting. She painted, that was all she did. She still paints, they still live together, he still goes fishing.'

'Aren't they bored?'

There was a screech of tyres, a brutal car horn. Angry sounds, although they couldn't hear the shouts and the curses.

'I'd put a line in. Catch little insignificant fish. I'd feel bad for disrupting their day. We'd put them back, and I always felt that the fish would have been happier if it hadn't been for me.'

Weston smiled. Imagined this woman reaching into his mouth.

'One day I caught a pike. We were out on a small boat on the lake. Early summer. A hot day, although not hot like this. Dad helped me haul it in. Two feet long, scared the shit out of me.'

Weston had his head resting on the side of the boat, a lazy warm afternoon. The buzz of insects, the sound of fish flapping in the bottom of the boat, water lapping against the side.

'You fall in?'

'Dad tried to get the hook out, but it was buried deep and, well, you know, the teeth. Pike's teeth. He didn't have a chance, not without getting his finger bitten off.'

'What'd he do?'

'He couldn't let it back into the water with the hook down its throat. He had one of those little rubber truncheons. Started hitting it over the head. You know, they're supposed to kill the fish with one crack.'

He turned to look at her again. Her back was still turned, still staring across the room. The same slide of black hair down over perfect skin.

'He couldn't kill it?'

'It screamed,' she said. 'A high-pitched scream. Over and over.'

'Do fish scream?' he said to her back. 'Fish don't scream,' he added.

‘I don’t know,’ she said. ‘This one did. He kept hitting it harder, it kept up, I don’t know, this high-pitched screech. It was horrible. That single black eye staring at me the whole time.’

Another screech of tyres outside, this time they could hear an angry yell. Tempers frayed in the heat.

‘What happened?’

There was a slight movement of her shoulders.

‘It died, eventually. The noise faded away, became a croak, then it stopped. The eye died, stopped looking through me. Dad took the hook out and threw it back into the water.’

Weston smiled curiously. She still didn’t turn. He knew that she was just about to leave. Their brief encounter had run its course.

‘I’ve never heard of fish screaming before,’ he said.

‘No,’ she said.

He wondered if he was supposed to be sceptical, if she actually cared whether he was.

‘Maybe it was magic,’ he said, desperate, perhaps, to not sound prosaic, and sounding all the more prosaic for his effort.

‘Maybe,’ she said.

She sat up, her back still turned, and looked across the yawning chasm to the bathroom door.

‘Maybe it was an enchanted princess, turned into a fish by an evil witch,’ he said.

She turned finally and looked at him. Her lips were closed, the face tired. I’ve told you something, her eyes said, now I’m leaving.

‘Of course,’ said Weston, talking to cover the silence, ‘that means your dad killed the princess.’

Weston smiled, but there was no more intimacy between them. The joke had just sounded like mockery. The Front Of House Café Assistant rose quickly from the bed and walked into the bathroom.

Weston laid his head back on the pillow and stared at the ceiling.

‘Your dad killed the princess,’ he muttered to himself. ‘Fucking moron.’

When she emerged from the shower, Weston was lying on the bed, eyes closed, earphones in. And so it was that the rear view of her walking naked into the bathroom was the last time he ever saw her.

Ben Hammond sat on the toilet seat, strumming a guitar while his children argued in the bath. Singing Dylan. He still sang Dylan. Tonight, *As I Went Out One Morning*. Twelve years since he had last seen Lake Weston, although he often thought about their time working the pubs of east London together.

'I don't like that one,' said his boy from the bath. He professed to liking Dylan. His sister and mother detested it with every fibre of their being.

'How come?' asked Hammond, breaking off the third verse.

'All that fairest damsel stuff. It's like, weird and old-fashioned and shit.'

'It's stupid,' said his sister.

Hammond started singing again, laughing as he sang, the way Dylan used to do, back in the 60's when he was still enjoying himself.

5

The warm summer stuttered on in angry bursts. No one seemed to be happy. The television and newspapers were filled with angry stories, barely an event going by without the words *heated exchanges* attached to it. London suffered more than most. Congested streets, stifling heat over the city. Angry fights in parliament over the continuing presence of troops in Iraq and Afghanistan; the threat of troop deployment to Iran; the never ending spiral of the Olympic budget; government sleaze, money not sex; a brief flurry of a scandal over the levels of public money going to management consultants; ID cards and ever-increasing, ever-enveloping, ever-suffocating anti-terror laws; twenty-eight days detention had become forty-two, then fifty-six, then ninety-two, now talk of indefinite periods at the Home Secretary's discretion. As if anyone trusted that. Protestors were being pushed further and further away from the centre of London, and while the detention law drew massive coverage and commentary and complaint, the laws the government claimed were being put in place to protect Westminster were being brought in under the cover of other bad news. Stealth laws, as the police tightened their restrictive grip over the capital.

Every day, every single day, a small area of the capital was closed off so that a suspect package could be dealt with. It had been ten months since there had been an actual terrorist attack. In that time there had been numerous plots foiled, hundreds detained, a few charged, almost a hundred suspect packages blown up. The terrorists were winning, that was the government cry. Only by crushing personal freedom could they crush those who sought to destroy that freedom, that was the paradox. *Freedom For All* shouted the government billboard everywhere around the country, the words shining in glowing red above a picture of a hooded man being led away by the security services. No one was quite sure how the irony was intended.

Lake Weston had one more engagement in London which had been keeping him in the city. A Tuesday evening at the Grosvenor, for the 15th Annual Children's Storywriting Awards. He had been nominated in three categories. Lent on to attend by his editor, his publisher, the publisher's marketing supremo, and his agent. Weston couldn't have cared less about awards. The industry twisted his arm.

A glittering affair with much sponsorship. Big names in attendance. Paid to attend in all cases. Not just a free dinner. More movie stars than writers, because movie stars sell, writers just write. Any British actor who had appeared in anything that could remotely be called a children's film in the previous twenty years and could be bribed into coming.

Weston was up for Best Children's Series For The Under-10s; Best Supporting Character, for the omnipresent Lucy Bargus, Fenton's mum, a woman he had completely based on Penny; and Best Book, for the previous year's entry to the series, *Fenton Bargus Takes On Corporate America*. The fact that it had missed its mark by some miles and was generally considered to be the weakest in the Fenton Bargus series to date – although only by those who hadn't read the upcoming *Fenton Bargus Takes On The Prime Minister* and the following year's *Fenton Bargus Takes On Manchester United/Real Madrid/Preston North End* – had not prevented it from making the list for Children's Book Of The Year. This was partly due to the fact that Fenton Bargus outsold most others and had some sort of inviolable label attached to it. However, the principal reason for its inclusion was undoubtedly that the publisher had paid for it. Had he known, Lake Weston might have been bothered.

The evening was long. Weston had come alone. He ignored the woman from marketing on his left, was not disposed to shout across a large table at people from the publisher that he barely knew, and was left with Eldon Strachan. It not being the place to discuss work, they had quickly drifted into silence and spent the evening listening to the speeches.

Weston's mind drifted off. When the backs were turned and everyone was looking at the stage, he studied the women across the table from him, studied the women on the adjacent tables. Compiled a list of the ones he'd sleep with if he got chance, put them into order. Made a top five. Drank too much wine. Mind rambled.

A tap on the arm brought him back, he looked up at the stage. Stephen Fry was opening the envelope, the TV screen behind showed *Best Series*

For The Under-10's. Strachan gripped his arm. Weston had previously won the award three times.

Fry looked up, a smile on his face. Eyebrow raised, a moment while the tension hovered over the audience, the master craftsman, then he said, '*Horrid Henry* by Francesca Simon!' The place erupted.

'Fuck,' muttered Strachan. He squeezed Weston's arm sympathetically and then poured himself another glass of wine. Weston switched off. Five seconds later he had already forgotten which of the awards it was that he hadn't just won.

A hand clapped on his shoulder and squeezed.

'Never mind, Lakey. Next one.'

He looked round at the smiling face in a bow tie and dark suit. Smooth hair, perfect teeth, he had no idea who the guy was.

'Thanks,' said Weston.

The hand was removed, the man walked on. Weston watched him go, regretting that he would never look that good in a suit.

The evening dragged on. Weston began to get drunk, a rare achievement given how much wine that required. Mostly he sat in increasingly stupefied silence. Strachan was engaged with the woman on his right, a new and vivacious addition to the editorial department. The award for best supporting character came and went, the evening built to the climax, the best children's book of the year. Strachan was nervous, Weston knew he didn't have a chance. Didn't care.

Sir Anthony Hopkins opened the envelope as Weston slowly turned his wine glass round, watching the reflection of the lights on the glass.

'And the winner is,' said Hopkins, once more taking his time, glancing up at the audience with the knowing smile, 'JK Rowling for *The Return of Harry Potter*.'

The place exploded. Weston looked up at the noise, roused from his waking sleep.

'Fucking hell,' barked Strachan, and then he caught Rowling's eye as she began the slow, self-conscious walk to the podium, and he embraced her with a huge smile and started clapping vigorously.

'Never mind, Lake,' he said through his bared white teeth, 'next year.'

Lake Weston had read the *Return of Harry Potter* and knew it to be infinitely better than any of the Fenton Bargus books, even the good ones, never mind the dredged-from-the-bottom-of-the-sludge awfulness of *Fenton Bargus Takes On Corporate America*. The next in the series was even less likely to trouble the voters. If there were actually any voters.

Late in the evening, the place had mostly cleared. Weston was standing wearily at the bar, talking to the man in the suit, who had turned out to be a marketing consultant.

'It's all a fix,' said Weston, voice tired. 'Why does anyone care?'

'It's not fixed,' said Hugo Pemberton. 'I mean, sure, does money occasionally change hands? Well, maybe, maybe it does. But does that mean that it's actually fixed?'

Weston turned and looked at him strangely.

'How else would you define fixing?' he said.

'You have to consider the angles of the corners of the box,' said Pemberton. 'If these things are bought, who pays the most money? The most successful publishers, putting the money behind the books they think are most likely to win. There are already built-in levels of success, even before you get around to deciding which book is actually the best.'

He raised his eyebrows at Weston. Weston wasn't sure that he would have understood what he'd just said, even if he'd been completely sober.

'So, fixing...?' he said. Becoming distracted, eyes wandering around the bar. A celebrity haven. More TV personalities than writers. Maybe he just recognised the TV personalities and didn't recognise any of the writers.

'Fixing is when you put a gun to a judge's daughter's head and tell him to vote a particular way or he'll be wiping his kid's brains off the wall.'

Pemberton burst out laughing, clapped a hand on Weston's shoulder.

'Don't look so shocked, Lakey. It's rare, I mean, really, really rare, that the kid gets wasted in that situation. Look, if you want to think of money getting paid over as fixing, fine, money gets paid over. Things get fixed. Did *Fenton Bargus Takes On Corporate America* deserve to get nominated for Best Children's Book Of The Year? Of course not, it was shit. We both know that. Roger handed over some money, the deal was done, your name went on the list.'

Weston's mouth dropped open. Pemberton pressed on, not prepared to believe that Weston hadn't realised that was what had happened.

'Why the face? *Corporate America* stank the place out, you knew that.'

'I, em...' he began, waved his glass in the air. Suddenly wished he was sober. 'It wasn't that bad,' he croaked. He coughed, tried to regain his voice. 'I mean, I thought the judges had this sort of attitude, you know, even something shit by him is better than most other people's best stuff.'

Pemberton looked at Weston curiously. Weston found himself sobering up quickly. Felt the wave of clear-headedness sweep across him. Pemberton squeezed his shoulder, shook his head, smiled.

'They say that to be a really good writer you have to completely lose all sense of reality.'

Somewhere the thought was formulating that Pemberton was just doing this to him because he was annoyed about *Corporate America*, the book. Marketing consultants had taken it in the neck, and much of the fodder for Weston's imagination had come from tales of the consultant's time at the publisher.

'I think it might be time for me to leave,' said Weston.

He lifted his glass, stared at it for a second, realised that even the thought of it brought a bitter taste to his mouth, placed it back on the counter and stood up.

'I don't know, Lakey,' said Pemberton, clearly not yet having achieved all of his stretch targets. 'You're unlikely to be back next year, so maybe you should savour it while you can.'

Walk away, thought Weston. Nothing is ever gained from taking up the offer of an argument or a fight. But while the wine might have turned bitter in his mouth, it was still having a say on his actions and his mood. Lifted his finger. Pemberton raised an eyebrow and stepped back a little.

'*Prime Minister*,' said Weston, 'that's the one. The best Fenton Bargus for years. It'll be on the list next year, and it won't need anyone, not Eldon, not Roger, not fucking you, to pay any bastard any money.'

Weston wanted Pemberton to be cowed by this, he wanted some acknowledgement that he was right, but he knew he wasn't going to get it.

Instead Weston was treated to an eyebrow that was raised even higher, followed quickly by a knowing look, the flash of awareness, a more prolonged look of superiority.

'What?' said Weston quickly. An ugly feeling in the pit of his stomach. Hated the fact that this guy knew something he didn't. This guy in a sharp suit, this cool-talking, five-grand-an-hour marketing slut, this infiltrator of the publishing business, this poisoned hypocrite wrapped in clothes of betrayal and greed, was taking him apart, piece by piece.

'You don't know, do you?' said Pemberton. 'I thought Strachan told you already.'

'Told me what?

Pemberton looked down the length of his nose, lifted the last of his whisky and water and drained it, then carefully placed the glass on the bar. His eyes looked quickly around the room then tracked back.

'Maybe you ought to speak to your editor,' he said.

Weston turned and looked across the room at Strachan, who was in serious low conversation with one of the senior directors. Weston stared long enough that Strachan caught his eye. A guilty look, no acknowledgement, no casual wave across the bar room floor.

Were they talking about him? Hushed tones in the corner of a bar at the dead end of the party. Where better to advance, or to crush careers?

He turned back to Pemberton, but Pemberton had already gone. He had lobbed his grenade and then walked casually away to the other end of the bar, where a couple of young women were propping up their end.

Weston automatically picked up his wine glass, finished the remnants of his third bottle in one vinegary gulp, his head snapped a twitch at the ludicrous acridity of the wine, then he placed the glass deliberately onto the bar and walked quickly over to where Strachan was huddled in a corner, discussing the fate of seventeen different writers.

From his position at the end of the bar, Hugo Pemberton watched Lake Weston walk purposefully over to Strachan's table. It had been unnecessary to wind Weston up like that, but it had been the final act in the short saga of ensuring that *Fenton Bargus Takes On The Prime Minister* never saw the publishing light of day, and so Pemberton had allowed himself the conceit of a few mind games right at the end.

He watched Weston slump into the seat next to Strachan, watched the executive excuse himself, watched Weston's mouth drop open. And then he nodded politely to the women and walked quickly from the bar. His time at Millhouse was finished. There were other publishers and other writers to fry.

6

Just after ten on a Tuesday morning in October. London and the long hot summer and the stress and the anger seemed a long way away. Weston sat at his desk, the laptop open in front of him, staring out across the Ullapool road to the heather on Ben Wyvis – what he could see of Ben Wyvis, through the rain and mist. Even the trucks and few cars on the road, a couple of hundred yards away, were clouded in spray. He had no heating on in the study, the room was cold. His fingers, which hadn't been flying across the keyboard in quite the way which he'd hoped when he'd got up at a little before six, were numb. Cold hands, he'd only just pulled on his jumper.

He heard the soft pad of footsteps behind him. Quickly closed the laptop and turned.

'Jesus, Lake, it's freezing,' she said. 'Can't you turn the damned heating on?'

He smiled and shrugged. Looked at his empty mug. Usually just warmed himself with tea. Before noon. Alcohol after.

She walked to the window and looked out across the bleak hills. She was wearing one of his t-shirts over her pyjamas and she hugged herself.

'That's why I left you,' she said. 'We're not heat compatible.'

He smiled. 'Bollocks.'

She turned round. Travis. She loved Weston's Highland lodge. Loved it enough, still loved Weston enough, to spend occasional long weekends there. Wine and strummed guitars, late breakfasts and walks up the hills at the back, down into the glens beyond, deer and pheasants.

'What are you writing? You closed that laptop mighty quick.'

He shrugged, made a dismissive movement with his hands.

'You know, what do I ever write? The name's Bargus, Fenton Bargus.'

'Yeah? And who's he taking on this time?'

Weston stared out at the mist.
'The illegal sex trade in women from Eastern Europe.'
She shook her head, he smiled and shrugged.
'Funny. I take it you're writing another one of your hopeful non-Fenton books that Strachan's going to use to fuck you up the arse?'
Weston held his hands out to the side.
'Just writing another Fenton,' he said.
'Whatever, Lake,' she said, walking past him, squeezing his shoulder.
'Maybe I'm writing *Fenton Bargus takes on the Home Office*.'
She laughed quietly. A soft laugh that he loved, a laugh that always crawled inside him.
'I'm going for a shower,' she said. 'Warm up. Mind if I put the heating on?'
'Sure,' he said. 'Why not? Warm the house up, then bugger off after lunch and I'm left sweltering in tropical heat for the rest of the day.'
She laughed again and started to walk down the stairs.
'Come and have breakfast with me in fifteen minutes.'
'Sure,' he said. 'Don't worry about it, I'll just drop everything.'

She took the call between the second and third cup of coffee, sat in the large kitchen, the rain now beating against the window, the heat from the hearth warming the room. A lazy autumn morning, Weston enjoying her company. Wondering why they weren't still married.
He sat back away from the table as she rose and walked to the window. She didn't say much, a few nods, a few affirmatives. He stared at her back for a while, and then absent-mindedly lifted another piece of toast which he didn't need.
She slipped the phone into her pocket and turned back to him.
'TV,' she said.
'You're going to be on TV?'
'No,' she said, irritation in her voice for the first time in four days, 'we need to put the TV on.'
She walked away, through to the small dark sitting room. Weston didn't have much time for television. Because he had the money, he had access to every channel on the planet, just in case he ever felt he needed it. Yet the TV was in a small room that in other large houses would have been the dumping ground for coats and hats, unwanted, unused Christmas presents and stuffed animals on the wane. Nevertheless, the set was fifty inch, high definition, flat screen. Stuck in a room for mice and dust.
'You're so fucking weird sometimes, Lake,' she said, voice still irritated, as she lifted the remote. The TV was on standby. 'When was the last time

you had this on? You know how many trees you just burned down by not turning the damned thing off?'

'What's with you all of a sudden?' he said. 'You're supposed to be the not high maintenance one.'

She threw him a sharp glance, then shook her head.

'Sorry, you're right. I...' and she shrugged away the sentence as BBC News came on in sharp, bright colours. Thick, grey smoke pouring from a building in Canary Wharf, the building with a massive hole, what could be seen of the remainder of the structure, torn and twisted metal. The film switched to the fire services on the ground, water pouring onto flames. Ambulances and police, people on stretchers. Bystanders as close as they could get. Chaos.

She listened to the report for a second and then hit the mute button, the presenter with no more information than she'd just been given over the phone.

Weston could feel his stomach crawl. Wanted to look away from it, didn't want to know about real life and death in London.

'Helicopter flew into the building, carrying a bomb which exploded on impact.'

She let the words hang out in the air.

'So it wasn't an accident?' said Weston.

She turned sharply.

'They accidentally had a bomb on the helicopter?... *Shit, that's a bomb? I thought it was my sandwiches. No wonder my teeth broke.*'

Weston held out his hands.

'When'd it happen?'

'Twenty minutes.'

'Twenty minutes ago? So they can't have investigated anything. It must be anecdotal evidence that there was an explosion, but you don't know what it hit in the building. Maybe it was just some guy out flying, had a heart attack in the cockpit, flew into a building, hit a gas main or something, big explosion. The media and government start screaming terror attack.'

She watched him until he had finished, and then turned back to the television. At some point there was bound to be someone with amateur footage of the moment of impact.

'You are so naïve, Lake, really. Or maybe you're just a liberal. Don't know which is worse. It's a shit world out there, and this is the kind of shit that happens. Helicopters don't just fly into buildings in central fucking London.'

He stared at her for another few seconds, looked at the TV, the Breaking News bar burbling quickly across the screen, and then turned and walked from the room. Had gone from enjoying her company to being glad she was leaving in under two minutes. Which was exactly what had happened most days when they'd been married.

Which was one of the reasons they weren't married anymore.

7

There never seemed any doubt. Not in the minds of the wise. It had been a bomb. Instant judgement on the part of politicians, the media, the public. It had become fact before there had been any proof. 10/2, 2/10, the papers weren't quite sure which way round.

Seventeen dead. Fifty-one injured. *Carnage Wharf* said the Sun over a picture of a bloody body, black from the burning. It took the Prime Minister little more than three and a half minutes, interrupting his shock and outrage and determination to not back down in the face of adversity, to mention how imperative it was that the police now had powers of indefinite detention. A further half minute later he felt the need to say that not all Muslims supported violence, which seemed a condescending remark too far, given that at that point, as far as anyone knew, the pilot of the helicopter had had a heart attack in the cockpit and flown into a gas main. However, such was the national presumption of blame, few found the Prime Minister guilty of any level of arrogance.

Normally this kind of story was of no interest to Lake Weston. He lived in his Highland lodge or his summer London residence, he dealt with his ex-wives, he wrote children's books, he drank too much, he listened to Bob Dylan and had sex with as many women as he could get hold of. Not that he met too many when living his solitary life in amongst fifteen hundred acres of heather not far past Garve on the Ullapool road. Fenton Bargus might have taken on corporate America and the Prime Minister, but he hadn't been about to get involved with terrorists or the state security services. *Fenton Bargus Takes On Al Qaeda* was some way off.

That, however, had all changed on the warm angry evening in London, when Hugo Pemberton had pushed Eldon Strachan into telling Weston what he should have mentioned several weeks earlier.

'Tell me,' Weston had said bluntly. 'What's Slime In A Suit getting at?
'It's about *Prime Minister...*'
'You're not going to pay for it to win any awards?'
A pause. Weston had stopped himself glancing back at Pemberton.
'We've shelved publication.'
'Excuse me?'
'We have been forced to shelve publication.'
'What? Why? Sales? It can't be sales. If it wasn't for…'
'It's not sales. It's the subject matter. But we're still doing the football story. So we need to concentrate on that, start pushing the envel…'
'The subject matter? The Prime Minister? What's wrong with writing about the Prime Minister? I can't write about the Prime Minister?'
'No!'
Strachan had been gripping his whisky tumbler with clenched, white fingers. A wine glass would have shattered.
'No, you can't. Jesus, Lake, look at the times. There are terrorists everywhere. The government pees its pants every time there's the slightest hint of anything. Anything!'
'This isn't serious, is it? Are you serious? It's a fucking kid's book. A kid's book. We take the piss out of the guy a bit, but we don't... I mean, it's a joke, it's just a joke.'
'Someone in government read it.'
'Who?'
'Don't know, doesn't matter. What matters is that Number 10 saw it, they didn't like it, they came along heavy-handed, they told us that if we went ahead and published, then you, me, Roger, everyone else at Millhouse, would be investigated and likely charged in connection with offences under the Terrorism Act 2006.'
'You have got to be fucking kidding me?'
'Part 1, Section 2, Paragraph 4b. It is what it is.'
'Didn't any of you stand up for this in any way whatsoever? This is censorship, for God's sake. State censorship. Doesn't that bother you?'
'You want to know the truth? I flicked them the bird, OK? Happy with that? Then they told me that if I didn't comply they would come down on us all like the Four Horsemen. They would be in your garden. They would be kicking down your doors, seizing your computer, seizing notebooks, seizing the contents of your fucking fridge. Is that what you want? You want your name all over the papers in relation to terrorism?'
'Who the fuck is going to think I'm a terrorist?'
'It doesn't matter. The suggestion would be out there, and you and Fenton would be screwed. So we did a deal. We agreed not to publish,

and to monitor what else you write, in return they don't fuck us over, they don't search your house, they don't tap your phone, they don't read every single fucking word you write on your laptop.'

'Monitor?'

The conversation had continued, that night and ever since, without ever coming to any sort of resolution. Except the obvious one. *Fenton Bargus Takes On The Prime Minister* was dead.

Lake Weston had retreated to the Highlands. He had ripped through the next happy instalment in the Fenton Bargus series – *Fenton Bargus Takes On Terry & June* – in under two weeks, and then had started work on his next great novel, the novel that would finally allow him to break free from the hellish chains of children's fiction.

Strachan had managed to make a deal with a new football team which had been established and immediately placed in the Chinese premier division, Beijing Galaxy. After initial reluctance, when he had thought that moving the story from Manchester to China might be relatively tough, Weston had taken little more than four days to make the changes. He had watched *Hero, Crouching Tiger, Hidden Dragon* and *Beijing Bicycle*, and had told himself that the story easily spanned the globe.

A few days earlier he'd had confirmation from Strachan that the Chinese had accepted the book, something which he considered hugely ironic. That the Chinese would approve his work, while his own government was scared by it.

Any time that he had spoken to Strachan over the previous two months he had said merely that he was playing a lot of golf, he was struggling with the new Fenton and that he would try to have it done by Christmas. He thought he was fooling him, but Strachan knew the code. He just didn't know what the latest adult novel from Weston was going to be about. He did at least know that it would never see the light of day.

8

Weston had arranged a meeting with a man named Morrison who he had found on the internet. He was writing the new novel in a great rush, pounding through the words. Stopping neither to spell check nor rake through the Thesaurus. Yet he realised that while the project might have been strong on character development and narrative drive, it was weak on substance and underlying message.

He walked into the Storehouse of Foulis, a small tourist trap selling local produce and homemade soup and cakes to the passers-by on the A9, between Dingwall and Alness. He hadn't given his real name to Morrison. Wearing the agreed brown jacket, grey cashmere polo neck. Morrison said he would be sitting by the window in a blue sports coat, reading the Independent.

The place was busy, as it always seemed to be these days. Weston glanced over at the man as he entered. Eating cake, cup of tea in his right hand. Weston did not acknowledge him, went first to the counter. Picked up a piece of lemon drizzle cake, ordered a cappuccino.

As he approached the table he looked out over the firth. The tide in, the waves gently pushing against the rocky shoreline. He sat down, placed his cup and plate on the table. Morrison regarded him carefully, then folded the newspaper and laid it to the side.

'Were you followed?' he asked.

Weston looked over his shoulder. 'That's a bit dramatic, isn't it?'

'It isn't a fucking game,' said Morrison gruffly. 'Anyway, I was followed, so it really doesn't matter if you were, I was just curious.'

'How do you know?' said Weston, looking around the room at the families and old women and truck drivers.

'You don't think they follow people who they consider threats?'

Weston stared across the table, taken aback by the immediate ferocity of the man.

'You're not getting into some flight of fancy with all this,' said Morrison. 'It's not just some book you're writing.'

'How did you know I was writing a book?'

He had an immediate horrible feeling of being out of his depth. He had arrived confident and curious, and within fifteen seconds the confidence was gone, curiosity replaced by an overwhelming feeling of inadequacy.

Morrison shook his head, poured some more tea into his cup. Weston stared at the brew. Thick, dark, no milk.

'You can use me for research for whatever it is that you're doing, or you can insult my intelligence, in which case I can leave and you can sit here and eat your cake in peace.'

Weston held his eye for a second, then looked down at the cake. Lifted his fork, took a bite. A mouthful of coffee. It wasn't an actual choice.

'Accepting that I'm a novice at this kind of thing, explain to me. You recognised me when I walked in, or you already knew? But I wrote to you using an assumed name.'

'When you first looked at my site you were logged into the internet using your own name.'

Weston couldn't stop himself looking surprised.

'You can check that?'

'Me and everyone with the right software who wants to. And governments always have the right software, don't they?'

Weston stared, then looked over his shoulder again.

'This is just... you know what I'm writing?'

'How could I?' snapped Morrison. 'But then, it doesn't take a genius. Why else would you be here talking to me? You're working on something that involves the imposition of the state on every single aspect of the supposedly free society that we have in this country.'

'Yeah,' said Weston, another glance over his shoulder. It doesn't take long in the company of a paranoid for the feeling to become contagious.

'Tell me about the book,' said Morrison.

'I'm not sure I want to do that,' said Weston.

'Fine,' said Morrison. 'You keep your secrets, I'll keep mine, and when I've finished my tea I'll get up and walk out and we'll never see each other again. That should confuse the guy sitting in the corner reading the Sun. Don't look round,' he snapped, as Weston's head began to move. 'Not that it matters, as they probably have the table bugged anyway.'

'How do I know you don't work for the government?' said Weston.

'Jesus, you're a piece of work, aren't you?' said Morrison. 'You come in here with your Miss Marple hat on, all *Ripping Yarns* and let's do a smashing book about government conspiracy and we'll be in Berlin in time for tea and cakes. Two minutes later you're worried that I might work for them. Well, maybe I do. But you know the really scary thing? The chances are that the government already know all about you and this book you're writing. You're aware of the Terrorism Act 2006, Section 31? How about Section 34? These people can tap your phones, they can look at your e-mails, they can hack into your computer, Jesus, they can do what they please. And it's all legal. CCTV cameras everywhere, nearly a tenth of the population on the DNA database, the technology to investigate every single thing about the individual that they could want, from what kind of toilet paper they use to what they had for breakfast and who they ate cake with at the Storehouse of Foulis. They can do what they damn well please, and the great British public, or the British people as everyone calls them now, have sat back on their ever-expanding fat arses, eating junk food, watching junk TV and reading junk press, and allowed it to happen. So, bully for you, you woke up and smelled the roses because you had some pointless kid's book spiked by the government. Well, hurrah...'

'How d'you know about that?'

'I have contacts, I hear things, I read things on the internet. It's a big world wide web out there. Big.'

'How specifically did you find out about it?'

Morrison still looked annoyed about Weston's persistence, though he had the deportment of a man who would permanently be annoyed about something.

'There's a guy at Millhouse, some small-time editorial assistant, who blogs on his Facebook page. He has five friends. Just another little office prick seeking his fifteen minutes, which he's never going to get.'

Weston stared angrily across the table, unaware that his mouth was open, that he was holding a piece of cake in midair. Had the junior editorial assistant been blogging about it before he'd even been told?

'Tell me about your book,' said Morrison.

A waitress walked by, Weston waited until she had passed.

'How do I know that you're not going to take my idea and make it into a movie, or another book, or something like that?'

'How do I know you're not working for MI6?' barked Morrison. 'How do I know that you're not going to suck me dry of all my ideas? How do either of us know shit?'

'All right, all right...'

'I don't make movies. The kinds of books I write don't involve fiction. There's enough frightening reality out there to not need to make any shit up. Having said that, if that's your thing, I'm not saying there isn't a place for it. So, tell me.'

Weston looked out over the firth. Didn't feel like eating the cake anymore. Watched a small white boat, the only thing moving out on the water, as it slowly hugged the coast on the far side.

'It's called *Axis of Evil*,' said Weston.

'Nice title.'

'Yeah. It's just, you know, about a group of Scottish counties that agree an alliance, and really it's just an alliance about cheese prices, but central government think it's darker than that, think they're conspiring.'

'Cheese…'

Weston hesitated. This was the first time he had told the idea to anyone. He liked it, he felt it had been going well. He hadn't thought about this before arriving for the meeting, but here he was, effectively pitching the book, and the man across the table didn't seem too impressed.

'So, you know, the cheese thing is an analogy. The book's about modern Britain. Celebrity TV, makeover shows, junk press, binge drinking, teenage pregnancy. Political party corruption, inner cities, banking excesses, increasing police powers, stop and search, tasers, ID cards, everything. It's a full throttle, grab the country by the balls kind of a thing. But the more I write, the more I've realised that it's the government thing that's making it work. As a book.'

Morrison nodded. Kept his eyes on Weston as he lifted his cup to his mouth and finished off his tea. He looked out to sea, noticing for the first time the small boat away across the water. He studied it for a while, long enough that Weston followed his gaze.

'How does it sound?' he heard himself asking with a writer's insecurity.

'You want me to be honest?'

He finally looked back at Weston. Weston had heard that phrase occasionally in his life. The one thing that he had learned was that it never presaged the words, *I think it's a wonderful idea.*

'Not really,' he said.

'You're trying to hit too many targets. Concentrate on the one. The biggest. Police powers, that's enough in itself. Your basic plot idea sounds OK, but don't go on about teenage pregnancy and litter and hoodies. There's worse shit than that in this stupid country.'

'Well, yeah, OK. I mean, that was what I was going to do.'

'Good. Right, I have to go. We should meet again, and we can talk further. I'll bring some stuff. Maybe I'll send you a couple of links to various sites you should be checking out.'

'I only just got here,' said Weston. 'Why don't we just talk now?'

'You saw the boat across the water there?'

Weston looked back at it, now sitting dead in the water, not far from the opposite shore.

'Yeah,' he said, with some curiosity.

'MI5,' said Morrison.

'No way!' said Weston, smiling. 'Come on, it'll just be a couple of guys in a fucking boat. MI5...'

Morrison leant across the table.

'You think the government want you to write this book? You think they want you meeting a guy like me? If they weren't on to you before, they bloody well are now, so you'd better get used to the attention.'

Weston sat back, withdrawing himself from the line of fire.

'Who's publishing the book anyway? Not that bunch of insipid surrender junkies that do your kid books. Don't answer the question, even if you know it, because if they're out there on a boat, they're listening.'

'From over there?'

Morrison looked across the table, head shaking, then stood up and started fastening his coat.

'You have, as they say in all the best movies, much to learn. I'll be in touch. Let's meet somewhere more remote next time. Good writing.'

He nodded and then turned and walked quickly from the restaurant. Weston watched him, then looked back across the water to the small white boat, resting still on a flat calm.

9

He wrote in a flurry for the next day and a half. Fingers fizzing, brain buzzing in time. The book becoming darker, more frightening. Sometimes he wondered if it was becoming too far fetched, the police surveillance techniques, the government manipulation and interference. Then he thought of Morrison and his apocalyptic visions, or he would take time out to read the stories of state terror. Or he would see a car driving more slowly along the A835 than normal, or a walker far across the glen, working his way over the heather on Wyvis, and he would wonder if they were now out to get him. Watching his every move. And maybe it had started with meeting Morrison, or just maybe it had been going on for months. Maybe since the first time someone in the government had read *Fenton Bargus Takes On The Prime Minister*.

Governments don't like writers. They are the people to foster ideas, the ones to try to lead the masses. Even now, the digital age, Blogger, MySpace and Facebook, the medium might be different, but there are still people writing, still people putting ideas into words. You start by taking away the writers and society more easily falls into place.

Alone in a large house in the Highlands for two days, Weston's imagination ran amok to the tune of Bob Dylan. *World Gone Wrong*. *Good As I Been To You*. The old songs. Simpler times. Maybe that's what the government imagined they could return to. Simple times, when people did what they were told.

His salvation from his increasing paranoia, such as it was, arrived late on the day after his meeting with Morrison. His cell phone rang. He jumped. It was dark outside and he was working solely by the light of the laptop screen. Darth Vader. He sighed heavily, lifted the phone.

'Penny,' he said. 'How are you?'

'Good,' she said. 'I'm glad you picked up.'

'What's up?' said Weston.
'Just passing and I thought I'd stop in,' she said.
He didn't immediately reply, allowing this information to sink in. People didn't really just pass Garve.
'Oh,' he said, 'OK. Where are you?'
Looked at the clock. A little over thirty minutes to midnight.
'I'll be there in five minutes,' she said.
She clicked off. Weston looked at the phone then back at the screen. Laid the phone down, saved his work, shut down the computer.
Immediately began to wonder, in the old way, if there was anything lying around the house that she shouldn't see.

He put the coffee cup down in front of her and sat across the kitchen table. How it had all started. They both knew it.
'Are you mad at me?' she asked.
Weston's life suddenly seemed submerged under a great government conspiracy, microphones under every table, a spook on every corner. For the first time in years, he realised that he was actually quite relieved to see Penny. A blast of normality.
'No,' he said. 'I mean, it's a little weird, but it's cool.'
'Good. It just seemed to make sense. I knew you'd still be working at this time of night.'
She seemed relaxed, not the over-tightened guitar string he was used to. She smiled, looked down at her coffee. *Oh crap...* The words came into his head. This is how it starts. She was normal. Attractive. Lips you could kiss all day.
'So,' he said, 'here we are. You just happened to be driving through the Highlands at midnight on a week day.'
She laughed, rested her chin in her palm. The Audrey Hepburn look.
'Got into Inverness just before ten. Wanted to come up and see the kids. I booked into the Thistle in Inverness, but here I am. Thought maybe I could stay for a couple of days, then go and see the kids on Friday.'
'Sure,' said Weston. 'Stay. I'll, em, make up the bed in the spare room.'
'I can do that.'
'All right, whatever. We can do it together.'
She nodded. Sipped her coffee. He was waiting for the twist. The rabbit from the hat. The twisted, blackened, boiled rabbit from the hat.
'Thought you saw the boys a couple of weeks ago?'
They were at Gordonstoun School near Elgin. Weston travelled over to see them every couple of weekends, although he was aware that as they got older and stumbled through their teenage years, visits from their dad,

who wrote books for seven year-olds, were becoming a lot less cool than they originally had been.

'I did. Just, you know, I wanted to speak to them.'

The crux. Weston leant forward. Cancer? Emigrating to Australia?

'What's up?' he said.

She took another drink. Looked out of the kitchen window into the dark of night, turned back.

'Maurice has asked me to marry him.'

The words crept out into the kitchen, hung in the cold evening air. Weston took the pressure off his elbows and sat up. Slightly disarmed now by her air of calm. He took a long drink of coffee. Glanced at the fridge. Maybe a glass of wine made more sense. He looked back at her.

'Who the fuck is Maurice?'

◉

The following day Penny went for a walk across the hills, while he cried off. She needed time to think. The previous evening she had told her ex-husband all about her new love, and why she had never mentioned him before, even though they had been involved for the previous six months. And then she and Weston had gone to the spare room to make up the bed, before ending up getting into it together.

He had cursed himself in the morning. She had been confused.

The flight of his fingers across the keyboard had been interrupted by an e-mail from Morrison. Various websites for him to visit. Blogs mostly. Weston read a few and realised how much it depressed him. Sorry tales of paranoia and desperation.

This was what he was becoming. He felt like he was making a good point, that he had something to say. Freedoms were being restricted, civil liberties were being treated with the utmost disdain. Writers had to stand up and say something. And yet, the more he read other writers, the more he stumbled into the black heart at the centre of any surveillance society, the more he realised that the people who populated the heart of it were the freaks and weirdoes and outcasts, the people that no one in mainstream society ever listened to.

He heard the back door open and close, the dull clunk of her boots, the jacket being taken off and hung up. His heart dipped. He'd enjoyed her being out the house, and now she was due to be there until the following day. Maybe her walk across the glen would have persuaded her to leave.

He had information overload, conspiracy theorists abounding. The British police state. The even more sinister and menacing EU police state. Everywhere he looked there were was someone claiming that all terrorist attacks were government sanctioned.

However, when he had been about to switch off and return to the increasingly ordinary lives of the protagonists of *Axis of Evil*, he had come across the name of a consultancy firm with links across government, a firm which did not seek to hide that it had originally been created to serve the European Union and whose grey anaemic fingers now stretched across every government department in Britain, private enterprise and big business, a pan-European consultancy conglomerate. Community Purpose. The root, one blogger had written with a flair for the predictable, of all evil.

He hadn't heard the stockinged feet come creeping up the stairs, but he knew she was there, standing in the doorway.

'This stuff is just freaky,' he said, without turning. 'You know we're always hearing about detention periods and all that kind of thing. You know that the police can just impound any of your stuff, I mean, they can come into your house and take anything. Don't need to explain, don't need a court order. And they don't have to give it back. Ever. They have that power. They can even take your fucking house.'

'What would you do then?' she said. He didn't turn. Felt his stomach turn, his soul crumple. The long walk over the glen may have got her out of the house for a few hours, but it had also given her the time to flick the switch. The old Penny, the usual, normal, regular Penny was now standing behind him.

'But the worst thing,' he said, 'there was a guy at the publishers. The usual, you know, consultant. Turns out the firm he works for, Community Purpose they're called, they're fucking everywhere. Government, the EU, the energy companies. They consult for other consultants. They're like some weird, shadowy Masons of the consultancy world. They're the Knights Templar of big business.'

She didn't say anything. He could feel the cold anger of her eyes burrowing into his back, he could feel the temperature of the room drop.

'There was me wondering how someone at Number 10 managed to get a hold of *Prime Minister*. How the hell did they even get to look at it? I mean, it wasn't like the book was a secret, but you know it's a pretty big series these days, and they tend to keep these things under wraps for as long as possible. How the hell did the PM's office get hold of it, that's what I was thinking.'

'You hadn't noticed that one of your ex-wives works for the government?' said Penny coldly from behind.

Weston turned. She was leaning against the doorframe, arms folded. Her face, her body language, were those of his dreams, when Penny would stand before him, complaining bitterly, before her head turned into that of a snake.

'Oh, for goodness sake,' he said. 'She's got some pointless management job at the Home Office.'

'Wake up and smell the cyanide,' said Penny bitterly. 'You sit there complaining about government, your ex-wife is part of it, but for some reason, she's above all that.'

'I never showed her the book!'

'She comes here all the time!' barked Penny. 'How do you know what she's doing while you're sleeping? While you're out walking, getting all that inspiration you always seemed to need? Or do you not need to escape from her the way you needed to escape from me?'

It never took very long. A few seconds foreplay, the briefest of physical exchanges. A lot of heat, quickly blown out. She would go off bitter and angry, he would start thinking about something else.

Except now she had him thinking about Travis. It wasn't that the idea hadn't occurred to him, but he had quickly dismissed it. He knew that she had an uninspiring job dealing with some aspect of public funding of the prison service, he knew she never had any contact with Downing Street. And he also knew that she just plain wouldn't do that to him.

'I'm going to make a cup of tea,' she said. 'You just sit there, the perfect host.'

I didn't fucking invite you in the first place, came to his mind, but got nowhere near his lips. He had given up the right to such heartfelt honesty the minute he had got into bed with the Devil.

10

Weston walked into the small room. Noticed the crucifix on the wall opposite the door, the first thing you saw. Looked around. There were seven different depictions of Christ on the cross, from Dali to a small wooden carving on the mantelshelf.

'I'm not a religious man,' said Jack Gilroy, stroking his grey beard, 'but it's good to surround yourself with the representation of one man's suffering for others. It gives one a solid grounding in perspective.'

'You're not religious?'

'No.'

'Then why would you believe that Jesus was suffering for anyone?'

The grey eyes stared out from behind the grey hair and the greying face.

'Like I said,' growled Gilroy, 'it's representative. You want tea?'

'Thanks. Milk, not too much, no sugar.'

Gilroy grunted, turned and walked into the hall. Weston watched him out of the room, and then went and stood at the window of the small council house outside Perth, and looked across the road at the other small council houses, trees and hills beyond.

'That's what they want you to think,' said Gilroy, stabbing his finger across the coffee table.

'Who?'

'All of them. Government, media, all of them. Even Morrison, even he doesn't see it, or is a fully paid-up member already.'

Weston wondered if he should have mentioned Morrison, but it was always good to get as many perspectives as possible. Recognised that he had stumbled into the world of investigative journalism, which was definitely not who he was or what he had been trained at.

'Doesn't see what?' said Weston. 'Morrison believes in everything.'

'But not the big one,' said Gilroy. 'Too wrapped up in his own importance, thinks MI5 have got nothing better to do than follow him around the Highlands. As if he can do any damage up there.'

'The big one?' said Weston. No patience.

'The EU for Christ's sake, man. The EU. All these laws, all these restrictions, they're not Britain's, they come from the EU. We're just falling into line. It's like they've taken the worst aspects of each country's police system and amalgamated them into one insidious Soviet-style, pan-European secret police force. It's frightening.'

'Yeah, I...you know, Morrison put me on to some of that stuff. I think. Maybe I just stumbled upon it by accident.'

Gilroy reached out with one of his massive hands, grey hairs on the backs of his fingers. And took another chocolate covered digestive.

'Morrison's not the issue. The EU, that's the issue. You're going to say, why don't these people make more of it? The press, the BBC, the three main parties, all of them. Big business, all of it. Corporate London.'

Weston nodded. Morrison had scared him, Gilroy somehow made him want to laugh.

'You think I'm an old fool,' said Gilroy, 'but you know, I don't give a shit. I'll give you one example, but I could give you three thousand.'

'On you go.'

'The trouble in Northern Ireland. Killed over three thousand people. The IRA murdered a senior member of the Royal Family, they killed a government minister, they tried to blow up the entire fucking government! And what restrictions did we have on society in the 70's and 80's? Detention for twenty-eight or forty-two or ninety-two days? No. Restrictions on protesting outside Westminster? No. Every government minister protected by machine gun wielding police? No. None of it. It was OK back then to kill government ministers. Now, you're not even allowed your own opinion. Regardless of how heinous we consider that opinion, we're supposed to be a democracy.'

'We were in the EU the whole time the Irish thing was going on,' said Weston.

'It's big picture, a long term plan,' said Gilroy, holding his hands out in explanation, having finally taken a bite of his biscuit, crumbs on his lips. 'They didn't have the treaties in place back then. They couldn't do all this stuff at once, could they? If they had said thirty years ago that you couldn't protest, that the government would strip pensions, that we would have unlimited detention, that there would be police powers to seize property.....need I go on. Take how this country has changed in the last three decades and imagine they had tried to introduce it all at once.'

He sat back. Weston looked uncomfortably across the coffee table. Gilroy did not have the bellicose nature of Morrison, he didn't look like every single thing on the planet annoyed him, but his sincerity and determination had Weston feeling just as much out of his depth. He leant forward, lifted a chocolate biscuit and took a large bite.

'Go on, eat the fucking biscuit while you can, Mr Weston,' said Gilroy darkly.

Gilroy walked him to the door. They had ended up talking about the old man's grandchildren.

Weston stopped at the door and tasted the fresh air. A cold afternoon, smelled like snow, but it was too early.

'Don't judge too harshly, Mr Weston,' said Gilroy as he shook his hand. 'I know what you're thinking. That we're all conspiracy theorists. But it's too easy to lump everyone into the same bag. Just because you question big government, doesn't mean you're the kind of deluded fool who believes the Yanks never landed on the moon. I don't care about any of that, I'm dealing with what's written in black and white. This country is nearly over, sir, and you'd better take heed of that. Put it in your book, or not, I don't care. Just listen to these words. Article I-6 of the EU Constitution. *The Constitution and law adopted by the institutions of the Union in exercising competences conferred on it shall have primacy over the law of the Member States*.'

He stopped for the significant pause. He ate Weston with his eyes for a second, and then smiled and took his hand.

'Just think about that as you head back up the A9. And any time you want another chat, don't hesitate to give me a call.'

Weston smiled and nodded. A warm shake of the hand.

'I'll be in touch,' he said, then he backed down the short steps and walked to his car. He stopped before opening the door and looked up at the sky again. By the end of his chat with Gilroy, he had felt strangely reassured, like he was doing the right thing. He felt invigorated, wanted to get home and get on with the book. A decent drive up the road, stop off at the usual hunting grounds for soup and cake and a cup of tea, get home after dark and then maybe pitch an all-nighter at the computer.

Get the book out there while there was still time, he thought as he buckled himself in. He smiled, realising that he was starting to buy into it all. The imminent destruction of the state, the inevitable Soviet-style government that was at hand.

Started the engine of his BMW, wound down the window and stuck a farewell hand out into the air. The CD player was coming to the end of

John Wesley Harding and, as he pulled away and watched Gilroy wave goodbye and retreat back into his house of crucifixes, *I'll Be Your Baby Tonight* jauntily filled the car. He sang along with Bob.

The explosion occurred just as he turned the corner. Still in first.

He was aware of the bright light to his left; the huge, the immense, the colossal all-encompassing noise as the great fireball instantly engulfed the small council house on a quiet street to the west of Perth.

He slammed on the brakes. The car rocked with the blast, immediately hit with debris and flying glass. Windows shattered in houses all around him, glass and wooden frames flew. Doors cracked, bits of garden fence cartwheeled. Something heavy landed hard on the roof of his car.

Weston stared, horrified, as the house of the crucifix burned. Huge flames. Breath caught in his throat. He could hear screams, a window shattered somewhere. And then, with that final belated act, the storm had blown over and the only sound was the burning of the house, the low rumble of flames.

A few people began to appear on the street. Everyone was either talking on the phone or holding up their mobile to get video. A woman in a red jumper, a teenager in black, another mother, baby in one hand, phone in the other. A car drove slowly past, the driver staring at the conflagration.

Weston watched them all, the horror still on his face, all the immediate questions of panic and subterfuge and conspiracy and fear stumbling around his head. Still didn't get out the car, just sat in awestruck terror.

He wanted to get away, wanted to drive quickly, be on the A9 in five minutes, on his way to Inverness. But would anyone have seen him leave the house? Would there be an endless stream of witnesses already on the phone to Sky News, saying that they'd seen a man leave in a black BMW, and here's the photograph of him and his number plate?

But the blunt horror of the situation gnarled up his stomach and refused to allow him any rational or reasonable thought. Had that been meant for him and the timing had been off, or had someone been watching, and had waited for him to leave the house?

He looked round at the car which had slowed, and which was now driving away. Another car had stopped, another was slowing from the opposite direction. He stared back at the flames, looked over the scene of carnage as people grew in confidence and more of them appeared from their houses.

No one seemed to be looking at him, no one seemed to be thinking anything of the black car. He had to blend in, if nothing else. He lifted his phone, flicked the cover, and held it up to take a picture of the blaze.

Bob had gone back to the start, *John Wesley Harding* rumbled quietly through the car. And, breathing still dysfunctional, hands shaking, Weston lifted his right foot which had been jamming the brake to the floor, put the car back into first gear and slowly drove away from the scene of the crime.

◉

He finally allowed himself to turn on Radio Scotland at nine o'clock to listen to the news. Almost at Inverness, a slow drive north with several stops.

The Scottish news opened with the continuing police investigation into the London terrorist attack from the previous week; that was followed with the latest American claims of military success in Iraq, the announcement timed to coincide and make a bigger splash than the news of the biggest car bomb in Baghdad in six months, the item that came third in the Scottish news. When the announcer moved on to the latest unemployment figures, followed by a report on an insipid debate at Holyrood concerning the badger plague, Weston began to feel a hand crawl up his spine, making the hairs on the back of his neck stand, making his hands tighten once more on the wheel, making his breath come in faltering gasps.

It came eventually, seven minutes in. Weston drove past the sign for Daviot as he listened to the words "*a seventy-eight year-old Perth man has died following an explosion at his home caused by a gas leak...*" Apparently there had been reports of the smell of gas in the area. No one from Scottish Gas was available to comment. No reporter on the scene, no follow-up, no interviews.

◉

Graham Barlow drove all the way to London in one go, so that he arrived there before Weston had made it to his home in the north of Scotland. His job had been to get rid of Jack Gilroy. There had been a time when the old man had just been another old fool, wittering on at the winds, no one paying him the slightest attention. However his website, and accordingly his views, had begun to make a little more noise, and after being quoted in a piece in the Guardian three months previously, suddenly he was being noticed.

The news on Radio Scotland had been right on two counts. Firstly, very few listeners had been at all interested in the story, and therefore they'd been quite right to make it so unimportant an item. Secondly, the house had exploded because of a gas leak. The gas leak just happened not to have been accidental.

Having remotely activated the leak of the odourless gas, Graham Barlow had stayed at a distance to make sure that everything went to plan. The explosion had not been aimed at Weston, although equally Barlow had not waited until Weston had left the house. The event was timed to occur when Gilroy first flicked a switch or lit his pipe after the gas leak had been initiated. After the fashion of his type, Barlow did not care whether or not there was any collateral damage.

From his distant vantage point, he'd noticed Weston leaving. However, as he'd been noting Weston's number plate, the explosion had ripped through the small estate and he'd made a minor error. And so, when it came time to file his report and pass on all the relevant information, the wrong licence plate was given. Consequently, a family of four in Weston-super-Mare suddenly found themselves being followed, while Lake Weston continually looked over his shoulder and never saw a thing.

For the time being, at least, he was in the clear.

11

They noticed he was distracted and, for the first time in a long while, it made him more interesting to them.

Weston's sons, Tom and Daniel, had long since tired of being the sons of a famous father. They had tired of his occasionally being recognised in public, they had been jealous perhaps; they had tired of their parents' arguments; they had tired of their father finding excuses to be away. There had been a time when they had thought their dad was the coolest parent on planet earth and then, as is always the case, that thought had faded and now he was just another sad, middle-aged bore who felt the need to visit his sons every couple of weeks.

Nothing to say. He had been a wonderful father to two toddlers, but now that they had grown up and were on more even terms, he was lost. The precise terms of reference that exist between parents and young children had been swept aside in a torrent of hormones and impending adulthood, and Weston had gradually lost touch. Now he came to Gordonstoun every couple of weeks out of duty. They wished he wouldn't.

'You all right, Dad?' asked Tom. The elder child. He had come out the other side of calling his father by his first name; Daniel was still there.

'Yeah,' said Weston, casually. 'Why do you ask?'

They were eating fish and chips in a small café in Hopeman, looking out over the harbour. A grey Sunday afternoon in November. Weston was already thinking about leaving, getting back to work, getting back into the car. Turning the music on.

'You seem distracted. Just, I don't know, different.'

Weston stared at his son. He hadn't really spoken to anyone since Gilroy. The odd shop assistant, the odd phone call. Hadn't spoken to Travis. A friend – he had one or two – had asked if he'd wanted to play

golf at Skibo, but he'd baulked. Even Penny had only called twice and he hadn't taken the calls.
'I've started listening to a bit of Dylan,' said Daniel.
Tom glanced to his side.
'Yeah?' said Weston, smiling. 'Which one?'
'Em, the long one. Just, you know, like a headshot of him on the cover.'
Weston shrugged, looking for a little bit more.
'Ends with a long song that sounds a bit like that George Harrison on the White Album.'
'*Blonde on Blonde*,' said Weston.
'Yeah. My mate...Alice... she got into it. It's cool.'
'Alice? Who's Alice?'
He looked slightly embarrassed.
'Just a girl. A friend.'
'OK. You know, I can give you a loan of some others if you like. I can download them.'
'OK. Yeah, maybe just one or two.'
The silence returned. The boys exchanged a glance.
'So, what are you working on at the moment?' asked Tom. He had wrapped up the fish and chips and was wondering when they could leave, get back to the school. They were missing a pick-up game of football. American football. 'Still on that Fergus book?'
'Fenton,' said Daniel. Tom hit his arm.
Suddenly Weston realised he wanted to talk. That he needed to talk. About the explosion. The incident that had put him off meeting anyone for a casual chat about conspiracy theory. At some stage he had realised that he had enough fodder, that the book had a momentum and narrative drive of its own. And it was nearly finished. It was current, relevant, pointed and cutting. And it frightened him.
If Number 10 were going to pull a book such as *Fenton Bargus Takes On The Prime Minister* because of some puerile humour and the occasional barbed political comment fit for a six year-old, what were they going to think of the *Animal Farm* of its age?
For that was how he had come to think of it.
But he had been working in complete isolation and the paranoia of total silence had been growing. He needed to speak to someone.
He hesitated. Stared across the table at Tom, longing to include him in his torment. But how could he? How could he bring his sixteen and fourteen year-old sons into this thing? Maybe they would be excited by the idea of the book, and they certainly would be interested in the death of old Jack Gilroy, but this was too much for them.

And, in the mind of the neo-paranoid, now that someone might be out to get him, what right did he have to drag his children into the mess?
With the hesitation came hope for Tom, thinking that maybe their dad was finally going to speak to them about something worthwhile.
'Yeah, just Fenton,' replied Weston disappointingly. 'Had some problems with the one that was due next year, had to do some re-writes with the one after that. They're wanting me to rush this one through.'
'Who does he take on this time?'
Weston looked a bit embarrassed then shrugged.
'Terry and June,' he said.
'Who are *they*?' asked Tom.
'Doesn't matter. I expect my editor will make me come up with some other title when it comes to it. It's just, you know, about middle-class English suburbia. It's just, well, you know how it is.'
The silence returned, the awkwardness swept back across the table.
Weston took a drink. Started tapping out *Working Man's Blues #2* on the table. Daniel watched his dad's fingers. Tom pushed his knife and fork slightly around the plate.
'D'you mind...?' said Tom, and he couldn't finish the sentence, just indicated the direction of the school with bent thumb.
Weston sat back, nodding. The best thing for everyone.

As he was driving away from the school, along the back roads behind Elgin, heading for the A96 to Inverness, he became aware of a dark Audi, blacked-out windows, not far behind him, heading in the same direction. Following him.
It tailed him all the way to Inverness. He thought of heading into the city and trying to lose it in the side streets, but Inverness isn't that big, and the likelihood was that his pursuer would know where he lived.
They didn't follow him over the Kessock Bridge. He wondered if someone else in a less conspicuous car was taking over the tail, or whether he had accidentally lost them.
Didn't even consider that the black Audi might just have contained another sorry parent leaving their child behind at school.

12

Three days before Christmas. Weston sat on the London shuttle, tapping the top of his small backpack. The completed manuscript of *Axis of Evil*. Hard copy. Small print, one hundred and thirty-three sides of A4.

A few weeks' more writing, editing, polishing, cutting. Another meeting with Morrison, a few more questions. Further berated by the man, for everything from the gap between meetings and for having the nerve to stumble unwittingly into such a nest of vipers as state security and the fundamental principles of democratic society. Surveillance, anti-terror laws, detention, seizure of property, ID monitoring, databanks, the expansion of Europe and the Brussels politburo. Perfect grist for the average children's author.

And now here he was at the nub, the quintessential point of the whole exercise. Book written. Finer points tuned. Facts checked, information gained from Morrison weighted as much as possible against reality. He'd had several chats with Travis, his great government apologist of an ex-wife, but had been mindful of her since Penny's blunt and suggestive implication of her having passed the *Prime Minister* manuscript to Number 10. He didn't believe it, but at least had been given reticence. He rarely had to start the conversations with Travis in any case, but had become more willing to keep them going.

Now, to whom did he show the book? Where did he go to try to publish? Did he just do it himself and get it out there, or did he first offer it to Strachan to see what would happen? It wasn't like the manuscript itself was illegal; it didn't make claims, it didn't paint anyone in government as evil or corrupt. It was the system that came under fire, the politics of the West itself.

Thoughts of doing it himself usually broke down when he came to the part where he had to sell it. Getting it printed, particularly with his money, was no problem. The black arts of marketing and distribution were where he suddenly found himself staring at hard work, and fields in which he was neither tested nor trained.

Earlier that week he had sat at his desk, looking out over the white hills. No snow, but two days of thick frost. They were saying it was going to be a cold winter, the reasons for it tied into global warming and the effect of big business on the planet. It seemed to Weston, now overdosed on conspiracy theory, that in the old days you used to get cold winters and they would be explained by the fact that you lived in Scotland. Now there had to be a reason, now every single day of weather had to be someone's fault, regardless of whether it was cold, warm or the kind of dreich, bleak drizzling nothingness that defined so many days in the Highlands.

He had made a list of everyone to whom he might show his manuscript. Ex-wives, people at the publisher, friends such as they were, conspiracy theorists; although the latter category was very small, consisting of two people, one of whom had been blown up by an accidental gas leak.

He had somehow managed to eek the list out to include fifteen names, and had then gone through each one and found as many reasons as possible why that person in particular shouldn't be the one in question. At the end of it he had been surprised to find Eldon Strachan with the fewest marks against him, aided by the positives of the possibility of him being able to help with the publishing process.

His agent, Geraldine Farmer, a harmless neophyte given the straightforward task of managing the career of Britain's second most celebrated children's author, ought to have been the obvious first port of call. Weston, however, had been gripped by conspiracy fever. He had wondered why, when his agent Valerie had moved to New York the previous winter, he had been given the fledgling, wet behind the ears, walking cliché for the new millennium in Prada shoes, when he would have expected someone with more experience. Now, though, fed with the food of the subterfuge junkies, he saw all kinds of reasons why he had been landed with someone trained in law, who didn't like to talk about her three years since leaving university, and who seemed to have barely the merest grasp of how the publishing business worked.

A clear and present MI5 plant.

He had invited Strachan round to his London apartment for a quick lunch. He intended locking him in the apartment until he had read the manuscript of *Axis of Evil*, front to back. He could then let him go without having to let the book out of his sight.

'Is everything all right, sir?'

Weston looked up. He hadn't been asleep, but his mind had been so far away that the effect had been much the same.
'Sure,' he said.
'You looked a little distracted,' said the stewardess. 'Can you fasten your seatbelt, please?'
Weston stared at her, looked at the illuminated seatbelt sign.
'Yeah,' he said. 'Of course, sorry.'
He fastened his seatbelt. The man sitting beside him stared at the back of the chair in front.

Strachan had politely accepted the invitation to Weston's apartment, while letting it be known that he had other engagements that afternoon.
They were sitting at the table in the small dining room. Weston had had the place cleaned the day before, as he always did before he arrived in town, and a cooked lunch had been delivered from a ridiculously expensive bistro not long before Strachan had arrived. Weston had pretended that he'd made it himself that morning.
'This is fucking delicious,' said Strachan. 'What the fuck is it? Cheese and shit?'
'Three types of cheese,' said Weston, smiling. He had no idea how many types of cheese there were in it. He had no idea if there was any cheese in it.
'You find it more and more often these days,' said Strachan. 'Writers who cook. WWC. It's a phenomenon. You lot have got bugger all else to do with yourselves, so you like, learn to cook and shit. Where d'you get this?'
'Nigella,' said Weston, trying not to laugh. Feeling strangely giddy at the absurdity of what he was about to do.
'Man,' said Strachan. 'Fucking Nigella. Posh TV fanny, that's all that is. Great tits though.'
Weston nodded.
'Every time I watch one of those shows, I imagine all the other TV chefs sitting at home getting really jealous and nasty. Sitting there with a bottle of Pinot attached to their face slagging off the competition.'
'You're probably right,' said Weston.
That was what he himself sometimes did and he wasn't even a chef.
Strachan took a drink of sparkling water, laid down the glass, placed his knife and fork on the edge of his plate. Weston felt the shiver in his guts. This was it. He knew that Strachan wasn't going to spend too long sitting around, scarfing lunch and discussing celebrity TV breasts.

'You know what I think?' said Strachan, dabbing at the corner of his mouth with the elegant cream serviette which had come with the pre-prepared lunch. 'I think you've got two books for me. You'll have knocked off the Fenton Bargus in two minutes, and you've been working on something else.'

Weston stared across the table. Eye twitched. Hated that he was so transparent. Not that it particularly mattered in this case.

'And now you've brought me here to pitch me the idea, sweet talk me, and see if you can get Millhouse to publish your latest attempt to break away from children's authordom. Well, Lake, I've got some news...'

Weston abruptly rose from the table, lifted the bag that was lying on the floor by the door, and sat back down.

'You're part way right,' he said crisply. 'First things first.' He passed a disk over. '*Fenton Bargus Takes On Terry & June*.'

Strachan laughed. 'That's funny. Might have to change the title, but I can see where it's going. Like it.'

Then he reached in and pulled out the slim manuscript of *Axis of Evil*. No title on the cover, a blank page, then the tightly packed manuscript within. Weston felt the nerves go, the determination flood in.

'Aha!' said Strachan, laughing. 'I'll get back to you in six months.'

Weston handed it over, a hard-hearted determination in his eyes.

'Untitled,' said Strachan. 'Nice. Is that because you can't think of anything? Or do you intend not giving it a title, and it's just going to be a blank white cover? Like *The Beatles*. That might not be a bad idea. Of course, someone's probably done it before. I mean, apart from The Beatles.'

He started to flick through the manuscript, gazing at words and names and phrases along the way, taking nothing in.

He looked up at the click of the key in the door. Weston placed the key in his pocket, stared with determination back at Strachan.

'What the fuck are you doing?'

Weston sat down and took a long drink, finished off his glass.

'I want you to read it,' he said. 'Now.'

'Are you nuts? I've got meetings coming out my arse.'

Strachan threw the script onto the table, shaking his head. He stood up.

'Sit down, read the manuscript,' said Weston. 'If you need to make some cancellation calls, on you go. Then get on with it, I know how quickly you can read. But don't skip anything, I'll be asking questions.'

'Have you just like completely lost your fucking marbles? Jesus fuck, Lake, what are you going to do? Pull a fucking gun on me?'

13

Weston spent the next three hours reading a couple of newspapers. The Guardian and the Independent. A few stories to whet the appetite of the average conspiracy theorist. He had never really believed anything that he read in the newspapers or heard on the news. Everyone has their own agenda, and the notion of truth is such an ambiguous concept in any case. But now he read every single story trying to work out the agenda of the writer, the agendas of those being quoted in the article.

It had pained him to fall back upon the threat to tell Strachan's wife about the regular trips that Strachan made to the home of another one of the authors on Millhouse's list. It had been very cheap, and Weston had had the decency to be offended at himself for doing it. He had also been worried that Strachan would regard him with contempt and call his bluff because, of course, he had no intention of speaking to Strachan's wife. About anything.

Strachan had made two calls. He had thrown a few cheap shots of his own, insults and innuendo. Weston was finished. There were moves at the company to ditch him. As much bluff and acrimonious bluster as Weston had given from his side. But Strachan was extremely pissed off and Weston suddenly realised the very obvious. That this was not a situation conducive to Strachan giving the manuscript a fair reading.

The two men sat and stared across the room at one another. Strachan had finally laid the manuscript back down on the table. Outside the day had turned dark, the traffic was at its peak and loud. The room was cold. Weston had only turned on a couple of small table lights. He laid down the second newspaper, having read everything of interest, completed the Sudoku and the Kakuro.

Strachan emitted a heavy sigh, lips pursed, fingers tapping on the script.

'What do you want me to do with it?' he said.
'What do you think of it?' said Weston. 'Does it work?'
'Fuck me,' said Strachan. 'A writer's insecurity. You use blackmail to kidnap me and hold me against my will, then the first thing you ask is for affirmation about your new book. You're a piece of fucking work.'
'What do you think of the book?' said Weston.
Trying to stay calm, detached, although his stomach was cartwheeling.
'It's brilliant,' said Strachan without enthusiasm.
'What?'
'It's brilliant. I mean it. I may not sound like I mean it, but then you've just held me against my will for the last three hours, so it's not like I'm about to start sucking your dick. But this is genuinely the best thing I've ever read of yours. Well written, pointed, acerbic, brutal, honest.'
The cartwheels in Weston's stomach had stopped. Replaced by elation. An endorsement from a non-sycophantic editor.
'Will you publish it?'
'Are you kidding me? Not a fucking chance.'
Weston sat back in his seat. Reality check. The answer he had been expecting, of course, but for the briefest of moments he'd had hope.
Horns blared outside, traffic revved or screeched. Someone shouted. The sounds of rush hour. Strachan shrugged.
'Can I go now?'
'Is that it?'
'I told you I wasn't going to suck your dick. You know we can't publish this. Give me a couple of days and I'll think about it, see if there's anything I can do for you.'
'Don't tell anyone,' said Weston, his voice coming out a little higher pitched than intended.
'Don't worry,' said Strachan. 'I could probably get arrested just for reading the fucking thing.'
Weston smiled. Didn't move. Began thinking strange thoughts of people getting arrested just for reading his book. Huddled corners of resistance. People passing the book back and forth, wrapped in brown paper. The kind of thing which would have happened in Nazi Germany or Stalin's Russia. People risking imprisonment just to be part of something grand, something which rebelled against the evil which had begun to control their lives. *Axis of Evil* would become an underground cult classic. It would grow and grow until the government was forced out of office. Forced to go to the polls, forced to give the public the choice of whether they wanted to live in this kind of society, and then they would be

democratically voted out of office. Pure democracy, as it was intended. As reintroduced into British society by Lake Weston.

'Are you going to let me out or are you just going to sit there in self-congratulatory, masturbating silence?'

◉

'I saw a bit about Bob Dylan in the Biggest Book of Records today.'

Driving home from school. Ben Hammond and son, his daughter staying late for a cooking class.

'Guinness,' said Hammond, 'not Biggest. Oldest guy to have an original album at No.1 in America.'

'Bob Dylan?'

'Yeah. It's cool, isn't it?'

'Isn't he dead now, though?'

'Bob? I took you to see him in Amsterdam last summer.'

'Oh. That was Bob Dylan?'

Hammond stopped at a pedestrian light, watched a family of six walk slowly across.

'Comedian,' he said.

'So if he's not dead, what does he do now? Like watches TV and stuff?'

'He tours mostly. Plays over a hundred gigs every year. He interprets his own songs for a live audience, on an average of once every three and a half days. He's been doing that for eighteen years.'

Realised that he sounded like a documentary. The family of six minced onto the pavement, the light changed, Hammond glanced at his son and drove off slowly along the road. Twenty's plenty.

'If it was me,' said the boy, 'I'd just watch TV.'

14

The following day a thirty-two year old nurse was arrested for standing at the end of Downing Street and reading out the names of all the British soldiers killed in the wars in Afghanistan and Iraq. It took fourteen officers to arrest her, although she put up no resistance. She was taken away in a black armoured van and charged later that day with contravening three sections of the Terrorism Act 2006. The following day the story was reported in none of the national papers.

Weston found out about it from Morrison's website, although it was unclear how Morrison had come by the news. Weston printed a copy of the report and put it in the new file that he had begun to compile. Already planning the follow-up to *Axis of Evil*, albeit for the moment he had no characters and no story. He had a theme and a target and that was good enough for a start. Carried away with Strachan's endorsement, he now felt as though he was on the brink of a new career. Political satire.

'You're on edge, Lake.'

Weston took another drink of wine, a long one, already on his third glass. Christmas Eve. Travis was looking as fabulous as always, borderline trashy in red. He raked his fork through the salad.

'You usually have a sort of Christmas good humour about you, even though you have to spend your day with your ex-family.'

'Not this year,' said Weston quickly. Looked at her at last.

'That's intriguing,' she said. 'What's up?'

'Maurice is up.'

'Maurice?'

'Penny's got a new shag. He's a dentist.'

'Holy crap! Do you think she thinks of you while they're doing it?'

Weston smiled, shaking his head. Finished off the glass. Knew that he should slow down, wanted to be sharp for later that afternoon, but couldn't stop himself. Tapped out *Rainy Day Woman #35* on the desk. An incessant drum. Trying to shift addictions, that part of his brain which he had transferred from alcohol to Bob Dylan. Travis was so familiar with the beat of his fingers that she recognised the tune.

'So, why are you in London?'

'A couple of work meetings. Seeing Eldon this afternoon.'

'And I thought we'd be going back to your place for a Christmas fuck.'

'Cheeky bastard.'

She finished off her first glass of white. Did not reach for the bottle. She was getting the train to Cornwall that afternoon to spend Christmas with her parents and her sister's family, all five annoying kids included.

'How about you?' said Weston. 'Usual horrible Christmas Day on the horizon?' A New Orleans street band played in his head.

'I'm not going this year,' she said, stone-faced. 'I'm going to have an aneurism on the way to the station.'

He smiled. Guard slipped. Leant over and lifted the bottle, shared the remainder between their two glasses.

'What's the meeting?' she said. 'Another one of your non-Fentons?'

He stared across the table, remembering what Penny had said, annoyed at himself that he should still be listening to that voice. He trusted Travis. He'd always trusted Travis.

'Yeah,' he said. 'Non-Fenton. Maybe getting somewhere this time.'

'Can I read it?'

The waiter appeared at the table.

'Everything all right, sir, madam?'

They both nodded. Travis was looking at Weston curiously.

'Would you like another bottle of wine?'

'No thanks,' said Travis, quickly. 'Some more sparkling water.'

Weston felt the yearning. He heard the wail of the harmonica on *Pledging My Time*.

'You've been very interested in talking about detention laws and our neo-police state,' said Travis, once the waiter had left.

'I'm not showing it to you,' said Weston, much more harshly than he had intended. 'Yet,' he added, trying to take the edge off. Too late.

He wondered if that was hurt in her eyes, but she waved it away quickly, lifted a piece of bread and broke it in half. Crumbs sprayed the table.

'So what are you doing tomorrow, then?'

'Going to the club,' said Weston. 'I'm not, you know, I don't have anyone specific to lunch with, but at least....' and he waved a hand.

Travis popped a piece of bread into her mouth and rested her chin in the palm of her hand.

👁

He met Strachan in Hyde Park. A specified bench. They had both thought it ridiculously John Le Carré, but had still made the arrangement.

Weston arrived first. The lunch with Travis had never really recovered. It was a cold afternoon. Crisp. The weathermen were predicting a mild front and rain for Christmas Day. Weston had dug up *Blonde on Blonde*, sat with his overcoat pulled tightly around him. Watching the tourists and the rollerbladers and old women in their Christmas misery walk by.

Strachan was dead on time. His last engagement before retreating to the country for three days. He sat down next to Weston without a word. Looked straight ahead, his eyes locking in on an extremely large couple.

'Would you really have told Mary?' said Strachan. 'That's all I want to know before we start.'

'No,' said Weston. 'I'm sorry, that was just shit. Forgive me.'

'I'll think about it,' said Strachan. 'So, I've given your problem some thought, asked around a bit.'

'But without saying too much,' said Weston.

'When you let me read the book you chose to trust me,' said Strachan. 'Don't question me again.'

Weston nodded. His stomach had not settled since lunch.

'Millhouse can't touch it. You're going to get your balls felt for this, and that's not what we do. The guys upstairs just wouldn't go for it.'

Weston knew that Strachan was one of the guys upstairs.

'I've asked around a bit, but no one's touching this stuff at the moment. Too sensitive, just not worth it. People just want to keep their heads down and come out the other side, happy and secure in their capitalist, safe democracy. That's life, Lake. The cry of the new millennium; what about me? That's all anyone's interested in. Stick your neck out, you just fuck up your life, plain and simple. Like that nurse who demonstrated outside Downing Street yesterday.'

'You heard about that?'

'Only because I've been sticking my big toe into this stuff. Why'd she do it? No one even picked up the story. Her life's down the pan, and for what? That woman must be miserable as fuck, nothing to throw away. Do you think she'd have done it if she'd been in love, had a couple of kids, a decent career?'

He looked at Weston for the first time. Weston caught his eye.

'It's our equivalent of the suicide bomber. Are you prepared to fuck up your life, possibly for no fucking good end whatsoever? Just to be a tiny part in a big picture? So, that's the question. Are you?'

Weston breathed deeply. Did he have that little of a life? He should have it all, of course. He had money and no responsibilities. He could do anything he pleased. He lived a life of wine and women. And so now, was this what he chose to do? Take on the government. Despite all that he had read, he still didn't believe that anything truly bad would come of it. He had written an anti-government polemic, but he still believed that he lived in a safe, democratic society. Despite the laws, despite the surveillance. Despite what had happened to Jack Gilroy.

'You've got two options,' said Strachan, when Weston didn't answer. 'You do it yourself. I'll give you advice, but I'm not getting involved and you need to know how fucking hard that's going to be. I mean, getting it out there. Alternatively, I've been making a few calls. Found a guy who publishes this kind of thing. Got a bit of a network, knows who to talk to. You'll need to pay for the thing, but I presume that's not a problem for you. Course, I don't know how much you'll be able to trust him with your money. You can meet him and decide for yourself.'

'Have you arranged it?' said Weston.

Strachan looked at his watch.

'He's going to be waiting in Starbucks twenty minutes from now. We should get going.'

'I thought you weren't going to get involved?'

'Once,' said Strachan. 'Just this once, to make sure you don't screw up too much. After that you're on your own with this guy.'

'What's his name?'

'Comes from up your way,' said Strachan. 'Morrison. Seems to be a bit of a thing in these circles.'

15

Morrison had smiled wryly when Weston entered the coffee house. Strachan hadn't mentioned the name of the writer to Morrison, but somehow he hadn't been surprised when Lake Weston walked in.

'So, is this book of yours worth the hype,' said Morrison, sipping on his black tea. 'Does it do what it says on the tin, or am I going to read it and think you're a pussy?'

Weston's heart had sunk at the initial mention of Morrison's name. Confidence had yet to recover. He stared across the table, wary of the viciousness of Morrison's tongue.

'I think so,' he said.

'Wonderful,' barked Morrison. 'I hope at least I get to read the thing before you expect me to publish it.'

Strachan, clearly not as intimidated by Morrison's rude exterior, leant forward and pointed a finger.

'Seriously, this book, *Axis of Evil*, is the best goddam fucking book I've ever read in my life. In my life,' he repeated.

'Well that's lovely,' said Morrison. 'Why don't *you* publish it?'

'In this climate?' said Strachan, an air of incredulity in his voice. 'Are you kidding me? This is explosive, you have to read it.'

'Oh, I will.'

'We have shareholders. I would get ripped to shreds if I put it out there. The government would be down on us like so much horse manure you couldn't imagine.'

'So you're looking for me to take the horse manure? I appreciate it.'

'There's a lot of money involved,' said Weston quickly. 'I'll pay for publication, I'll pay you an editor's fee, I'll pay for marketing. I want the book to be cheap and easily available. Everyone should read it.'

'Should they now? Is that the quote you're going to put on the front cover? *Everyone should read this book...The Author*. That'll suck them in. Actually, it probably would. Maybe I'll start using it on my books. *This book is staggeringly brilliant. And I should know, I wrote it...*'

'They said you were an aggressive pain in the arse,' said Strachan.

'Were you speaking to my ex-wives or the police?'

'You have ex-wives? Great, that gives you two something to talk about. You can compare maintenance payments and restraining orders.'

Morrison smirked, Weston glanced sideways at Strachan.

'How soon can you get it out?' said Weston, turning back to Morrison.

Morrison took a moment. Their third meeting, and Weston was still no nearer working the man out. Was he trying to figure out the margins and timescale, or was he just toying with them?

'I'll read it today. Let's say I like it and let's also push the boat out and say that it's not shit and doesn't need to be completely re-written. Over the next couple of days I'd do the proof read, copy edit the thing myself, let's not bring anyone else into it. Get it back to you, you make any changes that are required. We could be done before New Year, if you're prepared to put in a bit of work over the holidays.'

'Sure.'

'You don't need to affirm, I'm taking your enthusiasm for granted. While you're correcting the proof, I'll get a cover put together. In the New Year I can contact the printer, just get all the stuff straight to him if we're ready. They can get it typeset and the proof back to us, that might take a couple of weeks, then they're ready to go. Could have the thing by the last week in January, and then there's no reason why we can't immediately start selling on-line. The bookshops like a longer lead-in time, but if you want to throw money at them, we can get it in shop windows. A lot of money.'

'Not a consideration,' said Weston. 'I mean, not a problem. That seems really fast.'

'Too fast. I don't believe you,' said Strachan.

'Fine,' said Morrison. 'It won't take long to prove me right. If I decide to proceed. You lot are stuck in the slow, grinding machinery of big business. Me? I'm my own man. Show me the manuscript, I'll call you tonight or tomorrow. How long are you down here for?'

Weston shrugged.

'No plans. How about you?'

Morrison looked at his watch.

'Catching the Inverness from Gatwick in two hours fifteen minutes. I need to get going. Give me the manuscript.'

He put his hand out. Weston and Strachan glanced at each other. Weston hesitated. Morrison got to his feet, finished off his tea and stood looking down on the pair of them.

'I get people coming to me all the time with wacko book ideas. Some of them are shit, some of them are OK. Fact is, if I didn't get another one for ten years, I'd still have enough to keep me going. Now I won't deny that you're a bit different. You've got money, you're well known, I'm even prepared to admit that your book might be well written. Despite all that, I don't really care whether or not you give it to me. Your call.'

Weston looked up into the gnarled unshaven face. Hesitating before the big decision. The manuscript was sitting on the table, Weston's forearm resting beside it. Strachan watched the two men, curiously unsure as to which way it would go, as if Weston might suddenly get cold feet at the big moment of decision. Then Morrison leaned forward and lifted the script, opened his small bag and thrust it quickly inside.

'Well, that's that decision taken. I'll be in touch.'

He looked at Weston, nodded at Strachan, then turned quickly and walked out. They watched him go, quick strides, an imperious march across a busy road, as if the road belonged to him and the traffic would know to stop. No one beeped their horn, Morrison was lost in the crowd.

They stared out of the window, feeling that the hurricane had just blown over.

'He's a piece of fucking work,' said Strachan. 'Still, you know what?' He looked round at Weston. 'He was full of shit about how little he cared about it. But he wants it and he wants you. Badly. My friend, it's time for you to start watching your testicles.'

Weston hesitated with his coffee cup halfway to his mouth. He looked over the rim. Strachan started laughing.

'Not that, you stupid prick. Not him. Them. They'll be out to get you. The government.'

Weston closed his eyes and tipped cold coffee down his throat.

16

If anything it all happened even more quickly than Morrison had implied it could, principally because of Morrison's enthusiasm for the cause. His demeanour wasn't entirely an act. He was genuinely misanthropic, he genuinely thought that everyone in the country was being spied upon and shafted by the state, the actions of big government only a precursor to the inevitable and imminent Soviet style clampdown. However, it did not mean that his interest could not be piqued, his passion sparked.

He had been attracted by Weston's money, less so by his name. He already knew that Weston was considering publishing under a pseudonym, and he agreed that this made sense. Lake Weston was the writer of Fenton Bargus, and the public were never going to see past that. This had to be seen as something original and fresh from a first time writer, or perhaps something original and secret from an established political thriller writer or social commentator. Anything but the writer of *Fenton Bargus Takes On Terry & June*. The name of Lake Weston meant nothing.

The main thing, however, the thing that had really grabbed Morrison as he had read the manuscript on the afternoon plane from Gatwick to Inverness on Christmas Eve, had been the quality of the work. Wonderfully written, a bitter and punchy satire. An *Animal Farm* of the age.

And once he realised he had a perfect book on his hands, the money really mattered. The book retailers, the big chains, the distributors, the large publishers, they had the market tied up. Like all such enterprises, and despite all government claims to be looking after small businesses, it was as good as a closed shop. The big money took care of itself.

Morrison, the classic small publisher, had railed against this machine for years. More than two decades. Had started out optimistic and had watched it get worse and worse, the little guy squeezed more and more. But now, at last, he had the right quality of book coupled to a man who could afford for him to walk into every bookshop in the country and pay them the £1,000 or the £25,000 that it would take for them to accept the *Axis of Evil* posters and the *Axis of Evil* book dumps and the *Axis of Evil* window displays.

Up until this point in his publishing career, Morrison had been struggling along at the bottom of the third division. And now, all of a sudden, it was as if Albion Rovers had been granted an automatic place in the Champions League and Roman Abramovich had come in to bankroll them to buy any player they wanted from any league in the world.

Morrison's time was coming.

He pushed the brown envelope across the table. Weston tapped his fingers on it, glancing warily around him. They were in the café at the Culloden Battlefield Visitor Centre, a quiet afternoon in mid-January. A grey day, low cloud, raining out on the firth, the rain sweeping north. Morrison was drinking his seventh cup of tea that day. Weston his third coffee. No cakes, no pastries, nothing frivolous. Just caffeine and work.

'Can I look at it now?' asked Weston.

'What else would you do? Set it on fire and use it to light a cigarette?'

'I never tire of hearing that tone,' said Weston.

He lifted the envelope and slowly pulled out the A4 piece of paper. It was a mock-up of the cover of *Axis of Evil*, front, back, spine. A predominately light grey cover, the trunk of a tree running down the middle, snow covered hills in the background. A grim and sinister eye looked out from the tree, and above it, a bloody claw mark scraped across the bark. *Axis of Evil* was written in plain white type across the tree, and the author's name ran upwards, perpendicular to the title of the book. Robert Johnson.

'Wow,' said Weston. 'Wow,' he added a few seconds later.

'Fuck,' said Morrison. 'You sound like some under-impressed moron on *Changing Rooms* when they've discovered one of those poncey twats has covered their sitting room in flock.'

'Shit, do I?' said Weston. 'I love it, really. It's just kind of weird.'

'What is?'

'You know, usually writers, we get presented with a cover and the publisher says, this is the cover, what do you think? And we say, I think it's shit, and they say, oh, sorry, we thought you'd like it and we've already ordered 100,000 copies so it's too late.'

'And why d'you think I'm any different?'

'I don't know,' said Weston. 'But I'm paying for this. When you called to arrange the meeting you said it was for my approval, and I had a feeling, you know, that this is a genuine two-way thing. I can say no, I'd like something else, and you would.'

'That's nice,' replied Morrison. 'I'm glad you have such a sweet and naïve view of this process. So, do you approve?'

Weston smiled.

'Yes, I do.'

'Wonderful. Now, we need to talk about money for a PR agency. You realise that's how news works these days. None of the papers, none of the agencies, have any journalists anymore. They just pick up PR stories off the wire. It'll cost, but it's a clear way in for us.'

'OK. How much?'

Morrison smiled.

◉

A couple of weeks later, Weston received the e-mail with the proof of the cover of *Fenton Bargus Takes On Beijing Galaxy*. He hated it. He wrote to Strachan to tell him how much he hated it. Strachan wrote back to thank him for his input, but that marketing had done their consumer research and that this cover had proved to have had the greatest impact. He would take Weston's thoughts into consideration for the second print.

It was word for word exactly the same e-mail that Strachan had written to Weston for the three previous books, as well as to numerous other authors. He thought Weston enjoyed it. Weston didn't, but as it happened, for the first time in years, he didn't care.

17

Weston placed the proof copy of the Fenton cover on the table and pushed it across to Travis. She studied the Chinese writing, ticked-off the examples of Chinese culture that littered the cover, from a little red book to a bowl of egg noodles, and smiled.

They were having one of their wine drinking days. Barely after midday, already on to the beginning of their second bottle.

'You hate it?' she asked. 'It seems rather, I don't know...'

'Clichéd, stereotypical, racist and downright ethnically insulting?'

She smiled again. 'You have many Chinese friends, do you?'

'Not at the moment. And by the time this comes out, I'll have no Chinese readers either.'

She lifted the bottle and poured some more wine into his glass.

'So what else is up?' she asked. 'That non-Fenton book you were talking about just before Christmas? Ready to show it to me yet?'

He took a long drink of wine, licked his lips as he laid the glass down. Glad that he was already onto his fourth. Found it easier to lie when he had some alcohol inside him. She had always been able to see through him, just slightly less so when he'd been a bit drunk.

'It's a bust,' he said. 'Strachan was just pulling my pudding, as always.'

'I thought the way you were talking you'd taken it someplace else.'

'Can't,' he said. 'You know I can't, not without their agreement, and they're not ready to do that.' He shrugged casually.

'You need to make threats.'

'Maybe I will, but maybe I need to write something that I truly believe in before I go making threats on its behalf.'

'I thought you had this time.'

He looked steadily into her eyes and then out the window. The weather had turned cold again, the ever-oscillating patterns of winter. It would snow this time, properly. It would lie.

'So, can I read it?' she asked.

'Nope,' he replied firmly, turning back to face her. 'I *Jekyll and Hyded* it.'

'Did you? What does that mean?'

'Threw it on the fire.'

She was looking faintly bemused. 'I love it when I can't understand what it is you're talking about,' she said.

'They say that when Stevenson wrote the first draft of *Jekyll and Hyde* his wife read it and told him it was unprintable, so he threw the manuscript on the fire and started again.'

'Why was it unprintable?'

'Who knows? Because Jekyll was gay? Because it was too terrifying? Because it was shit? Of course, the thing is that Stevenson never mentioned anything about it, and Stevenson was the kind of guy who wrote about everything. *Travels To The Toilet With A Newspaper*, that kind of thing. The guy blogged a hundred and thirty years ahead of his time. But he never mentioned that he'd torched the first draft of *Jekyll and Hyde*. The story didn't appear until after he'd died and his missus mentioned it. So it could just be that it never happened at all and it was a bit of shameless self-promotion on her part.'

'*Hitler, My Part In His Downfall* type syndrome.'

He smiled and laughed. They stared across the table at each other. One of those moments when they wondered why they had let it all go. A few seconds, then she broke the gaze, feeling uncomfortable. She stared out at the cold afternoon. Bleakly romantic Highland hills.

'Anyway, I don't believe you,' she said, not taking her eyes from the view. 'And shouldn't you have said that you'd *Jekyll and Hid* it?'

He laughed again. Ran his hands through his hair, took another drink, followed her gaze. He was looking forward to the snow.

He turned back to her. Time to talk about something else. He had to move the conversation on without it being too obvious, albeit she could see straight through him. However, since his head was so full of *Axis of Evil* – the book, the typeface, the marketing, the cover, the print run, the website – nothing came to mind. And so he hid behind the only other thing that he could think of.

'Lunch?' he said. 'Got some fresh salmon in yesterday.'

Axis of Evil was printed and released with the speed of a biography of a newly dead celebrity. Morrison had irons in many fires, but he put them all aside for a few weeks, realising that he had been given an opportunity that was his to grasp.

In the last week in January, as the snow lay on the hills while the town and cities further south were drenched in neverending rain, posters for *Axis of Evil* appeared in the windows of every bookshop in the country. Two hundred thousand copies of the book were printed and shipped to Morrison's partner distribution company. Publicity bins were paid for, dispatched with the stock, and were up and available in bookshops within ten days of the lead-in posters being hung in the windows. As soon as the books were available, Morrison had full page adverts placed in every daily newspaper.

He loved the *Animal Farm* analogy, but the reputation of *Animal Farm* didn't happen overnight. Even the *Da Vinci Code* did not happen overnight. Books need to be read, their impact digested. It takes time. Morrison was determined *Axis of Evil* would transcend the conventions.

He took advantage of a slow month and threw everything at it that Weston's money would allow him to throw. A media blitz. The advertising equivalent of shock and awe. He had the PR company invent a couple of stories of government disdain for the book. A few fabricated or manipulated quotes, a completely made up story of the Home Secretary's outrage, all released to the wires as news. No one had time to check anymore.

Axis of Evil had hit the book shelves and everyone knew about it.

18

News-wise January wasn't as dead as Morrison would have liked it to have been. There was a trial of a man accused of brutally murdering an entire household. Five dead. It had race, it had blood, it had screams in the night. Like all the best crime stories, it had been news at the time, now it was news again ten months later. There was a celebrity Hollywood overdose which had ended with a tragic death. A run on one of the Scottish banks, fuelling anti-Scottish feeling among the English due to the fact that Westminster was bailing them out, combined with anti-English feeling from the Scots who blamed Westminster for the problem in the first place. House prices were finally crashing in the way the Daily Mail had been predicting for three years. Flooding in Gloucestershire and Somerset, sea walls breached in Norfolk. A missing child in Luton, which turned out not to be particularly newsworthy after all when the child turned up the next day. And according to the Daily Express, Princess Diana, apparently, was still dead.

Morrison charged in on his high horse, upset by it all, annoyed that the things that should have been at the top of the news were being ignored, or were fitted in between LA overdoses and tabloid murder.

He would also have liked the government to have been on the ropes, but the Scottish bank collapse aside there was little going on; or, at least, little that the opposition parties and the media wanted to talk about.

Morrison was enraged by the many millions of the taxpayers' money given to consultants, but no political party would ever stand up and demand an end to it. He believed that everyone scratched everyone else's back, and there was barely a piece of government policy that was not tied to and promoted by business.

It had become illegal to take your children out of school during term time. It seemed reasonable. But then it forced parents to take their holidays at peak times, when the prices were fixed high. The government had done something about children missing school, but they had done nothing about the parents then being ripped off by the travel companies. Because, Morrison believed, the legislation had been carried out with the connivance and encouragement of the travel companies. They were all in it together.

There were many other examples, and Morrison hated that the news every day was not dominated by these blatant examples of government corruption. Once *Axis of Evil* was out there and being talked about, it might be time for him to get to discussions with Weston about the follow-up, and government corruption would be the perfect place to start.

On-line orders had already begun, but the first bookshop copy of *Axis of Evil* was sold at two and a half minutes past seven o'clock on the morning of 31st January at the WH Smith in Victoria Station. And that day, as the shelves filled up, the books began to sell. No one had heard of the author, no one really knew what the book was about, but it was new, it was mysterious, and it was everywhere.

Lake Weston sat at home that day waiting for the phone to ring. He wasn't sure what he was expecting. That someone would read the first page and say, 'The writer's not some character called Johnson, that's Lake Weston that is! Fenton Bargus by any other name!'

He flitted between TV channels, flicked between BBC Radio 4, Radio 5 and Radio Scotland. Even tried Northsound.

Drank wine, became restless but didn't want to go out. Spent a long time standing at the window, looking out at the white hills. Some of the deer had come down and they milled around awkwardly in the snow, in the way that deer do, as if constantly waiting for something to happen.

He remembered the first time that Fenton had been mentioned on the radio. Driving home from the office, late afternoon, when being a full-time writer had still been a dream. It hadn't been a feature, just a passing comment by a presenter about what his kids were reading at that time. *Fenton Bargus Takes On The World*, by Lake Weston. The guy had been condescending and made some joke about Weston's name.

But that had been it, right there, driving along the A303 in the dark. Lake Weston had known. He had a future at this game, and the future was Fenton Bargus. And over the years, like everyone who gets what they want, he had begun to see that future as a curse.

The phone didn't ring all day. Apart from Penny, who wasn't calling to discuss the new anti-government thriller that was sweeping the country.

She was back to calling most days, even though she was now living with Maurice. She always had a reason, usually some manufactured worry about her teenage sons. That day she was concerned about whether they were masturbating and wanted Weston to give them some advice. Weston had given her the full benefit of his impatience and stress.

When it came, he nearly missed it. Fetching his third bottle of white wine from the fridge. He had been drinking non-stop since not long before lunchtime. Felt lousy. The house was untidy and stuffy. Dylan had been playing all day. On random, yet an endless stream of 80's drivel. It had been annoying him, but the inertia had gripped him more and more as the day had dragged on. An uncomfortable in his skin day, lost in fug, too much noise. The television and the radio and Bob all fighting each other. He needed space and fresh air and cool, clear water. But he was bogged down in mental sludge, crippled for the day by his addictions and the stresses of a new book that he had ploughed so much nervous energy and so much money into. Ridiculed or rubbished, castigated or scorned. Or worse, completely ignored.

He walked back into the sitting room, a midden of strewn newspapers and empty bottles, to hear Morrison's voice. Took a second or two to filter, then suddenly Weston was a great flurry of fumbling activity. Bob off, TV off, glass hastily put down, wine spilling to add to the mess.

'They're saying this is an *Animal Farm* of the age,' said the presenter. Weston smiled. 'But are you really saying that this government is on a par with the old-style Soviets? People make jokes about the Prime Minister, but seriously, Stalin killed twenty million of his own people.'

'Well, Alan,' said Morrison, 'if you want to sit back and watch while the government strips you of your soul, then on you go. Bank details, phone details available to over a thousand agencies, police with powers to impound private property indefinitely, police with powers to use tasers, a government that seeks to instil fear in the populace...'

'That's because people keep exploding bombs in the capital!' ejaculated Alan, the mild-mannered host. Weston smiled again. Morrison was capable of getting up anyone's nose.

'Maybe they do,' said Morrison, then darkly added, 'maybe they don't. But given that the government executes a foreign policy specifically intended to incite hatred and ethnic violence at home, can any of us be surprised if there are terrorists? We invade sovereign states, people react here at home in protest, violent or otherwise against the government, and then they say, told you there were terrorists. And it's funny...'

'I think we need to get back onto this book which you published today, *Axis of Evil*,' said Alan, cutting Morrison off. 'It seems to me in any case that it's more *1984* than *Animal Farm*?'

'Come on, Alan,' said Morrison, conversationally, 'we've been in the business long enough. It's all marketing. Is it like *1984*? Yes, it is. But you know what, the people already know we're in a *1984* situation. They already know Big Brother is watching. This goes beyond that. This is about how all these well-meaning public school fools pitch up in power full of good intentions, and before they know it, they have an armed guard, a chip on their shoulder and they don't want to hear any word of criticism from ordinary people because they suddenly think that that ordinary person is going to try and shove a bomb up their…'

'And who is Robert Johnson?' broke in Alan. Fingers twitching on the cut-off button.

'It's an author who prefers to remain anonymous for the moment.'

'A published author? Of our times? You mean, like Ian McEwan or Zadie Smith?'

'Yeah, like Ian McEwan or Zadie Smith.'

'Are there clues in the book as to who this author might be?'

Weston's stomach was churning, but he knew that if Morrison ever cracked, it would be later, when all possible advantage had been gained by anonymity and there remained only gain to be had by the reveal.

'Why don't you take a look?'

'And why has the writer chosen to be anonymous? Cowardice? Lack of faith in the material? Or is it just some pointless marketing plan?'

'Fucker!' barked Weston at the radio, leaning forward, taking a guzzle of wine. 'Don't let him away with that,' he growled, talking over the start of Morrison's reply.

'...and you're going to have to read the book closely before rushing to that kind of judgement. This is a dangerous government we're dealing with. They don't like this kind of thing. Who knows what they'll do.'

'Come after you?'

'Sure, they probably will. They can try.'

'The book breaks the law? If it breaks the law...'

'You know how many laws there are now, Alan?' said Morrison, raising his voice for the first time. 'Given that you can't read out a list of names at the cenotaph, given that you can't wear a t-shirt with a slogan embossed on it in the vicinity of Downing Street, given that you can't heckle a government minister, given that you can't organise a peaceful march virtually anywhere in the country, given that...'

Finally, with the nod from his editor, Alan flicked the switch. Morrison was gone.

'We have to leave it there,' he said quickly. 'That was Richard Morrison, publisher of the book *Axis of Evil*, which we may or may not be hearing more about in the next few days.'

A short radio pause, then the female co-presenter came in.

'And now back to the story of the man in Hammersmith who fell into a diabetic coma on the train and who awoke in a police van an hour later to find that he'd been tasered for failing to respond to police questions...'

'Holy fuck!' barked Weston at the radio.

Thereafter he started hearing the odd mention of the book. He went on-line to see if anything was happening, found a couple of passing references. Checked its Amazon ranking, the first refuge of the desperate author. The first time he'd looked it had been outside the top two thousand. By late evening it had charged into the top twenty.

Mid-evening, into his fourth bottle of wine. Felt tired and lousy, drunk with alcohol and nervous exhaustion. Had reverted to Dylan, mid-60's, comfort music. But even that sounded sickly, just another unnecessary noise in amongst the jumble. He needed a long night's sleep, a walk across the snowy hills in the morning, breakfast. He received three texts. One from Strachan congratulating him on the book launch and the way in which Morrison had managed to inflict it on the consciousness of the public. The second was from Penny, which he deleted without reading. The other was from Morrison telling him that he'd been invited onto that evening's Newsnight.

Weston looked at his watch. An hour and a half to go. He settled down in front of the television to wait, glass at his mouth, fingers on the remote, endlessly flicking between channels.

19

Paxman was in fine form. Vicious. He'd read the book that evening, he'd managed to get the Justice Secretary on to the show at the same time as Morrison, while telling neither man beforehand that they would be up against someone. Morrison had been delighted. The Minister had threatened to walk out, but his people had talked with Paxman's people, after which they had advised the Minister to do the show.

Morrison didn't have any people.

'Of course people have the right to protest,' said the Minister. 'We're a democracy, that's what democracy is. As long as the protest is peaceful and within the letter of the law.'

Morrison barked out a derisive laugh.

'What about the five students holding placards in Hyde Park protesting the continuing action in Afghanistan?' said Paxman.

Morrison had had another example on the tip of his tongue, but that one worked just as well.

'The police at the time judged that they posed a threat to the security of the public in the park.'

'Five students holding placards?' said Paxman. 'And a dog. Even the Chief Constable admitted that his men had been heavy-handed.'

The minister made a small gesture with his hands, as if that cleared everything up and it should be the end of the matter.

'Would you rather the police were lenient and people died, or that they were over-cautious and lives were saved?'

'Oh my God!' said Morrison. 'To hear this kind of justification in public is staggering. No one was going to die in that situation! And this is the kind of heavy-handed police tactics which we are seeing *every day*.

Every day. And always they hide behind this excuse, this thing that it's all for the sake of the public.'

'And isn't it?' said Paxman.

The minister looked like a man who, if he had been able to pull out a gun and blast Morrison's head into a bloody mess right there live on TV, would have done it. Off-set one of his people saw the look on his face, then walked into his line of vision and indicated a big smiley face. The viewer, if they'd been paying attention, only saw the relaxing of the tension in the Minister's face, the fidgeting of the corners of his mouth.

'We're supposed to be living in a free country,' said Morrison. 'With that comes good and bad, I accept that. How much street crime was there in the old Soviet Union? You know how much? Virtually none. It was almost non-existent. But that was because of the State apparatus, that was because they lived in a police state, where anyone who did anything, *anything* slightly out of the ordinary, was followed, investigated, crushed. Is that the kind of society we want to live in, because that is what this government wants? But if you address the real needs of society, then crime will fall without all this absurd…'

The picture went blank for a millisecond and then Weston was looking at a small man in a dead studio, away from the electric atmosphere of the studio in London.

'And welcome to Newsnight Scotland,' said the presenter, 'and thanks for joining us. Tonight we consider the latest moves by Donald Trump to build a multi-billion pound golf centre and housing...'

Weston threw his glass at the television, it hit the screen full on. The glass smashed, wine sprayed. The television screen remained unscathed.

The Prime Minister made a point of never watching Newsnight, specifically because he knew that Paxman and the BBC would want him to watch it. However, he had decided that he would take a look at the last ever episode, an event that wasn't going to be too far off. Paxman didn't know it yet. The controller of BBC2 didn't know it yet. But it was coming soon, and all that was left was whether pressure and incentives would be applied at the top, or whether the political will would be found from within his party to take the show off the air, considering the myriad laws which its subversive content now contravened on a nightly basis.

There was a knock at the door. The Prime Minister closed the last red box of the day, pushing it across the crowded desk. Another small stack of papers fell onto the floor, and he sighed heavily and sat back.

A lifetime of political service, and for what?

'All this crap,' he muttered.

The door opened, his nominal Chief of Staff, Marcus Bleacher, walked into the room. Long day, looking dishevelled. He closed the door behind him.
'Anything else?' said the PM.
'One more thing.'
Bleacher held up a copy of *Axis of Evil*. The PM looked at the eye in the tree, the snow on the hills. Too tired to think anything.
'If you're about to suggest some light reading to get me off to sleep...'
'You need to read this. They're saying it's the new *Animal Farm*.'
'A short book about pigs?' said the PM gruffly.
'They're saying that it does to this administration what *Animal Farm* did to the Soviet bloc.'
'And what was that, other than give fuel to the fire of the Cold War? Six generations of school children were fed Western anti-Communist propaganda under the guise of literature study. Did *Animal Farm* bring down the Berlin Wall, or was that politics and the forces of capitalism?'
'You should read it,' said Bleacher. 'The writer is anonymous, the publisher has just been on Newsnight. We've already started taking calls, the press are getting interested. We need a strategy.'
'Who's saying it's the new *Animal Farm*?'
'Well, the publisher for a kick-off. But whoever he is, because he just seems to be a small-time conspiracy theorist from the Black Isle, he's got plenty of money behind him. The book is everywhere. It's short, pointed. Brilliant as well, I must admit. If you got stuck on the tube for half an hour longer than normal this evening – and it's not like that never happens – chances are you'd have finished it by the time you got home. And the press are buying into the *Animal Farm* analogy. Personally I reckon it's more *1984*, but what do I know?'
He placed the book on the desk. The PM looked down at it, not wanting to touch the evidence in case it pinned him to the scene of the crime.
'We need a strategy,' said Bleacher again.
'Fine, I'll read it,' said the PM. 'What do we do?'
'Edwards and I have just brainstormed it. We can sit it out, let it pass. We could discredit the publisher, find the writer and do the same. If he's a solid character, then we get to work. Or we go in with the heavy artillery and wipe it off the map. There's enough in there to ban the book, ban the reading of the book, arrest the publisher, find the writer, send him to Belmarsh. Piece of cake. But then we leave ourselves open to the kind of accusations that he talks about here, so we need to be prepared. But it probably blows over at some point, and we apply the usual pressures to make sure that no one keeps the story going.'

The PM tapped his forefinger on the book as if finally acknowledging its existence and the problems that it was about to introduce into his life.
'I'll read it tonight,' he said firmly. 'Let me do that, we'll see what the press are saying tomorrow. And find me the author. It better not be someone that we've knighted recently or I'll take the bloody medal back and stick it up…' He let the sentence go.
Bleacher nodded and turned away, opening the door.
'And find out where the money's coming from.'
'I'll get a check run on his bank account right away.'
'That's the thing with this kind of thing,' said the PM. 'It looks like it's your country turning against you, people rising up in complaint, but you know what, it'll probably turn out to be funded by Al Qaeda, just wait and see. That's how this kind of thing works. They want you to think the electorate are turning against you, but it's all a plot.'
'Yes, Prime Minister,' said Bleacher, as he opened the door and walked back through to the outer office.

The press weren't slow to react, but neither did they jump all over it. Most editors were cagey about just how much of a story it was, waiting to see what the others were doing. They wanted two or three of their people to read it before jumping to any kind of editorial stance. Too wary of being hoodwinked by some charlatan conspiracy theorist with money to back him up and nothing else. Wanting to know that it was a book for the times, and not just any old piece of crap literature.
That night it wasn't just the Prime Minister sitting up late to read *Axis of Evil*. The wolves were out and they were biting.

20

The following morning Weston dragged himself out of bed a little after eight. Downstairs, television on, nervous and expectant. Flicked through five news channels, couldn't find a mention in the first few minutes, retreated. The government were announcing plans to build seventeen new hospitals in England and Wales. A major change in the organisation of the Health Service. *Strategic Health Care For All* was the mundane hookline of the document which the Prime Minister would be proudly launching at three o'clock that afternoon.

Bleacher had drawn up the idea for the health document at a little after two in the morning, as a way of making sure there would be something positive from the government on the news. He had seen the front page of the Independent, the only one of the majors which had decided to lead with the *Axis of Evil* story; he'd talked to some of the other editors, had seen the stories in the inside pages, read the review which the Times had rushed through, and recognised that there was trouble brewing.

There are contingency plans for such situations, but this instance called for one that bathed the government in a very positive light. No point in one of their failed terror plots or embarrassing revelations about the opposition or Royal family.

Each government department had a document intended for such situations, where Number 10 could be seen to be making a strategic re-launch, which in fact amounted to nothing more than repackaging money and announcements and deals which were already in existence. The trick, as always, was in the confidence of the delivery, the balls and the showmanship, and, Bleacher often thought, how many times you managed to cram the word *strategic* into the whole thing.

The beauty of the announcements was that they carried the same weight as a false claim against a celebrity. It was the initial story that was the thing. No one was ever interested in the truth, no one was interested in the banal explanation behind the sensationalism. The banner headline was all that mattered

Bleacher called the Minister for Health at 2:17am and announced the Code Yellow. The Minister had then awoken as many of his people in the middle of the night as was required to make sure that the Code Yellow was in place for the morning news and that everything would be in order for the mid-afternoon press conference.

This was exactly the kind of thing which Weston had put in *Axis of Evil*, but turning off the television and stumbling back up the stairs to the shower, the inside of his mouth stale and bitter, he didn't have the clear-headed thought to consider this. Had he left the television on for a minute longer, he would have seen the words *Axis of Evil* blazoned in enormous print on the cover of the Independent.

Instead he stepped into the shower, resolving to have a day far removed from the previous one, which had been spent in abject poverty of spirit, soaked in wine, sitting amidst expensive squalor.

Ten minutes under the water, the last two with the hot tap turned off, under the blazing and stinging cold. Cleaned his teeth, gargled twice with mouthwash, dressed for the great outdoors, drank two large glasses of water, took three headache tablets, popped an apple in his pocket, pulled on his walking boots, and stepped out into the cold of a snowy, bleak bitter day in the Highlands.

Realised five minutes up the hill that he had left his phone in the house. Stopped, looked back down the glen at the meandering path of his footprints, and decided that he needed the complete break. Clear head. No alcohol, no news, no human contact. No Dylan.

And only the presence of an iPod in his pocket would test his resolve of any of those.

◉

It had begun. *Axis of Evil* was news. Metro and the Standard followed with reviews on that second day, the others lining up for the day after. The Times had led with the opinion, and the others would follow suit: whoever it was who had first said that *Axis of Evil* was the new *Animal Farm* – and no one knew who that was – had been dead on the mark.

'*A breathtaking novel which fires a nuclear weapon at the heart of duplicitous government...*' the Times had written, in a review full of lines which could be culled and put on the cover of the second edition. Morrison had even smiled when he'd read it.

◉

Morrison had known all along that they needed the media on their side. The Opposition were never going to join in the fight, as they were more or less in bed with the government. To him, neither side really cared who was in power. They had their expense accounts, their London apartments, their homes in the country, their advisory roles with big business, and it didn't matter which side of the house they actually sat on. No one believed for a second that, if the Opposition ever got back into power, they would dismantle the state apparatus which all previous governments had assembled.

They needed the media, and thanks to the money which Weston had thrown at the project, while the Opposition were sitting uncomfortably on their hands, the media were piling in on their side in droves.

Sometime during the morning the momentum had begun to build on the question of who the author might be. Morrison fielded all the calls he could, developing a nice line in intrigue, ruling no one out, playing on the fact that the media loves a mystery.

When it became clear to the news editors across the media board that everyone was after the same thing, the rush became a stampede. Authors and publishers, agents and editors were all given the call. Non-stop, all day.

Somehow, though, no one imagined that the writer would be a children's author, even a hip, trendy, fêted children's author like Lake Weston. There were a few calls sent in the direction of Eldon Strachan, but mostly the work went the way of Bloomsbury and Harper and TimeWarner and Headline, the hacks desperately wanting the writer to be some grandee of the business, to give the work even more gravitas than it already had.

Strachan had been ready for it, and had simply and angrily denied that it had been the work of any of his authors. He found that the phrase 'Would you bunch of wankers just fuck off?' more or less did the trick of covering up his awkwardness at the lie.

21

Weston walked up over the first ridge, down into the next glen, up to the top of the next ridge. The walk was gorgeous. A clear, bright, beautiful day. Snow stretching for miles, the contours of the hills lost in the blaze of white. The deer stood out starkly. He stumbled across a capercailzie mincing through the heather. Two eagles circled high overhead.

He had lost the nerves of the previous day, had begun to think about the future. If his identity wasn't discovered, did he come out of the woodwork at some point? Did he write his follow-up? Did he kill off Fenton? *Fenton Bargus Takes On Malarial Meningitis*. Or did he just walk away from it all? Do that thing which he had so often thought about, take himself off around the world? He had the money, he had the freedom.

By the time he'd reached the second ridge, a couple of hours had passed, he had eaten his apple, he was hungry and he was listening to *Desolation Row*. He was always capable of lasting longer without food and alcohol than he was without Dylan.

He stood at the top of the ridge and looked down at the small village below, picturesque in the snow. A few houses, the primary school, a farm at either end, the shop on the single lane road running through the village, the small hotel, The Highland Arms, where he knew he would get as good a lunch as he would anywhere in the north. A large herd of deer lingered in the field to the left of the village.

Weston removed his earphones and thrust them into his pocket. Turned off the music. Listened to the stillness. A slight wind against his ears, nothing else. He could see a yellow car driving silently much further up the glen. A bird of prey sat on a fence post away down the hill. The cold nipped his skin, a cold that he could smell. The torpor of the previous day had been completely banished. He felt alive and awake, filled with enthusiasm and determination.

He suddenly felt like running down the hill and diving headfirst into the snow. Or cartwheeling. Zorbing. He felt like Fred A-fucking-staire, felt like he could go dancing down the hill, then pirouette into the hotel restaurant, a huge smile on his face, and order venison steak and the coldest, coolest glass of fresh water they could get him. No alcohol, no drugs, no crap to screw up his head.

He smiled at the thought that at any moment he was about to burst into *The Sound of Music* and there was nothing he could do about it, and then he started walking briskly down the hill, his boots stepping in fresh snow.

The hotel lobby smelled wonderful. Warm and smoky from the fire, thick red carpet, paintings of hillsides and deer and rivers on the walls. There were two armchairs sitting beside the fire, a copy of that day's Scotsman on the table. He waited to see if anyone was going to appear, and then walked over to the table and lifted the paper. *Axis of Evil* had not deserted his head, but it had been pushed back under the weight of the glorious scenery, the clean air. He had managed to escape the obsession of the previous day, the compulsive neurosis that had stapled him to the seat in front of the television for the entire day.

The Scotsman led with a story about the number of Scottish soldiers who had now been killed in Afghanistan, with three other cover stories beneath it. A fatal car accident on the A9 near Dunkeld; further questions over illegal campaign payments to the latest leader of the Scottish Labour party; and a small, cagey story with the headline, *Maverick Scottish Publisher Takes on Westminster*.

Weston's heart gave a small skip. He quickly scanned the story, wondering if he was going to come across his own name buried in the mix. Two paragraphs on the front page, continued on page six. He opened the paper as footsteps padded into the lobby.

'Hi there,' said the woman in an apron, standing in the doorway.

Weston quickly looked over the rest of the story. No mention of him, no photographs, just an image of the book cover. He looked up.

The woman was in her twenties, stunningly attractive. Her words finally filtered in and he realised she was American.

'Hi,' he said. 'Sorry, just looking at the paper.'

'That's all right. You have a reservation?'

'No, no. I was just wondering if I could get lunch?'

'Of course. Through here, if you just want to give me your jacket. We're not exactly busy today.'

He smiled and walked forward, undoing the buttons on his coat. Felt a further sense of elation at the fact that his book had already made the front pages of a Scottish broadsheet.

'It's cold out,' said the woman, and Weston smiled and thought, Canadian, not American.

The snow started again while he sat at the window of the restaurant looking out at the cold hills. Chicken soup to start, then the venison steak he had been thinking about as he'd walked down the hill. The menu had been refreshingly bereft of persillade and rouille and extravagant descriptions to cover up plain food. A basic, wonderful Scottish Highland menu, with no need for exaggeration or embellishment. He thought he could just sit there all day, although at some point between the venison steak and the apple pie, he realised that he was going to have to get a move on very soon if he was going to get home before darkness fell. And for the first time in several hours he began to feel flat and lonely, solely at the thought of walking back into the house, the living room still a mess of empty glasses and bottles, the air still stagnant with worry and stress, the television sitting in the corner demanding his attention.

22

Bleacher's plan had worked for a few hours, but momentum had begun to build. Everyone wanted to be the one who unearthed the author's identity. If the writer had been known straight from the off, he would have been on all the shows going for the day, on the sofas and the soft chairs, but as a punchy news story it would have been without legs. The mystery of the writer's identity added another level of intrigue, and while every news editor in London implored his people to unearth the author of *Axis of Evil*, most hoped that neither they nor anyone else would find out for several days, and the story could build.

The Prime Minister looked in the mirror, brushing imaginary dust from his lapel. Dark blue, sombre pin-stripe. Smiled broadly, checking his teeth. Closed his lips, the face relaxed. Bleacher walked in behind him.

'We're on,' he said.

The Prime Minister turned.

'This is going to work?' he asked. 'I'm going to be pissed off if they start asking questions about that damned book.'

'I...you know, I can't guarantee that. But you're prepped if it happens.'

'We know who it is yet?'

'We think so. We'll talk about it after you get through this. And we've also had a couple of people at Justice going through the thing, and it looks like we'll be able to move pretty quickly.'

The PM turned away from the mirror and looked directly at Bleacher. He narrowed his eyes and then smiled slowly.

'Good,' he said simply. 'Come on.'

He walked quickly out behind Bleacher, remembering to straighten his shoulders and stand two inches taller as he went.

'But Prime Minister, is there actually anything new at all in these proposals?' asked the man from Sky.

The PM placed his hands on the lectern. Firm jaw, expletives kept in his head. He would be having a word with the media magnate's representatives some time soon. He was getting fed up with this guy.

'Listen,' he said, and Bleacher stared at the floor behind the PM, 'real government is not about flashy announcements. We are here to let the British people know what we're about and where we're going with the major issues. The British people need to know that they can trust their Health Service. This is why we're here today at this wonderful hospital, a shining example of what the future holds for the British people in health care terms.'

He pointed his finger at the next journalist. ITN. The words had tripped easily off his tongue, the effort as always just in making sure he didn't complete his sentences with the words, 'All right, you bastard?'

A recent report on the hospital in which he stood had indicated that it was indeed a beautiful building. It had also noted that the main beneficiaries of the project would be the American company who had built the hospital and who would be raking in millions from the taxpayer for decades, that the deal had not even benefited the government in the short term, and that a non-PFI build would have given the taxpayer a saving of 76.8%. The PM was ready for the question, but the pack was keen to move on.

'This was all organised in a bit of a rush, Prime Minister...'

'A lack of communication at the Department of Health,' said the PM quickly, nodding at the Health Minister standing behind him to his left.

'So this has nothing to do with trying to detract from the *Animal Farm* story which has been building all day?'

The PM gripped the lectern. The Health Minister stared at him, head bowed, eyes raised. One photographer managed to get a beautifully demonic shot of the man, an instance of hatred and loathing, the red of the lectern briefly reflected in his eyes. The following day no editor chose to use the picture, as the story wasn't about the Health Minister. 'Get me one of those of the PM!' someone barked at him.

'I'm sure that will be addressed by this government at some point in the very near future, but we did not come all this way to this outstanding medical facility, which represents wonderful value for the taxpayer, to discuss literature of any sort. I'm sure the British people are far happier to know that their Prime Minister is striving for the things that are important to them – better health care, greater opportunities for children, better policing.'

'So have you read the book, Prime Minister?'
Bleacher looked warily at the PM. He could bluster and he could fudge and he could waffle like all the best politicians, but when asked a straightforward yes or no question which didn't stand elaboration, it was always very obvious when he was lying. *Don't say no*, thought Bleacher. They can tell.
'One of the things which struck me as being so impressive, as I toured this new facility, was the optimism of patients and the overall feeling of wellness. I think it shows a new optimism in the country and in the British people, that they have confidence in their government and optimism in this government's ability to change Britain for the better.'
Bleacher stared at the PM from one hundred and thirty-five degrees. To completely ignore the question and to use the word *optimism* three times in the answer was slightly incriminating. But at least it was on-message. If you said *optimism* often enough, someone would have to put it in print at some point, the public would eventually feel optimistic and would keep spending money and keep voting for the party which induced such positive feelings for the future.
'Did you read the book, Prime Minister?' asked another voice.
The PM looked down at the woman, full eye contact. Flinched a little and stared over the pack.
'No,' he lied, 'I didn't read the book. And I have no intention of reading the book. Now, I'd like to talk about the new Accident & Emergency Ward which opened last week, and which I hope you all had the chance to tour this morning...'

23

The snow continued to fall, Weston stayed rooted to his seat. Too warm, too comfortable to go anywhere. There had been a few others in the dining room, now he was alone. He sat with his chin in his hand staring out at the road. There had not been a car passed in fifteen minutes, the snow was lying more thickly.

The fire in the dining room cracked and fizzled, warm soporific noises of winter. Weston's brain atrophied in the narcotic laziness of the afternoon. While his enemies marshalled their forces, he did nothing. He had launched his missile and now he sat back, unsure if they would respond, not knowing if his enemy even knew who it was who had fired upon them. And so he did nothing while the forces of darkness gathered unopposed.

The waitress returned to the room with the credit card machine and lifted Weston's card from the edge of the table.

'What are you going to do?' she asked, looking out at the snow. They had discussed the weather intermittently over lunch.

'Not sure,' he said. 'D'you think I'd get a taxi up here?'

'Think you're screwed,' she said.

He looked at his watch, then back out at the dying of the day.

'We have a room,' she said. 'Quite a few as a matter of fact.'

The receipt juddered out of the machine. He met her eyes.

'You're probably good until about the middle of July actually,' she said, smiling. 'We can launder your clothes overnight, give you a toothbrush.'

Weston returned the smile. 'Sure,' he said, 'that sounds great.'

He had been wanting to ask. She handed him his card and receipt.

'Well, come through when you're ready and we'll get you sorted out, Mr Weston.'

She smiled again, lifted his empty coffee cup and then turned and walked out the room. He watched her go, the black cotton of her skirt swaying in the winter warmth.

The snow fell, carried on the wind whistling down the glen. The deer huddled in groups in a cold winter field.

◈

The PM stood at the window, looking down on Downing Street. He could remember the days when the public had been able to walk along this road. Innocent times, dangerous days. Everything had been painted in comfortable shades of grey, unlike these dark days when it was all black and white.

Bleacher was standing behind him waiting for an answer to his question regarding the briefing the PM had to read before meeting the President of Pakistan in a little over half an hour. Finally the PM turned.

'We need to talk about the book first.'

'We wasted the NHS announcement,' said Bleacher bluntly.

'I know,' said the PM, 'we need to discover whose fault that was.'

Bleacher stared at the floor.

'You know who wrote the book?' he asked sharply.

'Yes,' said Bleacher, glancing at his notes. He'd been told, but he didn't like the answer, so he had brought along another messenger.

'There's someone from MI5 outside waiting to speak to you, Prime Minister. But I thought maybe it could wait until after...'

'Bring him in,' said the PM gruffly.

Bleacher hesitated, then walked quickly to the door, opened it, leant through and summoned someone silently with a quick jerk of the thumb.

The PM stared out of the window, the office door closed again. Sometimes he wondered if it was worth the effort. Sometimes he wondered if the country deserved him.

'Speak to me,' he said gravely.

'Prime Minister, we think the book was written by a children's author named Lake Weston,' said the MI5 representative.

The PM turned at the sound of the young woman's voice. She was in her late twenties, blonde hair newly cut in a short bob.

'You probably know his name from the Fenton Bargus series.'

The PM grunted. 'I met him a few years ago. Something we did on promoting children's literature. In Edinburgh, before the Festival.'

The MI5 agent looked blank. Bleacher had long ago stopped being surprised by his boss's total recall.

'You're sure it's him? I read this book. It felt more like it had come from a serious political writer. One of those people who sees himself as a social commentator. As if that's what the country needs.'
'We already had intel on him. The book has been published by a man named Morrison...'
'I heard that bastard on the radio this morning.'
'Given the nature of his enterprise, the pamphlets and books which he releases, we've been keeping an eye on him for some time. Weston has met with the man four times since the middle of November. On the third of January, Weston made a transfer of two point seven million pounds into the account of the Dingwall Press.'
'Which explains where the book's advertising budget came from...,' said Bleacher, chipping in.
'Why wasn't Morrison already off the streets?' said the PM.
'Judgement call,' said MI5. 'It would've been a thin conviction, he would've been back on the streets soon enough, and he'd have had even more of a gripe. Better to leave him out there and keep an eye on him.'
'It sounds circumstantial. Maybe they're friends. Maybe Weston wants to support the man in his work. We still need to look at him for handing over the money, but it's not the same as him writing the book. When we do this, it needs to be the right person. I don't want any fuck-ups.'
'There's software we use, pretty old hat. You throw in a passage or two of the work you want to check, and then you input work from known writers, and the software will throw up the closest match in terms of sentence structure, frequent use of various words and phrases etc. It can take time for it to work, particularly in a case like this where you're dealing with the potential for it to have been done by any one of about a hundred thousand people in the country.'
The PM breathed out heavily, Bleacher stared at the carpet. He hadn't had time for the *keep it brief* speech.
'In this case, there was no need to check thousands. Given the other intelligence we had at our disposal, and given that we already thought Morrison and Weston were working together, Weston was the first one we tried. Came back as a 98% probability.'
The PM stared at her, an intense gaze, burrowing through her head.
'So we're pretty certain, sir,' she said, unable to stop herself from saying anything further.
'OK, thank you. Wait outside,' he added, and then turned away and walked to his desk, slumped down into the black chair.
She looked at Bleacher who indicated the door with his eyes and she nodded and quickly left the room, closing the door behind her.

The PM raised his hands in a gesture of hopelessness.
'So, what?' he said. 'Taken to the cleaners by some kid's author. You really think it's this guy? What's his motivation?'
Bleacher coughed, stared at the floor.
'He wrote a book in his series which made fun of the office of Prime Minister. The PM figure was kind of a cross between you and Blair. Well, to be honest, it was a cross between you, Blair, Saddam and Winnie the Pooh.'
'Enough commentary. What happened?'
'We leant on his publisher through one of our people. Made sure it didn't happen. To be honest, the legislation is so tight these days we could have prosecuted, but we tried not to threaten that route. Didn't need to in the end, they were pretty happy to go along with it. It looks like the author wasn't quite so enthusiastic to toe the line.'
The PM tapped his forefinger on the desk. Irritated. Thinking.
'The President of Pakistan?' suggested Bleacher gently, looking at the clock. They had lost the opportunity for decent preparation.
'The press don't have this yet?' asked the PM.
'No, sir. They will have the software, and presumably the intelligence to run the same checks as MI5, but they'll be starting from a position of cluelessness and so will by necessity take much longer to find out.'
The PM nodded, slapped his hands on the desk with a gesture of some decisiveness and then stood up quickly.
'I want an action plan by 8pm. You take the next four hours out to think about it. Get some people together, hang on to that spook that was just in here. Has she got a name?'
'Probably.'
'Who did the work on the Pakistan briefing?'
'Shelley.'
'Get him for me. You get to work on Weston.'

Weston took a walk in the snow. Walking off lunch, knowing that there would be little else to do in the evening except repeat the experience in the warm cosiness of the dining room. Beginning to feel detached. Had felt the freedom of escape that morning, but now, nine hours later, was beginning to miss his phone, couldn't help wondering how many calls he had missed.
He wanted to call Morrison, but his number was in Weston's cell phone not in his head. A call to Strachan wasn't out of the question, but the chances of the man still being in the office past five o'clock, which it would be by the time he returned to the hotel, were nil. Like so many

other things in modern life, the convenience and simplicity of the mobile phone was also its curse. He knew virtually no one's number.

He kept to the road, walking back down the glen for half an hour, before turning back and trudging into the teeth of the blizzard. Just Bob for company, although the charge on his iPod had started to go and he knew that he wouldn't have him for much longer. Realising that he could potentially be without Bob for the walk home the next day over the two ridges, he rationed himself to the thirty-three minutes of *Nashville Skyline* before returning the earphones to his pocket and walking back into the wind.

Returned to his room, where a fire had been lit in the hearth. A warm room of rich reds and browns, thick carpet. He didn't turn on the lights, but walked to the window and looked out at the snow, the light from the flames throwing erratic shadows around him.

He went into the bathroom and hung his coat over the bath, took off his trousers and hung them over the heater, walked back into the room and hung his jumper and socks by the fire. Turned on a table light and slumped down into a large comfortable chair, TV remote in hand.

A quick flick through the channels, he came to Channel 5 News. They were talking about the US Presidential race. A reporter was discussing Obama's trousers with the earnestness of a true political pundit.

He felt tired. Lots of food and fresh air. Did he want to sleep now? Bad timing. He was wiped out and liable to sleep through dinner.

The cover of *Axis of Evil*, the beady eye in the grey tree, appeared on the graphic behind the presenter's head. Weston snapped awake.

'They're calling it the *Animal Farm* of the day, an instant classic, the political book of the age. But could you be contravening the latest Anti-Terror legislation just by reading the book and just how long is it likely to stay on the shelves...?'

24

There were five people sitting round the table. The PM, the Minister for Justice, Bleacher, the MI5 agent Shockey and Bleacher's number two, Edwards, the man Bleacher was grooming as his successor. (The time was not too far away when he would leave Number Ten to publish his diaries.)

'Shockey?' said the PM. 'What's your first name?'

'Geraldine,' she said.

The PM scribbled something on a notepad, leaned on his elbows.

'Minister,' he said, looking at Justice. 'You've studied the book?'

'Yes, Prime Minister,' said Justice. (The Justice Minister liked to refer to himself simply as Justice, for the Marvel comic book superhero effect.) 'They've found violations of ten articles of the Terrorism Act 2006. Of those ten possible charges, eight are borderline, the kind of thing that usually goes untried because it's tough to get a conviction. However, there are two blatant and serious breaches of the Act, which make prosecution not only possible but also imperative. We need to deal with this as quickly as possible.'

'The publisher and the author?' said the PM, and Justice nodded. 'We can ban the sale of the book?'

'Yes we can.'

The PM stared at Bleacher. 'How do you think that'll play?' he asked.

Bleacher tapped his pen on the desk.

'I'm not sure it's entirely necessary,' he said. 'Not yet, at any rate.'

'Go on.'

'We all know how counter-productive a ban can be. How do you turn the shittiest piece of artistic crap into a hit? Slap a ban on it. Creates curiosity, everyone wants to know what's the deal. And given the level of interest which we already have here…'

'So we let it keep on selling?' said the PM, his voice edgy.
'We let it sell out,' said Bleacher. 'We found out that Morrison ran an initial print run of two hundred thousand copies. That's a shit load of books, but you know, there's a fair chance that most of them have already gone. It's like Harry Potter out there.'
'They've been sending orders out from the distribution depot all day. Practically empty already,' Shockey chipped in.
'You have someone at the depot?' said the PM surprised.
'Yes,' answered Shockey flatly.
'He'll just reprint,' said the PM.
'He won't be able to,' said Bleacher, 'once we've arrested him.'
'When are you going to do that?'
'As soon as you agree the way forward.'
The PM tapped a rabid forefinger.
'That won't help it blow over quickly,' he said. 'Presumably he'll be able to organise his work, a reprint, from inside custody. And how long are we going to be able to hold him?'
'He's a one man band,' said Bleacher. 'He works alone, he lives alone, he eats alone. No one will mourn or protest his being taken into custody. And when we hand him over to the Americans…'
'His website is in flagrant violation of several articles of US terror law. They have become very interested in him.'
The PM looked at Edwards, the first time he had talked. Handing Morrison over to the Americans, while an obvious move, had been his idea.
'So,' said Bleacher, 'within a couple of days, Morrison will be a non-person. The book will be read, the stink will not get any worse than it has been today, and slowly it will fade. *Axis of Evil* will become just another piece of literature, read and forgotten.'
'And what about Weston?' said the PM. 'We'll need to get him out of the way. We can't hand him over to the Yanks.'
'We don't arrest Weston,' said Bleacher.
'We give him a knighthood?' suggested the PM darkly.
'We fuck him over. Ruin his reputation. If he's too scared to come out and admit he wrote the book, then we use that to our advantage. While he's lurking in the background, we fuck him up the arse with underage sex allegations. Seems he works with children a lot, it's not too much of a stretch. We close down his accounts, we repossess his house, we turn the guy into a walking sleezoid bum with no one to turn to. And if at some point in the future he pops his head up and says, *It was me who wrote the book, that's why they're saying these things about me...*you

know what? No one will believe him, because the fact that Lake Weston is a child-molesting drunken fuck will be imprinted on the consciousness of the British people.'

There was near silence in the room. The movement of the clock on the mantelshelf. The sound of Justice's breathing. The click of Shockey's slightly nervous fingernails.

The PM sat back and stretched his arms out. Locked his fingers, cracked the bones. Finally he smiled.

'Do it,' he said.

'Good,' said Bleacher. 'Now, we need to ensure that his name doesn't get out in relation to the book. At the moment, no one has any idea that it might be him. We need to keep it that way.'

'Who else knows other than Morrison?' asked the PM.

Bleacher looked at Shockey.

'We think Weston's editor at Millhouse, although we're not sure of his part in it all.'

'You'll deal with him?' said the PM.

'Yes, sir,' said Shockey.

The PM looked around the table, glanced at the clock. The fire was being fought.

'Right,' he said, 'I hope you all know what you're doing.'

The PM looked down at some paperwork on his desk. The meeting was over. Bleacher looked at the others around the desk and nodded. Slowly they rose from their chairs and headed out of the PM's office, on their way to start the ruination of Lake Weston.

◉

Weston had only a main course for dinner. The salmon, lightly poached. Boiled potatoes, steamed vegetables. Unsophisticated and not after the modern fashion, but all the more delicious for it. He had allowed himself a single glass of Pinot Gris. The dining room was busy, and he wondered where all the people came from on this winter's night.

He had picked up a paperback in the bedroom – the biography of a World War II naval captain – and sat alone in the warmth of the dining room, the clink of idle chatter around him, reading the story of the man's formative years in Edwardian London.

Occasionally he allowed himself a single Dylan song, the equivalent to nipping out for a cigarette. From *Blind Willie McTell* to *When The Deal Goes Down*, from *Oxford Town* to *Every Grain of Sand*, little excerpts of addiction to keep him going.

She appeared with his coffee, just as he had removed his earphones and started a new chapter. They smiled. He wondered if she worked fifty hour shifts. Like a junior doctor.

'What do you listen to?' she asked, taking a quick glance around the room to make sure she was free for a few seconds' chat.

'Dylan,' he said, shrugging. He'd had so much abuse for his addiction over the years that he had grown used to apologising for it.

'Wow,' she said. 'I love Dylan.'

Occasionally he also received that reaction. He returned the smile.

'Yeah?'

'Sure. I saw him in Vancouver in, I don't know, 2004 maybe.'

'July,' said Weston. '21st. That's the last time he played *One Too Many Mornings*. That's a great song. I expect he'll play it again sometime.'

She smiled curiously at him.

'That's, em, freakish...'

'I did this thing. You know, looked at his set lists, worked out the last time he'd played each of his songs.'

'Oh my God. So how many times have you seen him?'

'I generally don't tell people in case they think I'm weird,' he said.

She laughed. 'Oh, that's OK, I'm already there.'

Weston joined her laugh. Recognised the signs.

'One hundred and fifty-seven,' he said slowly.

'Oh my God...'

'A lot of that, I should say, was one tour when I followed him around North America, saw every night of a sixty-one date tour.'

'Man, why did you do that?'

'Writing a book. Of course, my editor didn't want to publish it, but I had fun. Met a few people on the road.'

'You meet Dylan?'

'Nah. Don't really want to.'

The voice came from the other side of the small room. 'Excuse me!'

She smiled at Weston and then turned and walked quickly away. He noticed this time that she'd changed her skirt from earlier.

The sex was disappointing. Not disastrous, but not as good as they had both imagined it was going to be. When it happened, when she came to his room at ten-thirty in the evening, it was almost as if they were doing it because that was what was supposed to happen. There were orgasms, there was sweat, but there was little passion and no fun. By midnight she was gone, and Weston was alone again, clutching to the remnants of the charge on his iPod, listening to the full sixteen minutes of *Highlands* and making sure he turned it off before he fell asleep.

◉

The police came for Richard Morrison at 2:38am. He'd been expecting them, and he wasn't at all surprised that when it happened it should be in the early hours of the morning. He knew they liked to work on the basis of upsetting the equilibrium of their victim.

Morrison never saw criminals, just victims. Victims of police injustice or, if they had committed what he would class as a genuine crime, victims of society. He had been waiting to become a victim of injustice for several years, and knew once he had appeared on television celebrating the release and the cause of *Axis of Evil*, then the police would not be far behind.

So they did not find him fast asleep, in his pyjamas or naked. He was sitting at his computer, writing furiously, working. Setting up the next print run of *Axis of Evil*, the money already dispatched, the delivery from the printers to the distributors already organised. Blogging, vlogging, writing e-mails, predicting his own downfall.

Richard Morrison, however, for all his cynicism, for all that he mistrusted the power of the state, for all that he thought the state controlled and manipulated society, still imagined that he would be released. He knew he had rocked the ship, he expected to be punished, to be beaten possibly, to have absurd charges brought against him, but for all that, he still expected that at some point he would walk out of police custody, into the waiting arms of the media, one day in the not too distant future.

And that was his mistake.

He did not resist arrest, but at 2:39am he was brought to his knees by means of a taser, the first of seventeen blows. At 2:47am he was dragged from the house and bundled into the back of a police van. Seven police officers stayed to carry out the search.

◉

Eldon Strachan went to bed feeling reasonably content. He had spent two days waiting for the roof to cave in, but for the moment it appeared to be holding. And while he was no great publicist, with no great eye for a story, he didn't think that *Axis of Evil* would have any legs. There would be a few days of curiosity, and then people would just start getting annoyed that the two principals in the case were keeping close counsel, and they would move on. The twenty-four hour news channels were only ever five minutes away from the next terrorist attack, the next airline disaster, the next rise in interest rates, the next collapsing bank, the next overdosed celebrity, the next dead politician, the next African genocide, the next stock market plummet, the next housing crisis, the next murdered teenager, the next celebrity marriage, the next missing child, the next footballer's headbutt. They would move on, and while the story of *Axis of Evil* would stay on the backburner for a while, eventually it would be forgotten.

There were no new classics, that was what Strachan thought. The times had changed from the days when the classic books were written. There hadn't been so many books to read, there had been little else to do other than read books. With no challenges from other media, the times had been ripe to create classics. Not anymore, not in this short-term memory, instant gratification culture. *Axis of Evil* could create all the fuss today, the media could place all the labels on it that they wanted to, even buying in to Morrison's *Animal Farm* concept, but it would last until the next *Animal Farm* came along, or the next *1984* or the next *Pride and Prejudice*. The age of the classics was gone, and nothing, not even a book as well written as *Axis of Evil*, was going to change that.

Eldon Strachan went to bed contented, and slept comfortably, his wife lying next to him in M&S red and white striped pyjamas.

Strachan awoke in the back of a police van, chained at his ankles and wrists, drowsy and nauseous, mouth dry.

His wife, Mary, doyen of the gossip columns and bringer of food to thirteen cats, never woke up.

25

Weston pulled back the curtains and looked out over the snow-covered hills. A glorious, cold winter's morning in late January, a weak winter sun, the snow bright, untouched, perfect.

He felt better about going home today, a new determination to sort everything out. The front room, his diet, his drinking, Fenton Bargus, the next great political novel. More walking in the hills, less drinking wine and wallowing in self-pity. Downstairs, breakfast, pay the bill, stop at the small shop to buy an apple, a chocolate bar and some water, then head out onto the hills. Be home not long after lunchtime.

He felt awkward going down to breakfast, but when it came to it, and his full Scottish was being placed in front of him, his last night's love had been replaced by a chatty man in his mid-fifties, keen to talk about the previous day's snow, its place in the pantheon of great snowfalls over the last fifty years, and how more was expected that afternoon.

Weston walked into reception forty minutes later, more relaxed than he had arrived at breakfast. His clothes had been laundered overnight, they had provided him with a small toothbrush and an overnight airline-style bag. He was clean, fresh, well-fed and ready to head out into the snow. Only the low level of the charge on his iPod stood in the way of a relaxing and enjoyable stroll back over the hill.

She was at reception, checking out an elderly Japanese couple. Their eyes connected briefly, she looked back at the man's credit card as the machine whirred. Weston stood and stared at the stag's head which protruded far out into the room, great antlers almost reaching to the ceiling. He hadn't noticed it when he'd arrived, or any of the other times he'd walked through.

'Mr Weston,' she said, as the old couple walked past him, the man wheeling a large blue suitcase behind them.

'Hi,' he said. She smiled, he placed his card on the counter.
'Did you enjoy your stay?' she asked, an awkward attempt at pleasantry.
He didn't answer, looked curiously at her. She raised her eyes, finally the tension was broken and they both smiled. She laughed.
'Sorry, that was dumb.'
She took the credit card out and re-inserted it into the machine. Pressed another couple of buttons. He watched her hands, the movements of her fingers. The fingers that had encircled him the previous night.
'We didn't make a very good job of it, did we?' he said.
She looked up and smiled again, a sympathetic look.
'Not really.'
'Next time,' he said, a remark which he thought sounded a lot more stupid than it actually was.
'Next time,' she said kindly. 'This card doesn't seem to be working, sorry. Was this the one you used yesterday?'
'Yeah, it should be all right,' said Weston, unconcerned.
She tried again. Weston turned and looked out the front door. A car started. The Japanese. Away to slither off down the road in search of the next Highland photo op.
'Nope,' she said. 'Sorry. You don't have another card we could try.'
Weston curiously lifted the card then shrugged his shoulders.
'That's weird,' he said. Took out his wallet, passed over another card. The next credit card in the line. He had five. He had forgotten why he had five credit cards, and his accountant had told him not to on many occasions.
The machine gave three short beeps, she took the card out and stared uncomfortably at him.
'Sorry, no luck.'
'That's...eh...OK, I'll, eh...here, try this. You take Maestro?'
'Sure, that shouldn't be a problem...'
The next card went into the machine.

Twenty minutes later Weston walked out of the small village shop. Concerned at last, an uncomfortable feeling in his stomach. None of his cards had worked at the hotel, not even the debit card which operated by taking money from an account which he knew to be in credit by over twenty-seven thousand pounds.
His new Canadian girlfriend had been sympathetic and had refused to take the sixty-eight pounds and fifty pence cash which he had on him as part payment, accepting in good faith that he would return the following day to make amends. They had talked about him calling his bank from

the hotel, but the awkwardness of their short-lived relationship meant that he didn't want to be standing around the lobby for half an hour waiting for someone to take his call.

Weston had left the hotel feeling no more than embarrassed, but assuming that the problem had been with the hotel's card processing facility. A couple of equally twitchy minutes in the shop had changed his mind. He had only spent eight pounds, so that he could easily cover the cost, and had tried one credit and one debit card. Neither had worked.

And now, as he stepped off the road onto the snow-covered, unbeaten track, he began to wonder why all of a sudden none of his bank cards were working. He wasn't naïve, he wasn't melodramatic, he wasn't stupid, he wasn't one for exaggerated histrionics. But without looking for conspiracies or soap opera or unwanted drama, the only reason he could think that his cards had all been stopped was that two days earlier he had released a book which had denounced the government and all that it stood for, and now they had discovered who he was.

How many people or organisations had the ability or authority to blackball someone across the banking and credit card board? Credit card fraud maybe. That's what his accountant always talked about. He had been effectively incommunicado for the past twenty-four hours, maybe something had happened that wasn't sinister, wasn't apocalyptic.

It was a possibility, but the timing wasn't, the timing was something he couldn't get out of his head. This had happened as the book came out. Had they known it was him all along? Hadn't Morrison insisted that he was followed at all times?

His stomach churned. He removed his gloves, felt the stinging cold on his fingers, fiddled with his iPod, battery almost done.

The pleasant walk across the snowy hills no longer held any pleasure. Now he just wanted to get home. Get his messages, take his calls, check e-mails, speak to Morrison, find out what was going on. Call the bank, try to discover the nature of the problem.

He turned to *World Gone Wrong*, which seemed the most appropriate song out of them all for the moment, and put the earphones in place. Two songs, the kind of quick fix he had survived on the previous evening, trying to save some power for later.

He set off into the hills, his boots sinking into fifteen inches of snow. The iPod died one and half minutes later.

👁

It was a dark, dank cell. Cold. The kind of place which never felt the benefit of heating. So surrounded by thick walls, so deep within the building that no warmth ever reached it, even on the hottest August day. A lifeless room. No spiders in the corners. No rats.

There was a single plain wooden chair in the middle of the room. Sometimes the chair was empty, sometimes someone was tied to it naked, sometimes someone sat in it in the dark, fully clothed, not tied by ropes or handcuffs, but bound by fear. Total darkness. The occasional drip onto the head or arms of what might have been water.

Eldon Strachan was fully clothed, ankles tied together, arms and torso bound to the chair by rope. He was neither gagged nor blindfolded. He had long ago given up shouting, and such was the darkness, the blackness of the walls, a blindfold would have been completely superfluous.

Like all people in this situation, he had lost track of time. He was lost on every possible level. He had screamed for a while. He had cried. He had panicked. He had fallen asleep. He had peed himself. He had screamed and cried again.

When the door opened and the lights were turned on, he was hunched over on the chair, upper body supported by the ropes.

This wasn't a single naked low-wattage bulb suspended from the middle of the ceiling. This was a roof full of spotlights, and in the light the walls were painted white. The light was blinding, especially to someone who had been sitting in the dark for a number of hours.

Strachan squinted into the light, could make out the single figure of a woman, then had to close his eyes. With the sudden light the fear and anxiety returned, a great rush of adrenaline and terror, his heart thumping, mouth instantly dry, his breath coming in uncomfortable jerks.

She stood and watched him. She was wearing a dark trouser suit, her hair tied severely back from her forehead.

She wasn't smiling.

He waited for her to say something, or for the sudden strike across the face or head. He waited for the torture. Every nerve alive and expectant. His soul broken and defeated already, he wasn't thinking of how he could get out of this situation, his thoughts were all of the pain that was to come. But more than the fear and the promise of suffering, it was the silence that unnerved him. This bleak, dark wraith standing before him in horribly grotesque quiet.

'Where's my wife?' he blurted out eventually. 'Where's Mary?'

'She's dead.'

He opened his eyes, bottom lip hanging down, instant tears, he peered into the light. Choked.

'What do you mean?'

'She's dead. It's hard to think of another way to put it.'
He choked again, the first tear squeezed itself from his eye.
'Why? She was......why?'
'The police may have been a little heavy handed.'
He kept opening and closing his eyes; eyes now damp with tears. Becoming accustomed to the spotlights. Getting a better look at the brutal woman standing with her arms folded in front of him.
'But why? What....?'
He couldn't find the words. He had gone to bed with his wife, they had lain together while she had read her mid-life crisis chic-lit and he had quickly looked over a manuscript from one of the members of the Arctic Monkeys. They had turned out their lights within five minutes of each other, and then he had woken up in police custody, his head throbbing, sick to his stomach. How could he possibly think straight?
'We need to know how many people you told about *Axis of Evil*?' said the woman coldly.
'What?'
Axis of Evil? Had it crossed his mind in the previous few hours of blind, aching panic? Not for a second. He had assumed kidnapping and ransom. Maybe terrorists, because weren't there terrorists everywhere?
'*Axis of Evil*,' said the snake-like voice, the words whipping out. 'It was written by Lake Weston. We know you read it. We need to know with whom you discussed it. Who else read it?'
He could not imagine that this was why he was here. Not *Axis of Evil*.
'What about Mary?' he said. 'Mary.'
'She's dead. Who else did you tell about *Axis of Evil*?'
The voice cut into him, sharper than the grating ropes on his wrists.

26

From the ridge above the glen in which he had spent the night, Weston had a fantastic view. The Highlands at their magnificent best, a grand, sweeping vista, snow covered hills and mountains, the grey blue of the lochs. The dark silhouette of birds against the sky.

Away down the glen he could see a police car, heading slowly up the road to the village. The road had yet to be cleared of snow, the police car hardly seemed to be moving. He watched it for a few seconds, and then turned and trudged over the top of the ridge, down into the next wild, uninhabited glen, a great valley of white.

He owned much of this land, a concept that still felt quite alien to him. They were just hills. Beautiful, ever-changing. How could he actually own something like this? How could anyone?

He felt slightly uplifted by the austere beauty of his surroundings, a panacea for his concern over the credit cards, the absence of Bob. He was once more just out walking. His pace picked up, until he was almost running. Sliding and slithering downhill, using his hands when he slipped, laughing and smiling, a child-like pleasure in the moment. As the ground evened out, he broke into a full run through the snow, exhilarated and flying, until he slipped and stumbled and fell, laughing, into a great heap in a three foot snow drift.

He lay for a second in the snow, staring up at the sky. Blue sky. The colour of the sky from his youth. No planes in sight, but there were two long contrails crossing each other, so that the sky looked like a giant Scottish flag.

There were clouds far away to the west. They would arrive before too long and the flag would be obliterated.

He sat up and looked up at the blank white of the next part of the climb, he raised himself to his knees, then to his feet, dug his boots into the snow and started on the final uphill stretch before he could start the long walk down to his house.

◉

At that moment, Weston's phone was ringing. By the time he got home, the phone would be showing seventy-three missed calls. There would be one hundred and fourteen messages. Not that he would get to see them.

The man searching the dining room looked over at the phone. He had been in the house for a little over two hours, the phone had rung seventeen times. There had been a variety of ringing tones, but mostly it had been, as it was now, the Emperor's theme. Having looked at the phone several times, he knew that it would be Penny calling again.

He grunted and then returned to going through endless piles of invoices and receipts and general household paperwork stacked in the drawer under the television.

◉

That morning, Penny actually had a reason for calling. The Daily Mail had been sitting open at page 5 since 8.27am. The story was in most of the dailies, although Lake Weston was not the type to make the front pages. He may have sold nearly ten million books worldwide, he may have been wealthy enough to buy a large Highland estate, his books may have been present in one in three British households, but he didn't command the papers in the manner of even the most vague C-list celebrity. The Pop Idol winners, the X-Factor runners up, the Big Brother failures, the one-hit wonders and the soap stars.

So the fact that one of Britain's foremost children's writers was wanted in connection with an accusation of sexually assaulting a minor was of some interest, but not enough to knock Jordan or Amy or Britney off the front page. Or even the new literary sensation, *Axis of Evil*.

The Metropolitan Police had issued a short statement, stating that Weston was wanted in connection with allegations made by the parents of a twelve year-old girl. They were at pains to stress that they just wished to speak to Weston at this point, and that charges would not necessarily be brought. They queried Weston's location.

No newspapers or media outlets were leant upon by the government, the story was just sent out into the world, like a leaf blowing off a tree in autumn, to see where it would land. And generally, as the small, insubstantial item landed on news desks fairly late in the evening, with no time for anyone to chase the story, it landed on page five or thereabouts. A photograph of Weston, an image or two of a couple of Fenton books, a short biography included to report that Weston had been twice married, was rumoured to be an alcoholic and that the quality of the Fenton books had gradually been slipping over the previous two or three titles in the series, added to the basic story. Most editors then embellished the tale by suggesting that the reason Weston had been writing children's books all these years was because he was a sick, child-molesting, paedophile.

It was a theme, just as Bleacher and the Prime Minister had realised, which would pick up its own momentum as the day progressed.

While Strachan sat in his brightly lit room, facing up to the apparent death of his wife, and Weston trudged up the hill towards his home, anxious to get back to see what had happened in the world during his twenty-eight hour absence, Richard Morrison sat on a plane, tired and hungry and sore. Unlike the others, however, he was well aware of what was happening to him.

Perhaps in films conspiracy theorists were tracked by men in suits and sunglasses, and perhaps they managed to escape and tell their stories. But not in real life. In reality there weren't long car chases, there weren't sharp suited men wearing Armani sunglasses on damp and miserable afternoons. In real life the apparatus of the state was big and all-powerful. And he was in the process of being swallowed.

He had been beaten repeatedly, kicks and sticks, and now he had been on a plane, blindfold, for several hours. They wanted him out of the way, and they were taking him as far away as possible.

Richard Morrison had seen the arrest coming, he had seen the beating and the humiliation. But this he hadn't foreseen. Instant, brutal, total subjugation and defeat. Generally in life he believed that there was always a way, always an answer. But for the first time in a long, long while, as he sat slumped on the plane in the dark, the drone of the engines, the judder of an overhead locker the only sounds, he knew that he was about to be proved wrong.

27

'Billy's dad says that Dylan was never the same after the motorcycle accident.'

Ben Hammond looked curiously at his son. He had taken the day off sick – which was easy enough being self-employed – called his son in sick at school, and was taking him on a sneaky trip to the Star Wars exhibition. Bumping along on the Tube. Had found a seat. Reading the adverts.

'Billy's dad said that?'

'Yeah.'

'Well, Billy's dad's a Muppet.'

'But didn't Bob have the accident after *Blonde on Blonde*? You said he never did anything better than *Blonde on Blonde*.'

'There's two things,' said Hammond, leaning forward. 'First, after he climbed Mount Everest, d'you think Sir Edmund Hillary ever climbed a higher mountain?'

'No,' said Robert, uncertainly.

'He'd reached the peak. He couldn't go any higher, so he just had to go off and climb other mountains, different types of mountains. It's the same with Bob. He'd made the best rock album of all time. Period. How can you make a better album than the best album ever? Answer me that.'

'I can't.'

'Exactly. Second thing. Come off your motorbike and have an accident, get laid up for a couple of weeks, well that's one thing. Unless it's really serious, and this wasn't, it's not going to change your life. However, at about the same time as the accident, you know what happened to Bob?'

'No...'

'He got married and had kids. One minute he was living the 24/7, rock 'n roll, drugs, booze and sex lifestyle, the next he was living on a farm and changing nappies. Now that, my young Padawan, will completely screw with your id, no matter who you are.'

He smiled at his son, then looked up and read the Mastercard advert for the thirteenth time.

'Is that what happened to you, Dad?' asked Robert.

Weston stood on the top of the ridge above his house and looked down over the broad glen. The A835 winding its way towards Ullapool, the cold slate grey of Loch Luichart away to his right, the slow rise of Ben Wyvis on the other side, up to the great plateau, the broad and unspectacular mountaintop which could be seen in every direction for miles and miles. All pristine, all white.

His house lay several hundred feet below him, the broad high roof covered in snow. The path down here was rockier, steeper, more dangerous than on the previous descent.

A movement caught his eye. A quick flash in the morning sun. At the side of his house. He stood frozen for a second and then suddenly, with no coherent thought, dived sideways into the snow and started crawling towards the cover of a rock.

He lay behind the rock, panting from the adrenaline. He breathed hard, wiped the snow from his face. Felt the cold dampness of the snow creep under his sleeves. Head down, face resting just above the snow.

Why was he here, cowering and hiding six hundred feet up the hill from his house? Who was it likely to be at this time of day? Postman? UPS maybe. But whoever it was had been at the side of his house, they had been looking for something, someone.

Mind suddenly on fire, all those thoughts which had been lying dormant. Morrison had warned him. He had said the authorities would not like it, that they could publish the book anonymously if they chose, but they had to accept that MI5 were already watching, and it wouldn't take them long to put two and two together.

Weston had thought Morrison was exaggerating, playing the role of the paranoid conspiracy theorist to the full. He might have allowed himself to get sucked into it briefly when in his company, seeing spooks and shadows in every corner, but in the cold light of normality, away from the glare of the man's paranoia, it had seemed absurd.

Now the dark thoughts rose up like bile from his stomach. His credit and debit cards had all been cancelled, there was someone snooping around his house.

He turned to lie on his back and looked up at the sky. Clouding over, the pale blue sky slowly disappearing as the grey swarm arrived from the west. Body tense, thoughts progressing to terrifying, logical conclusions. They were out to get him.

He turned over and edged along to the end of the rock. Stopped himself just as he was about to stick his head round the side. He was wearing a grey woollen hat, and now he covered it in snow as best he could, pressing the snow down hard onto his head, hoping it would stick.

Another pause, deep breath, he inched his head out beyond the rock until he had a good view down the hill to his home.

He watched closely, waiting for any movement in the vicinity of the house or garden, or on the road leading up to it. A more careful examination than previously, when he had looked at the house for a few seconds before diving into a snowdrift.

No movement, the area around the house a mass of white. Too far away to see if there were any footprints in the area or any tyre tracks leading up to the house. The light was now too flat, the sun gone, the sky getting duller and more sullen by the minute.

He kept his head still, he watched. Eventually he withdrew all the way behind the rock and rested his head on his arm. He couldn't lie here all day. He couldn't lie here until he imagined that the government weren't going to be interested in him any more.

He closed his eyes and tried to bring the cartwheels of his insides under control.

The world famous, Booker prize winning author was rather enjoying all the attention. The media had gradually come to an agreement over the list of which writers were most likely to have written *Axis of Evil*, although they had not necessarily been able to agree on the favourite. There was at least some agreement in omission, in that none of them had suggested the possibility that Lake Weston might be responsible.

Of the authors contacted by the media, some were pleased to get the attention, some were amused, some were jealous or resentful of the publicity machine which had accompanied the release, some were rude, some played along, some were happy to imply that yes, maybe it had been them who had written this instant book of the times.

The famous author had had a smile on his face since the interview had started. He had been nominated as favourite to have written the book by at least three media outlets, and the murmuring was growing that he was the most likely. One of them had run the writing style diagnostic, and although it had only arrived at a 55% chance, which was well outside the usual parameters, they had chosen to accept it as near-confirmation. 55% had seemed good enough a statistic on which to run a story.

'So, you're denying that it was you who wrote *Axis of Evil*?'

The author smiled again. 'Like I said, I wish I had. It's been a while since I managed such perception in one of my own books, I'm afraid.'

'But there's this statistic in the Mirror today which states that there's a greater than fifty percent chance it was you who wrote it.'

The author laughed.

'That's really not a story. If you were to take, say, my first novel as the basis for that test, and then test my latest novel against it, you would probably find there was a 99.7% chance that I'd written the novel. Just over fifty percent really doesn't mean anything.'

A pause. The presenter looked at his notes, knew that he didn't really have anywhere else to go with this. His co-presenter itched to get her turn, the editor was giving her the signal to bide her time.

'You've read it then?'

'Yes, last night.'

'And what did you think? Worth the hype?'

'Definitely. A wonderful piece of writing. Incisive, daring political commentary.'

'You think it will have any effect on government policy? Really, when it comes to it, it's just a book, so why should it?'

'You know,' said the writer, getting into the meat of it, the reason he had come on the show, 'I do wonder, can the government ignore it? Of course they can. But this is about public opinion, this is about the groundswell of grass roots political movement, it is the kind of thing which we need in this country to truly engage in the political process.'

He's beginning to grandstand, thought the editor and he pointed a finger at the female co-presenter, who had been sitting on her hands waiting to swing the first punch.

'And I find myself most grateful,' the author continued, despite the fact that he had seen the pointed finger, 'to whoever the writer is, for making me realise that it is time that we all, not just the writers and commentators and prophets, we all engage in this...'

'So you're saying,' said the woman, cutting him off with some enthusiasm, 'that categorically, it was not you who wrote this book?'

The writer paused, looking curiously amused.

'Yes, I am saying that. I thought I'd said that already'

'I don't know that you actually said the words. I mean, you didn't say the actual words, *I did not write Axis of Evil*. But you're still insisting that that is the case?'

'Yes.'

'So will you say that you did not write this book?'

'I thought that was what I was saying...'
'But will you say the words, so that our listeners can hear them, that you did not write this book? Otherwise the British people are just going to believe that you're avoiding the question with the kind of tangled elusive language which you employ so well in *Axis of Evil*.'
Her co-presenter gave her a raised eyebrow. The author shrugged hopelessly. It was just like the media, he was thinking, to take something good humoured and completely screw it up. From having a bit of fun and enjoying himself, it had taken a little more than ten seconds for him to think that he wanted to tell the stupid woman to bugger off and to walk out the studio. Now, of course, if he actually refused to say the words, then he would be adding fuel to the fire.
'I did not write the book,' he said humourlessly, the death of enjoyment obvious in his voice.
'Which book?' she shot back.
The author stared across the chasm of the studio.

Although he was no longer sure which thoughts were real or imagined or had been placed there by his interrogators, Eldon Strachan wondered if this was the end for him. If he would ever get out of this chair, if he would ever be allowed to lie down anywhere.
His own thoughts were all about lying down. On a bed, on a field of grass, on a cold stone floor, he wouldn't have cared. He was exhausted, he hurt everywhere.
He had no idea how long he had been sitting on his own. Two hours or ten minutes. A day, a week, half an hour. All he knew was that every time he almost fell asleep a shower started above his head and drenched him with water. Either ice cold or stingingly, painfully hot. And as his tiredness had grown, so had the frequency of the overhead deluges.
In fact, he had not been there that long. A little over twelve hours so far. But it wasn't about the length of time. Eldon Strachan had endured the longest twelve hours of his life. And it wasn't going to get worse before it got better. It was just going to get worse.
The door opened, he barely lifted his head from his chest. His eyes couldn't open very wide in any case, now that he had been beaten repeatedly about the face. The lights were on, he clenched his eyes as tightly as possible. His whole body tensed, already anticipating the pain that was to come. He panted, short gasping breaths of panic.
The woman's clipped footsteps approached. She stood before him. Silence, but for the sound of his tortured breathing.

He didn't want to look at her, didn't want to open his eyes. But the mere presence of her was sucking him in, forcing him to lift his head.
His neck hurt. It was an effort to look up, an effort to open his eyes.
'Who else knows that Lake Weston wrote *Axis of Evil*?'
Her voice was as clipped and sharp as the sound of her shoes.
He could feel himself start to cry again. Tears of frustration and desperation. He was in a territory that was not his own, he had been plucked from normality and stuffed brutally into this netherworld of torture and pain. The laws of publishing, the laws of normal everyday life, did not apply.
His head lolled forwards onto his chest. He heard her footsteps back off. He heard the sound of the water, and then the soaking burning touch as it showered onto him, hotter than it had been before. He screamed and huddled forward, automatically making himself into as tight a ball as possible, taking the brunt of the pain on his neck and the top of his back.
The water stopped suddenly. He let out a sobbing gasp, the skin on his back stinging horribly.
'Who else knows that Lake Weston wrote *Axis of Evil*?'

28

Weston had stared round the side of the rock fourteen times in a little over half an hour. He was cold, hungry, needing to go to the bathroom. There had still been no sign of any movement. His mind rambled between grand conspiracy and imagining he was being a total idiot.

He fixed some snow once more to his hat, held his breath and poked his head around the side of the rock. A longer look than many of his darting glances. He studied the house, he finally allowed himself a breath.

He looked along the glen, down to the road. East and west. Up the hill on the other side, the foothills of Wyvis. It was time. He couldn't lie there forever.

As he stood up he felt the first flake of snow land on his face. He lifted his head to the grey sky. All trace of blue had gone, the snow was coming. He shivered and once more started the walk down to the house. One eye on the path, one on the house, searching for movement.

He slipped a couple of times, but the landing was soft. The snow started to fall with greater intensity, visibility worsened. Proper snowfall, large white flakes. He was close enough that the house always stayed in sight, but the top of the ridge behind him vanished.

Through the small gate at the back of the garden, he walked tentatively up the path. Everything blanketed in snow, no footprints. He slowed further, looking for the twitched curtain, the slight movement, anything slightly different from the norm.

He came up to the house and walked round the side. He stopped, heart jumped. There were the footprints, a single set. The doubts which he had allowed to grow as he'd lain behind the rock, the possibility that he'd imagined seeing someone, had now been banished.

'Fuck, fuck, fuck...'

He looked over his shoulder, turned back. Followed the path of the footprints, up to the side window, back to the front of the house.

'Fuck, fuck, fuck...'

He pressed himself against the wall and edged along to the window. Stood just short of it, then quickly turned and peered into the room. Tensed for the shock. It was the small television room, and it looked like he had left it the previous morning. Newspapers and wine bottles.

He pressed against the wall. Looked around, back up the hill through the snow, down the glen to the road. Then quickly he ducked down and crawled through the snow, beneath the window. Elbows out, shunting himself forward with his feet, keeping his body low. Kept crawling, unnecessarily, until he got to the front of the house.

He stopped. Looked down the driveway. A single set of tyre marks, up and back. Another deep breath, closed his eyes, rested his head on the back of his hand.

'Come on, Lake, get it over with.'

He peered round the side of the house. There was no vehicle sitting outside. Several sets of footprints led into the house. For the first time he felt annoyed. Several people had come to his home. Had they gone inside? Were they, at this moment, drinking his wine, eating his food?

'Fuck this,' he muttered.

He got up quickly, walked to his front door, brushing snow off as he walked. Hard to tell how many sets of footprints there were leading to his house. Five, maybe six, maybe more. A great jumble. Up the steps, he tried the front door. Had to fumble for the key in his pocket. He opened up, stepped into the house. Stopped and listened.

There was nothing, no immediate sounds of anyone else, no obvious indication that someone had been in the house. The hallway was bright – wooden floor, pale rug, walls magnolia and hung with modern art, large paintings of swirling colours – but he switched on the light.

'Hello!' he called out, and then rolled his eyes. What answer was he expecting? *'Hi, we're up here! It's the CIA! Don't mind us!'*

He kicked his boots on the doorframe but did not take them off. Stopped again, listened to the silence. Looked up the stairs.

Deep breath, swallowed his nerves, walked quickly through the hall into the kitchen. It looked the same as he'd left it. A mess of plates and empty bottles. Back out into the hall, a glance up the stairs and then through to the front room. The adrenaline was fading, he was getting the sense that no one was here. Maybe someone had come to the house, but it didn't mean that they had come inside.

Back out into the hall, remembered that he needed the bathroom. Locked the door behind him, didn't fancy the idea of someone bursting in on him with his trousers undone. Lifted his head, thought about his phone. Where had he left it? In the television room, thrown onto a coffee table in amongst the debris.

He flushed the toilet, washed his hands, stood hesitantly at the door for a second, then quickly unlocked it and pulled it open. He stepped out into the hallway.

Still nothing but the cold silence of the early afternoon.

He noticed a newspaper lying on the hall table. He stopped, stared at it from five yards. Felt the sudden flutter of nerves down his spine, the crawling in his stomach. He hadn't left a paper there, there hadn't been a paper there when he'd come into the house two minutes earlier.

He walked over, eyes wide, glances over his shoulder. It was a copy of the Independent, folded open at an inside page. The date at the top of the page had been highlighted in green. That day's date.

Weston lifted the paper warily. The small black and white picture of himself stared back at him, under the headline *Children's Author Wanted by Police After Child Sex Allegation.*

He swallowed. He felt the most unbelievable sense of fear and foreboding. His skin crawled, his heart thumped. He felt nauseous, thought he might be sick.

His eyes drifted quickly over the report. The parents of a twelve year-old girl had reported that Weston had abused their daughter at a school he had been visiting. A succession of derogatory remarks about his books, then remarks about his character. A few implications about this being the tip of the iceberg.

His mouth was dry. He reread it. He quickly glanced at the front page of the paper, checking the date, checking the main storyline.

Feeling empty, feeling that his insides had been ripped out, he laid the paper back down on the table.

'Slightly sensationalist reading, but where would the newspapers be if they had to stick to the truth?'

Weston turned and looked up at the man in the dark grey suit who was standing at the top of the stairs.

'Who the fuck are you?' he said.

With the appearance of the man he had been expecting, his nerves died, his heart calmed. Always better to be faced with your fear.

'We're MI5,' he said. 'Although, given that we're trained to lie and our whole existence is predicated on subterfuge and deceit, how can you

believe anything I say? If we're not MI5 then I'm lying, if we are MI5, then you can't believe me.'
'Who's we?' said Weston bitterly.
'Oh, you know, there are seven of us,' said the grey suit. 'Just wrapping up our search up here. More or less done.'
Weston didn't move. The suit had the upper hand, in so many ways.
'Was it you who planted that story?' he said, indicating the paper.
'Nah,' said the suit, smiling. 'That's not the kind of thing we do. I take that story as genuine. Your sort always get found out in the end.'
'What the fuck does that mean?' snapped Weston.
The suit looked at his watch as a group of men and women emerged from the bedroom door and gathered beside him. The suit smiled again, while pointing at the overhead light in the hall.
'In a few seconds that light is going to go off,' he said.
Weston looked up at the light. Suddenly the nerves and discomfort were returning. He felt surrounded, his own house seemed claustrophobic.
The gang of seven stood on the first floor and watched the light. They all waited, as if something mightily more significant than a light going off was about to occur.
The light went off.
The grey suit clapped his hands together and started walking down the stairs, the others behind him.
'That, what you just witnessed there, my friend, was your electricity being cut off... that's the kind of thing we do.'
He came to the bottom of the stairs and walked slowly over to Weston, his entourage behind him. A van pulled up outside the front door, the tyres crunching through the thick snow. While he stood in front of Weston, the others slowly walked to the front door and out into the cold. With the door open, winter's chill flooded into the house.
The suit stopped, his nose no more than a couple of inches away from Weston's face. Weston's jaw clenched. He could smell the mint on the man's breath, the warmth of the air from his mouth. Expensive white teeth. His eyes, a sharp dangerous blue, burrowed into Weston, who wished he had the strength to stand up to him.
He held the man's gaze but felt no conviction. He was aware of his own weakness in every fibre of his body. Every muscle, every nerve.
'No electricity, no phone, no power...'
'There's a generator,' said Weston, a doomed attempt at defiance.
'You might find that you need fuel to power your generator.'
'I have fuel...' said Weston, but the words drifted off as he said them.

'As I was saying. No power, no fuel, no phone, no money, no operational bank accounts – and by the way, that's also the kind of thing we do – black-balled financially, and now that the word is out that you sexually abuse young girls, the black-balling is going to grow.'

Weston swallowed again, was aware of how loud a noise it made in the silence. The front door had been closed.

'You can't do this,' he said. Awful, pointless words.

'Every single thing that we've done, *every single thing*, is within the law and to counteract the activities of a suspected paedophile.'

'But...,' he began, but there was nowhere for the statement to go.

'Now you're going to give me the money which you have on you.'

Weston's eyes widened. He swallowed loudly again. His nerves broke out all over his face.

'I don't have any money on me,' he said.

'Just over three hours ago you went into a village shop seven miles from here, you purchased a drink, a sandwich, some gum and two pieces of fruit. You received change from a twenty pound note, and close examination of CCTV footage shows that there were at least two further notes in your wallet. Give me the money.'

At last Weston took a small step away from him. He had some money around the house, but how did he know that these people hadn't just taken it? Yet, still he did not see the full implication of what was happening. He still imagined driving along to the bank or the police station to sort everything out, finding a phone and calling Strachan or Morrison or Travis. Or even Penny, he would even gladly talk to Penny at this moment.

'No,' he heard himself say. 'You've taken enough already.'

The man from MI5 reached inside his jacket pocket, swiftly pulled out a hand gun, cocked it and pressed the barrel against Weston's head. A fast, simplistic, brutal action.

'Give me the money.'

It was all show, of course. He knew that he would get crucified back at the office if any physical harm came to Weston. But he also recognised the discomfort in his opponent.

Weston, his hand suddenly shaking, reached inside his coat and pulled out his wallet. He started to open it, but the man from MI5 snatched it from him, then he put the wallet and the gun back inside his coat.

'You can keep the change,' he said.

He smiled again at Weston, then turned and walked to the door. He opened it, Weston stood and watched as his life walked out the front door. The man stopped and looked back.

'The police were here earlier looking for you,' he said. 'I expect they'll be back fairly soon. You can be here to greet them, or you might want to get the fuck out of Dodge. Your call.'

'I'll go to the press,' said Weston suddenly. A weak defiance, but he had to show something.

'On you go,' said the suit. 'I'm sure they'll be keen to hear the confession of the paedophile children's author. Might even knock *Axis of Evil* off the literary front pages.'

'I'll tell them I wrote the book, that that's what this is all about.'

'Good luck, my friend, but I doubt they'll believe you.'

'There are others who know,' said Weston.

The smile again, this time while the eyes burned a hole in Weston's head. Weston stared at the darkness in the pits of his eyes.

'If you're looking for Morrison or Strachan, you might have trouble getting hold of them. Otherwise, I'm sure the press would be very convinced by your story, so why not give it a go. I could recommend one of my contacts in London.'

Weston closed his eyes. Finally recognised that it was time to shut up. Every road that he took, the barriers were down. Crushed and defeated.

'No? Well, let me know if you change your mind.'

Weston didn't open his eyes. He lowered his head. Heard the door closing, the footsteps outside.

When he finally opened his eyes as the van reversed, the weight of the morning, the weight of the last ten minutes, lay crushingly on his shoulders, and tears of desperation had begun to well up in his eyes.

29

The Prime Minister laid the newspaper to the side and leant back in his seat. He fiddled with the knot in his tie, tightening it slightly.

'I've got the questions, Prime Minister,' said Bleacher.

The PM was distracted, staring into space, his right hand now straightening out imaginary creases in the tie, his left hand sitting idle on the desk. Finally he turned and looked at Bleacher.

'Nothing of substance,' said the PM, a statement rather than a question.

'He's majoring on ID cards again,' replied Bleacher.

The PM grunted. 'For God's sake.'

He leant forward and took the file from Bleacher's hand, then he opened it and quickly scanned over the list. Prime Minister's Questions.

'Didn't their guy say something totally absurd about identity theft two years ago or something?'

'December 2006. It's in there. You should use it.'

The PM flicked through the paperwork, paused to read the comment. He smiled humourlessly.

'I don't see anything about the book? What are the press saying about it today?'

'No one has tabled a question on *Axis Of Evil*, but you should still be ready. I've written a couple of one-liners you can use if you need them. They'll work best if you can let them rip. Should get a laugh.'

The PM grunted and started flicking through the file once more.

'The media have zeroed in on a couple of names. The usual suspects, and not our guy. No one has even suggested him.'

'And the other thing?'

The PM looked up. Bleacher pursed his lips and looked out the window. Then he turned back to the PM and stared steadily at him.

'There is no other thing, Prime Minister,' he said.

The PM returned the gaze and then finally nodded.
'Give me five minutes with this,' he said, and then he sat forward and folded the file open at the first page. Bleacher walked out the room.

The plane touched down in the Caribbean at 12:05 GMT, a cool early morning in Cuba. Richard Morrison had drifted fitfully in and out of sleep, finally waking up with the uncomfortable jolt of the landing. He rested his head back against the side of the plane. Still blindfolded, still handcuffed. He hadn't been fed, hadn't been allowed to use the bathroom.
He had awoken desperate to pee. He felt stiff and sore and cramped. Needed to move. He had lost all sense of how long he had been in the air. Hadn't been able to stretch his legs.
The plane started to slow. He thought he was going to wet himself.
'Hello,' he said, looking to one side. He had barely heard any movement for the entire length of the journey and he wondered if he was alone in the cabin. 'Hey! I need to take a pish.'
He moved his head in the direction of the slightest noise, wondering if anyone else was there. He squeezed his legs together.
'The plane is taxiing to a halt,' said a detached male voice close by. 'Do you think under normal circumstances that you would be allowed to leave your seat and go to the bathroom?'
Morrison stared in the direction of the strange mid-Atlantic accent.
'These aren't normal circumstances,' said Morrison.
Silence. Morrison shifted his head around, searching.
'So, can I use the toilet?' he said.
The plane slowed. The sound of the engines dying, the brakes and the antiquated steering, the final shudder of the cabin locker.
'Hello?' said Morrison, with irritation.
The blow to the side of the head was swift and precise and silent and Morrison didn't know anything about it. As the plane came to a standstill, and the doors were opened to the cool Caribbean morning, his head was slumped forward on his chest, a trickle of blood in his hair.

Weston had a Hysterical Five Minutes. He had coined the term for his own amusement when he'd lived with Penny. Once, near the end, he'd even let it slip out. Penny's Hysterical Five Minutes, were most definitely hysterical, but had usually lasted a lot longer than five minutes.
Weston just about kept to within the time limit. A frantic, desperate dash around the house, lifting phones, checking in cupboards, fleeting seconds of silent screaming, standing still staring out of the window in despair,

expecting the police to come crashing up his driveway at any minute. All his money was gone. Passport gone. Laptop gone. Phones disconnected. Electricity off. Mobile phone gone. The car keys had been left hanging, and he had dashed out to the Land Rover. The men and women of MI5 had helpfully left the bonnet open, so that Weston wouldn't have that fleeting second of hope as he tried to start the car. Battery removed, alternator removed, wires cut.

He ran back into the basement of the house, up the stairs into the kitchen. Breathing hard, heart pounding. Panicking. Opened the fridge door. Milk and wine and water spilled out onto the floor, splashing his feet, his trousers.

'Fuck!' he barked, then stepped away, slamming the door shut.

He staggered back and leant against the kitchen counter. Head in hands, trying to get himself under control.

'Think for fuck's sake.'

He let out a long breath. The moment of total panic had passed. He stared at the magnetic Dylan calendar on the fridge which the boys had given him for Christmas. Early 60's Bob, smoking a cigarette. Chic Bob.

'What would you do?' he said.

Dylan stared back from behind the haze of retro-cool cigarette smoke. What would anyone do?

He rubbed his hands quickly over his face, hand through the hair. Were the police likely to be coming, or had that been another red herring let loose by the man from MI5? If he had even been from MI5. But it had been there in the press. The paedophile children's author.

Despite himself, despite the absurdity of it, he started thinking back to visits he'd made to schools over the previous year or two. Had there been a kid who had construed something the wrong way?

The power of the press. Even Lake Weston, the one man who absolutely knew for sure that it wasn't true, suddenly wondered if there was anything in it. He knew he hadn't done anything, but at least it had him questioning whether someone else thought he might have.

Dylan stared back at him from the door of a fridge that was filled with running gloop.

'I can't think. I need to get the fuck out of Dodge, right enough.'

He nodded at Bob, then walked through the house to the front room, finding within himself the measure of control and good sense that was required. A nervous glance out the window. Thick snow, swirling. A blizzard had descended. He could barely see fifty yards down the road. Hoped that this snow would keep the police away.

Whatever was in the press, whatever was going on in the attempts to ruin his name, he could worry about later. For the moment, he had to worry about escape. If he was really to be taken into police custody, if he was really to get his photo taken being led into a police station, handcuffed and hunched over, that would be the end of his career. The phrase *no such thing as bad publicity* did not extend to talk of paedophilia.

'Get packing,' he muttered, as he walked upstairs.

The snow was falling, winter was in full parade, and he was going to have to leave his house, get off the beaten track and try to avoid capture in the hills and glens. He was at least fortunate enough to know the land.

He first went to the bedroom window. Another check of the blizzard, another look down the fifty yards of visible driveway. How could they come out in this? Why would they come out?

He raced round the house. A torch, waterproof matches, canteen, a small metal pot, sleeping bag, one man bivouac, one change of clothes, nothing heavy. Trousers, t-shirt, underwear.

Befitting his wealth, the camping gear was all hi-tech, modern, extremely lightweight and had never been used. All those trips he'd intended to take late at night, to sleep wild in the reaches of his domain.

He returned to the kitchen. Hadn't removed his jacket. Searched the cupboards for any food he could take, although he didn't want to load up. How long did he imagine he would be living in the wilderness?

Two tins of soup, half a packet of crackers, half a packet of chocolate digestives. Five teabags. Never did keep much in the pantry.

The backpack was crammed full. He pulled the chord, wondered what he'd forgotten. Looked outside at the raging storm, the snow collecting in mini-drifts against the window.

Dylan stared back at him, tousled black hair and cigarettes. Weston was booked on a flight from Heathrow in mid-March to take in three Dylan concerts in Uruguay and Argentina. Even earlier that week, with his concerns and angst over *Axis of Evil*, Dylan in Buenos Aries had seemed a long, long way off. Now it seemed a complete impossibility.

He hadn't seen him in concert since the previous summer. A warm night in Berlin. *Don't Think Twice* and *All Along The Watchtower*, *Thunder on the Mountain* and *Absolutely Sweet Marie*. An ok evening. Mundane Dylan. Since he'd been working on *Axis of Evil*, he hadn't ventured to the States the previous autumn, not taking the flight he had booked to Austin, Texas, not using the ticket he had purchased on-line. The privilege of wealth.

He snapped his fingers.

'My old MP3. Holy crap.'

He ran out of the kitchen, up the stairs two at a time. If there was one thing he needed as he set out on a long walk into the snow, it was Dylan, and the iPod that lay silver and useless in his pocket was dead. Into the big front room, he dived over to the desk drawers. They were packed, crammed with the endless amounts of paper which so dictate modern life. Bank statements and credit card statements, life insurance and sales figures. He filed once every two or three years.

Knew he was leaving, threw papers onto the floor. Found what he was looking for stuffed in at the back.

Flicked the control, the panel illuminated. It was playing halfway through *Death Is Not The End*. Full battery. He felt the addict's relief.

The doorbell rang. His breath caught in his throat.

Stood still, heartbeat nought to sixty. Deep breath, tried to compose himself. Edged his way to the window, peered out. Police Land Rover parked in the driveway. Snow falling on the windscreen. He hadn't heard it as it had crept in through the blizzard.

There was a knock at the back door. From the front of the house, the doorbell rang again. The panic which he had only managed to get rid of a few minutes earlier, now rushed back through him, a fevered drug coursing violently around his system.

He stood rooted. Frozen by fear, scared to make any noise in case he betrayed himself.

If he could believe MI5, then the police had already been here and had turned away. Perhaps they would do so again. Stand still, not a noise, not a movement, get out when he could.

'Mr Weston!' came the call from outside the front door. A few yards back. The officer had stepped into the middle of the driveway. 'We know you're in there, Mr Weston. We have a warrant for your arrest.'

Weston knelt on the floor, rubbing his forehead. Desperately trying to sort out his options. There was only one police car in the driveway, so they hadn't arrived mob-handed. He could sneak past them in the house, then make a break for it. Out into the blizzard.

Leaving footprints in his wake.

Hand himself over. Go down and open the door before they broke it down. He hadn't done anything. Was there any need for the innocent to feel guilty? Somebody was out to get him, but he would get a lawyer. Strachan or Morrison or even Travis would help him. Someone.

And all the while the media would crucify him, his lawyer would tell him not to say anything publicly, and the denials of his lawyer would be treated with utter contempt and disbelief by everyone who heard them.

And if he ran, what then? Accused paedophile on the run...

Heart pounding, chaotic head, he couldn't possibly think of all the implications. He needed peace and quiet, he needed time. He needed to be back at the hotel in which he'd spent the previous evening. Or a police cell. That would give him plenty of time for reflection.

He lifted his head at the sound of another car on the driveway. The slow creep through the snow. A slight squeal of brakes. A door. Two doors. Footsteps crunching in the snow. Voices. A woman's voice. More police.

He edged along the floor towards the window then very slowly lifted his head. A quick glance, then he pulled himself back down until he was lying flat on the floor.

Not police after all. Worse. Television.

He stared at the ceiling. One hand running through his hair, the other desperately clutching what was about to be left of Bob Dylan in his life.

'I can't give in to this.'

He crawled on his hands and knees, then stopped, staring at the carpet. He couldn't hand himself over, not when he had no idea what he was facing. He had to get out. He needed to get hold of the bag in the kitchen and then do something, anything to get past the officers at the back door.

'Professor Weston, in the library with the typewriter?' said a voice from the door.

Weston looked up. A police sergeant was standing in the doorway. A big man, arms by his side. Regulation flak jacket bulking him out even more. Brutal face. He filled the door. In the silence Weston could still hear the voices outside.

'Came in the back,' said the sergeant. 'The Chief Inspector likes to give people a chance to open doors. I usually don't bother.'

'You've got him, Sarge?' said a voice from the hallway.

'Aye,' said the sergeant, taking a step into the room. 'Down on his knees. Where he belongs.'

Weston stared up at him. Mouth dry, heart still hadn't slowed down. Heard the front door open, the scurry of footsteps. Urgent voices. The television camera being brought into his house.

Was he breaking news? Lake Weston, paedophile, breaking news? Was someone somewhere, on television or on a website, carrying this live? Lake Weston about to get arrested in his own home for a crime that he had never committed, broadcast to the planet.

'You'll come quietly, Mr Weston,' said the sergeant, another step towards him. 'Sounds like the TV people are here.'

'Everything under control?' said a constable, coming in at the sergeant's back.

'Aye, Michael, it is. Put the man in cuffs. Mr Weston, would you like a hood for when we walk past the cameras?'

The constable paused, as he disentangled the cuffs from his belt. The sergeant raised an eyebrow at Weston. Hard face. Thin lips. Had stopped drinking two years previously, but thirty years of it prior to that had left its mark on his worn, bitter, ugly face.

Weston stood up. The constable approached.

'I'm not the one who needs my face hidden,' quipped Weston.

He visualised the driveway, he visualised the Police Land Rover and the television van. When he had first walked into this room with its fantastic panoramic windows overlooking the glen and the mountains, some part of him had imagined smashing through them. Running full pelt, forearms up to protect the face, crashing into the glass. Had wondered if the glass would be so tough that you would just bounce off.

It was time to find out.

'Funny,' said the Sergeant. 'Cuff him, bring him downstairs.'

Weston hesitated for a second. The sergeant started to turn away. From out in the hall he could hear footsteps on the stairs, the raised voice of another police officer. The TV cameras were approaching, stirring up angst and anger as they came. The blizzard roared, the snow fell against the window.

The constable approached, hands outstretched. Weston looked into his eyes, betrayed himself with a flicker of a look. For a fraction of a second he recognised that the constable knew what he was about to do.

Weston turned quickly. Three paces to the window, quick stuttering steps, one long stride. Arms up to protect his face, still clutching his little piece of Dylan, he leapt at the window.

They were in the kitchen. Robert was doing his maths homework, Ben Hammond was emptying the washing machine. Mother and daughter at the supermarket.

'You know what I hate, Dad?' said Robert, looking up, pencil in mouth.

'What?'

'Maths homework,' he said.

'Yep, fair enough. You know what I hate?'

'No.'

'When you put a duvet cover in the washing machine, then when you take it out, all the other washing's gone inside it, and you've got to fish around for it.'

Robert stared at him across the kitchen. Kicking his legs under the table, avoiding the four times table.

'Is that a Bob Dylan song?' he asked.
Hammond smiled. 'This isn't about Dylan.'
Robert shrugged and looked back at four times seven. Was quickly bored.
'Does Bob Dylan empty his own washing machine?'
'Don't know.'
'Does he have a washing machine?'
'Don't know. Expect so.'
'Twenty-eight,' said Robert quietly, and scribbled on the paper.
Hammond looked round curiously at his son.

30

Weston sat huddled against a tree. Exhausted, freezing. Knew that he had to keep on the move. Sitting still just allowed the cold to creep through his body. He was shivering, his body consumed by cold in the way that it is when you can't imagine ever being warm.

Now that he had stopped running, his ankles ached. One a dull pain, an ankle that he just wanted to rest on a seat and not put any weight on for a few days. The other was sending constant shards of screaming pain through his leg.

Dylan filled his ears. His last respite. *Man In The Long Black Coat*. Head resting against the tree, face screwed in pain, eyes open. Looking back the way he had come. Realised that his footsteps through the wood were more dangerous, that they would take longer to be obliterated by the blizzard.

As he had run from the house, out over the hill, he had run full pelt into a walker, winding his way back down off the hills. Had laid the guy out flat, had more or less run right over him, a prop forward steamrolling a full back.

That was the last he had seen of anyone. The closest policeman, he assumed, had run into the walker, or something else had caused him to lose his way. Now however, he had no idea if they had given up, or whether they were following his tracks at a measured pace.

And so he had not been sitting against the tree for long. This was a five minute break, a dubious five minutes he knew. The music drowned out all sound, giving him no chance to hear any approach before he saw it, and sitting down had allowed the pain in his ankles to fully show its severity.

The song faded and he clumsily turned the music off through gloved hands. Thanking some higher power in which he did not believe for having the good fortune for earlier putting his gloves in his pocket.
He was refreshed by Dylan, the way others are refreshed by nicotine or chocolate or alcohol. Or water. He stood up and the benefit of his addiction vanished in one searing blast of pain from his right ankle.
'Fuck,' he ejaculated at the cold forest air. 'Holy fuck.'
He fell back against the tree, sharp intakes of breath, hurried and desperate grasps at air. Stared back through agonised eyes at the path he had left through the snow leading straight to him. He couldn't stay there.
An hour earlier he was just a guy being wrongly accused of a terrible crime. Now he had resisted arrest and assaulted three police officers. Lake Weston, celebrity children's author, was going to be front page news, and this time at least some of it had the potential to be accurate.
A deep breath, bracing himself against the pain. He wanted to have the earphones back in, to turn the music up loud. It was all he could think of, it was the only pain killer he had. But he couldn't block out the afternoon like that, not with the police on his tail.
'Fuck it,' he said, summoning up some mental image from somewhere. He had to be a movie action hero, the type of guy who had to put up with crap and hurt and pain, and would just get through it.
He pushed himself away from the tree, grimacing, a loud blurt of tortured anguish, and staggered further into the wood. Leaning against trees, pushing himself off, driving himself forward, lurching on.

The blizzard could not last. Maybe for an hour it swirled and raged around him, sweeping in from the coast. Finally he noticed, as he lifted his head for the first time in several minutes, that at last the white hills stretched away from him, that he could see further than twenty yards. He looked over his shoulder at the receding storm. Still white and thick behind him, but clearing slowly.
Noticed the first hint of blue sky away to the west, out over the sea. Just like Scotland, he thought grimly. It would be summer some time in the next fifteen minutes. Then it would be raining before the hour was up.
He had begun to wonder how they would come after him. If they would come after him. How much of a priority would he be? Maybe that depended on the lies that had been told in the first place to instigate the newspaper stories and the visit from the police.
Dogs? A helicopter? Teams of officers sweeping across the hills? However it went, he wasn't going to be able to hide for very long, regardless of how well he knew the terrain.

He looked around him as the countryside opened up. No other sign of civilisation, not a house, not a telegraph pole. However, he knew the road would not be far over the hill to his right. He had been walking wounded for an hour. He might have managed to elude his pursuers in the storm, but it didn't mean that he'd covered much ground. The road would be close, just as Ben Wyvis would soon be in sight on the other side of the glen. The question was whether he risked attracting attention to himself on the road, risked thumbing for a lift.

Forty minutes later he was lying behind a small, snow-covered mound, next to the Ullapool to Dingwall road. Had decided that he would only stop cars with foreign number plates, as those drivers were less likely to have read a British newspaper or watched the British news. It was a risky and insubstantial supposition on which to base his next move, but he had nothing else.

He had been lying by the road for ten minutes, out of sight. The road was still heavy with snow, the plough yet to come this far and cars too infrequent to have made a great difference.

He had been passed by nine cars in all in the first ten minutes or so of lying in the snow. Only one of them had had overseas number plates. He had risen quickly from his hiding place, the car had driven past, too fast in the snow. Dutch. A look of impassive disinterest on the driver's face.

He wanted to turn the music on. Couldn't afford to have any of his senses overtaken like that, however. He needed to focus.

Another car, another glance over the wall of snow, another white British number plate coming his way. This time he wondered if the driver noticed him poking his head over the white parapet, but the car did not slow. Realised he had to be more careful. Just eleven minutes in, cold and sore, and he was already re-evaluating his strategy. This wasn't the summer, there weren't going to be a hundred foreign cars along every hour. The one that had passed could be the one for the day.

He lay back from the edge, listened in the stillness. No wind, Highland calm, the dead silence of snow. The skies were bright although still with a light covering of high cloud.

Another thirty minutes, another seventeen cars. Legs aching dully, a dead pain accompanied by occasional shots of a knife thrusting into his ankle. Shivering, hurt, uncomfortable. Needed to be sitting down in a warm room, legs up. Wanted to be someone else, someone other than the cosseted author, the man with the comfortable life. Someone who could stand pain and discomfort.

A car, heading west. Senses awakened, pain instantly forgotten. This was the one. A sixth sense from nowhere. He edged up, looked along the road, through the hole in the snow. A white number plate, black letters. Still a short distance away, but he knew it wasn't British.

It was time. The first time he'd limped out, when the Dutch car had passed, he had been confident. Now, with more time spent fretting in hiding, he rose with trepidation.

He struggled up and waved a desolate hand at the car. Saw that it was a young woman, the plates of the car German.

'Ruddy perfect,' he thought. 'Hey!' he called out, unnecessarily.

The car slowed immediately. His ankle jerked with pain, he tried to keep the look from his face. Wasn't about to try and invoke sympathy. Just wanted a lift somewhere, to get off the road and off the hills.

The car stopped, window down. White Audi A3 Cabriolet.

'Hey,' she said. 'Are you all right?'

She spoke English with a vague pan-European accent.

'Sure,' said Weston. He indicated the hills. 'Out walking, got caught in the blizzard. Went over on my ankle a bit. Can you give me a lift?'

'Yes. I am going to Ullapool though.'

As if Ullapool would be the last place anyone wanted to go. Weston smiled, despite the pains shooting all over the lower half of his body.

'That's great,' said Weston. 'I've got a hotel there.'

He winced again. At the lie. There was no need to lie. He opened the car door and eased himself in.

'You look in pain,' she said.

'I'm fine. Just twisted it,' he said.

He didn't look at her. Pulled the collar up on his coat, closed the car door, was subsumed by beautiful warmth.

She was thirty, short brown hair. Thin face, wide mouth. Freckles. A boyish look about her. She moved off along the snowy road.

'You walked from Ullapool this morning?'

He stared along the road. Suddenly nervous. He was not used to this, the basic lie to a total stranger. What story explained him so far from the town, walking with sore ankles? Where was his car or his backpack? Where was his tent? Already felt like he could get into a tangle of lies, and she wasn't even trying to put him under any pressure.

'Got a lift some of the way along this morning,' he said eventually.

She glanced at him, looked back at the road.

'What about you?' he asked uncomfortably, wanting the conversation to be about something else.

'I work for a German travel firm. I drive around Europe, find places to stay, hotels to book, routes to take.'
'You came to Scotland in January?'
'Sure. Everyone knows about Scotland in the summer. Too much rain and too many insects. My boss wanted me to come and see what was wrong with it in the winter.'
'How's the list?'
'Coming on.'
She smiled, didn't look at him as there was a car coming in the other direction, and they had to squeeze past each other in the narrow lanes that had been carved through the snow.
'Plough,' said Weston.
'What?'
'Snow plough up ahead,' he said, pointing at the large yellow truck heading their way.
'Oh, OK. Maybe that's one less item on the list.'
They passed the plough in silence, sprayed with salt. The driving became easier. The silence lasted. Weston slumped lower in his seat. Closed his eyes. The hurt showed on his face. She tried not to look at him as she drove, stopped herself asking questions until they got close.
'Which hotel are you staying at?'
They had come down the hill and turned right, arriving at Loch Broom and the last of the drive along to Ullapool.
Weston had tried to block out the pain, but he couldn't. The dull ache was there, the shooting shafts of agony kept coming. Trying to breathe normally, trying not to make himself any more memorable than he was going to be. He wanted her to drop him off then forget him.
'Not sure,' he said automatically. 'Just drop me at the pier.'
She glanced at him curiously. Having come down to sea level, the snow was much thinner on the ground, the gritted road damp grey rather than white. He realised the peculiarity of the remark, but wasn't thinking, didn't really care. She could drop him off, he would walk away, she had served her purpose. Once in Ullapool, he just needed time to think. He had enough change in his pocket for a cup of tea, not a lot else. Any feelings of hunger were in any case being completely overwhelmed by the pain.
No more conversation. She picked up on his awkwardness, became curious and a little fearful. Recognised that there was more to him than a man who had been out walking and had gone over on his ankle. But then, wasn't this why she travelled? To meet interesting people, to experience

a sense of danger. Europe could be so safe, that was what her colleagues who travelled through Asia and Africa said.

'You know the town well?' she said.

'Not really,' he said.

'Maybe you could show me around,' she said anyway. Gave herself a small thrill with the suggestion. Suddenly felt absurdly nervous.

'I don't have the time,' he said bluntly.

She drove slowly up the one way street. Past the closed gift stores, the small cafés still hopefully open for business, the few shops, the bank, the fish & chip bar. Arrived at the pier, she pulled into the small carpark. Finally looked at him properly. He still had his eyes closed.

'You sure you'll be all right?' she said.

He opened his eyes, stared harshly at her, took in his surroundings. He nodded, then quickly opened the door and stepped out of the car. She didn't want him to go. He had adventure attached to him. The words were there, but she didn't say them.

It didn't matter. He didn't get far.

He leant on the car door, put his weight on his right foot. It felt as though he had been shot in the ankle. He collapsed in an ugly, agonised crumple, a loud yelp of pain let out into the cold afternoon. The smell of the sea.

She ran round the car. A couple of people on the street stopped to watch.

'What was that?' she said, bending over him. 'Are you all right?'

He smiled weakly through the grimace, a rueful, disembodied laugh. Face pale.

'Come on, get back in the car.'

She got behind him and put her hands under his arms. He levered himself back up, leaning on the side of the car. She pushed him. She was slight, little strength in her. He made most of the effort, all the weight on his arms, pushed himself up onto the seat.

She closed the door. Caught the eyes of a passer-by. Recognised that everyone watching assumed the incident to be drink related.

Got back into the car, looked at him. The white, strained face. Immediately he had begun to think that perhaps, if he handed himself in, he might at least get his ankle treated. Or maybe it was time to get to a hospital, and if he was handed over to the police, then so be it. It would be better than this.

Which wasn't necessarily accurate.

'I should take you to a hospital,' she said.

He looked straight ahead. Away to the right there was a newsagents, a small billboard outside. He looked at the headline, written out in black. It wasn't about him, not yet. It read *New Banking Crisis Leads To Fear Of Run*. Some other time he might have thought it clumsily written. This time he just saw his own name on it. Tomorrow's headline. *Suspected Paedophile Arrested.*

'No,' he said. 'I'll be OK, just give me a minute.'

'Let me take you to your hotel at least. You can barely move.'

The crashing, outrageous pain, the pain that had nearly made him black out, was beginning to ease off, the dull, dreadful ache returning.

'I don't have a hotel,' he said dully.

She nodded. 'I know.'

He glanced round at her.

'Lies that bad?'

'So should I take you to a hospital?'

He shook his head. He stared straight ahead, she stared at him. Trying to evaluate the man. Wondering what she was committing herself to. Maybe this would give her a story that she could tell to all her colleagues who spent their time in Africa.

'I...my room, you could stay in my room. Stay with me, if you like.'

He finally turned. She hadn't intended to sound so uncertain.

He didn't answer. It seemed too perfect. Picked up by a woman who then offered him her room. Suddenly he saw the security services written all over her face.

Another bullet ripped through his ankle.

31

Darkness had swept in over the hills. He sat in the car, eyes closed. No longer looking over his shoulder. She was checking into her hotel room, he wasn't thinking about how long she was taking. What other option did he have? She could have been CIA, MI5, MI6. She could even have been Stasi or KGB, it didn't matter. The alternative wasn't checking into an expensive Highland lodge. The alternative wasn't normality.

Let Me Die In My Footsteps. Eyes closed, he allowed early Dylan to smother him, quiet vocals, acoustic guitar. Music the only sound, the only sense. Music as an analgesic, the power of the mind. If people could be cured by placebos, if the brain could be fooled into thinking that the pain wasn't there, why not allow the pain to be eased by the same thing that so often eased his stress? If it was effective against angst, it could be effective against pain. Music therapy.

It wasn't working.

The door opened, his eyes snapped open at the rush of air. She was leaning over him, staring. Waited for him to remove his earphones.

'Sorry,' she said, 'I was getting a couple of things.'

He looked drawn, pale, ill.

'What were you getting?' he asked, more accusation than intended.

She held up a walking stick with an ornate stag's head handle.

'It'll draw too much attention if you stagger in, leaning all over me.'

He stared blankly. She took out two cups of coffee from a small bag and set them on the dashboard. Then two boxes of pain killers and a tin of spray for freezing the skin.

'We'll drive around for twenty minutes. You take the pain killers now. The strongest I could get over the counter. Take four. Spray your ankle. You might be able to take the edge off. Drink your coffee. Get in a frame of mind to walk into the hotel. When you do it, you're going to have to lean on nothing more than the stick and walk as easily as you can.'

She stopped, looking at him for some confirmation.

'I just thought, if you go in now...'

'No, no, it's good. I like it.'

She nodded, handed him the small bag and walked round the car.

'You want me to spray your ankle?' she asked as she sat down.

'Ankles,' said Weston. 'I should be all right.'

Bleacher stood looking over the Prime Minister's shoulder. A perfect view of where the PM's hair was thinning. They were reading a hastily compiled report on that day's banking crisis. Bullet points, so that it could be easily digested by the PM in under two minutes, but bullet points which failed to address the complexity of the issue. Bullet points which laid out what had happened that day and in the previous week and a half, but bullet points which failed to mention cause and effect. The years of fiscal mismanagement from every single financial institution and figure in the UK which had led to the current emergency.

'How long does the Chancellor last after this?' said the PM.

His first comment. A true politician, thought Bleacher. Fuck the poor bastards who would lose all their money, fuck the recession which was looming over the country like a tsunami. None of that mattered as much as political fallout.

'That's up to you, Prime Minister,' said Bleacher. 'There will be a rush to see him go. However, getting rid of him won't make the problem disappear. So, you take the sitting duck out of the firing line, we may get someone to replace him as Chancellor, but whoever that is...'

'I was thinking of promoting the Health Secretary,' the PM chipped in.

'Very well,' said Bleacher. 'But if you do that then he is inviolable on the crisis up until now. Putting it very simply, you're not.'

The PM turned and glanced at him.

'We've had a strong economy for years,' he said harshly.

And we all know what that was built on, thought Bleacher.

'Leave him,' he said instead. 'Let him take the flak, see how it pans out.'

'He's going to get his arse ripped off.'

'Fine. We just need to leave it there as a line of defence for as long as possible. Before they get to your arse.'

The PM glowered at him, then once more read quickly over the report.

'Bloody hell,' he said eventually, screwing the paper up in one hand. He threw the ball of bad news at the wall and walked over to the window. 'At this rate, by the time Lisbon comes into effect, we'll be the poor, desperate whipping boys of Europe. The whole point is for us to be equal partners, not Cyprus. We'll just get our arses kicked.'

'What you do now is the important thing,' said Bleacher.

'And what is that?'

Bleacher stared across the chasm of the room. Why is it that election to high office immediately deprives a person of the ability to think for himself, he wondered? A complete inability to make decisions without someone telling you what they should be. Which was why Bleacher was quite happy where he was. He could walk down the street and no one noticed him, he never received the blame when things went wrong.

And yet he ran the country.

'Absolutely nothing,' he said.

The PM grunted. Turned away, walked over to the drinks cabinet. He glanced at the clock to make sure it was after five o'clock.

'Tell me about Weston,' he said shortly.

Bleacher had been enjoying the distraction of Lake Weston. However, he realised that as the media got hold of the new banking meltdown, no matter what they did at Number 10, Lake Weston was not going to be on anyone's front page the following day.

'It's in hand,' said Bleacher.

'Do we know where he is?'

Bleacher didn't reply.

The PM turned sharply.

'Well, where the fuck is he?'

Bleacher stared at the PM, nodded his head, turned and walked quickly out of the office.

Weston lay in the bath, his pained ankles soaking in the warmth. The hurt in his left ankle had almost completely gone. His right ankle now throbbed gently, but nowhere near as badly as it had an hour earlier.

She had helped him out of his clothes and into the bath, and he hadn't been in any position to complain about it. Not that he would have.

There was a knock at the bathroom door and she walked in without waiting for him, holding two glasses of white wine, the glasses clouded over with the chill of the liquid. He smiled weakly. She handed him the glass, closed the door over with her foot, put the lid down on the toilet and sat down.

'You're very German,' he said.

'Nudity?' she asked.

He nodded. Took the first sip of wine. Cold, very dry, very smooth.

'This is a nice wine,' he said.

She looked down his body. More bruises than those on his ankles, but they were the worst of it. Both swollen, the right having ballooned. He had left it in the water for a short while, and now had it perched on the edge of the bath.

'How do they feel?' she asked.

'Sitting here, a warm bath, alcohol and pain killers, not too bad.'

'Neither of them is broken.'

He took another long drink of wine, laid his head back, closed his eyes. Any time he thought of what the morning would bring, he closed his mind to it and determinedly thought of something else. For the moment he was fine, relaxed, pain levels controlled. All the crap that he had to face, everything that life was currently throwing at him, it could all wait.

'It will be very painful in the morning, however,' she said. He opened his eyes. She wasn't smiling. 'Should I call for a doctor?'

He shook his head.

'You are going to tell me why not.'

He couldn't tell whether or not that had been a question.

'If I tell you, then you could get into trouble if someone finds me. I don't tell you, then I'm just a guy you picked up at the side of the road.'

'You think I am better not to know?'

'Yes.'

She suddenly drained her glass in one very quick gulp.

'I need to go to the restaurant for dinner,' she said. 'I will order room service for you when I get back.'

She stood up, tipped the glass back to get the dregs.

'See you later,' she said. She walked out. He watched her go, her black jeans tight across her backside. The curve of her hips, the movement of her buttocks. The bedroom door closed, the key in the lock. He wondered if this was the moment when the men in black would come in and gun him down, or thrust a bag over his head and haul him off.

Silence. He rested his head back against the bath.

'It would probably be too much of a cliché if I just fucked her,' he said to himself, smiling ruefully.

His foot slipped off the rim of the bath, hit the tap and splashed brutally into the water.

'Fuck!' he yelled, the pain shooting once more up his leg.

◉

She wondered if he might be asleep by the time she got back to the room. The dining room had been wonderful, what she had been told to anticipate from a hotel in the Highlands. She had eaten smoked salmon and roast venison, drunk a half bottle of red wine. She was unsure about the man in her room, but she had dulled her uncertainties with alcohol.

The waiter had been cute, but she had had to accept that there was nothing happening there. She hated going back to the place of lodging of the itinerant waiting staff. They never had any money, their places always depressed her. Usually she just took them back to her room. Fucking her way round Europe, that's what they said about her at the office when she wasn't there. She would have cared if she'd known.

Nevertheless she lingered in the restaurant and in the bar afterwards feeling slightly uncomfortable about the man waiting for her. Some time after ten she reluctantly took herself back up the stairs. A little drunk. Let herself into the room, expecting quiet, possibly the uncomfortable sounds of someone sleeping in pain.

Weston was watching the news. Eleven minutes past ten and they were still talking about the banking crisis. Live footage of people queuing up outside banks for the following day. She stood just inside the doorway, her eyes on the television. He looked at the remote, on top of the television. Four and a half yards away, that was all. Could have been a mile. The story of Lake Weston, paedophile, had been listed as second item on the news.

Suddenly nervous, thinking he would betray himself if he leapt painfully from his seat, he sat rooted, waiting for the report to change. They had told the banking story in the first thirty seconds, and here they were, still talking ten minutes later.

He glanced back at her. For the first time he wished that they had framed him with something else. Hadn't really thought about it before now. He had just been running, not thinking. Now he felt the shame of what they were accusing him of. They had known what they were doing.

His suspicions of her had gone. She was the only thing saving him from capture and the opprobrium of the masses.

The reporter in the field, standing in Generic High Street, Generic Town, wrapped it up, the news switched back to the studio. Weston's mouth was dry. The news anchorman mentioned the name Lake Weston and child abuse in the first sentence of the next report.

'You people panic at anything,' she said, and turned away into the bathroom. She closed the door just as Weston's picture came up on the screen. He wondered if she was referring to the banking crisis.

Weston relaxed slightly, but watched the report in horror as his name was publicly dragged through the mire. Wondered what Strachan was thinking of all this.

Listened to the sound of a long pee from the bathroom. Imagined her sitting on the toilet, jeans at her ankles. Grateful that they had not exchanged names.

By the time she emerged, they had already moved on to three more British Army deaths in Afghanistan. She stood and watched for a second and then walked over to the television and turned it off.

'The news is always depressing,' she said.

She stood in front of the television. He was in a bathrobe, both ankles perched on a soft stool in front of him. Slim, attractive, face no longer showing the pale strain of pain that it had for the first couple of hours.

'Are you hungry?' she said. 'We should order room service.'

He nodded. She walked over to the phone, lifted the receiver and the menu folder which was lying on the table beside it, and ordered the first two items on the list.

They made love starting at 11:13pm and finishing twenty-nine minutes later. He was uncomfortable to start with, forgot his pain at some point, felt sore when they had finished. It was better than he had expected. She had not been disappointed either. They had laughed at the end.

She liked to keep count. Weston was her two hundredth and forty-first lover. He assumed that she wouldn't have slept with him if she'd known he was an accused child sex offender.

Eldon Strachan had lost all sense of everything, except pain. He had lost connection with everyone. He didn't miss anyone anymore. He didn't wish he was at work, he didn't wish he was at the club having a meeting over fresh lobster and a bottle of Pinot. He didn't wish for the open spaces of his occasional sailing weekends down at Kingsbridge, he didn't wish he was sitting in the pub with his two oldest friends, drinking a pint of Thatcher's and watching the Test Match.

It wasn't that all hope was gone. He had moved on from the loss of hope, from the rush of despair and the tearful derangement of pessimism and desperation, to complete emptiness.

He felt nothing, nothing at all. He was merely existing, lying on a cold stone floor. Fitful, uncomfortable sleep, no dreams. He wasn't hungry, he wasn't thirsty.

He was alive, but that was all.

Occasionally he twitched.

Richard Morrison was being processed. When he had been put on the plane in the UK there had been a reason why it had happened. Now he was just a guy. Just a number. Just another person who the guards had to watch, just someone else who was fed sparse food, allowed to exercise for fifteen minutes a day, and who would, at some point in the possibly distant future, receive a visit from a lawyer or a prosecutor.

Richard Morrison had been swallowed up.

Of the three men who had known about the writing and publication of *Axis of Evil*, Lake Weston, the one who was actually responsible, had so far got off most lightly. Not that it seemed that way to him at that point in time, but while on the down side he had no money, had been forced to flee his home and was having his name falsely dragged through the media gutter, he was spending his second night in a row in a beautiful old Highland hotel, had had sex with women on consecutive nights, had fed well on Highland broth and Norwegian caviar, and had drunk the better part of a bottle and a half of wine.

Morrison would have given anything for it. Strachan had forgotten what wine tasted like.

Weston was sitting at the window, legs down for the moment, looking out at what he could see of Loch Broom. A dark night, no moon. Cold. Maybe more snow in the air. She was watching him from the bed.

He could feel her eyes.

'What about tomorrow?' she said.

Head on the pillow, hands dragging the duvet to her neck. Felt the cold in every bone. Wanted him to come to bed.

'Where are you going?' he asked.

He was giving her nothing. Nothing to attach herself to, nothing to make her like him, nothing to hang on to.

'Up the west coast. Booked into a hotel in Durness in a couple of days. Not sure where I'll stop tomorrow. Another day and back to Inverness.'

He didn't say anything. He was trying to calculate, but felt as if he was doing it from a position of having no idea what the numbers looked like. He wasn't trained to run or hide. He wasn't trained for any of this.

He needed somewhere to go and someone solid to turn to.

Eldon Strachan. He would be pissed off at him, but he would believe him at least. He had to get to London.

'You come with me?' she said.

He finally turned and looked at her. It would be so easy. A few days touring the north. He could keep his head down, rest his ankle. Maybe the story wouldn't blow over, but it might at least die off a little. And at some point, possibly, he would work out what the hell he was supposed to do in this situation.

But he couldn't. He couldn't walk away, he couldn't take a holiday. Not now, while his Rome burned.

'I need you to give me some money,' he said coldly.

'How much?' she asked without hesitation. As unsure of herself as he was. A loan seemed straightforward, just an uncomplicated business transaction.

He hadn't thought about that, hadn't expected the answer.

'Two hundred pounds,' he said. That would get him to London, get him some food, get him a night or two somewhere cheap if he needed it.

'Do I get it back?' she asked. Didn't care at all about the money.

'I'll send it to you when I get access to my accounts again.'

He stared through the semi-darkness at her, finally turned away. This was how he was getting through this, with the belief that he was in a horror two or three day period. At some stage, some time soon, the truth would come out, it would all be over and he would have access again to everything he owned. Money, house, car.

'And I'll need a pair of scissors and a razor,' he said without feeling, without gratitude.

32

She was gone when he awoke, daylight filling the room. He snapped out of sleep like he'd had a bucket of ice water flushed over his face. Briefly wondered if she had just got in her car and driven away, then saw her clothes from the day before still draped over the chair.

Head back on the pillow, as the pain from his right ankle travelled up his body to meet him. He winced, opened his eyes, looked to the bedside table to see if the pain killers were there. He'd left them in the bathroom, along with the spray. Head back down, not yet ready to limp out of bed. Was aware that his ankle was even more puffed up than before.

He had been awake for twenty minutes, lying still in the warmth, staring at the ceiling, when the door opened and she came back into the room. She was carrying a couple of bags, which she laid on the end of the bed, away from his feet.

She looked down at him for a short while, a dead gaze. The distance between them had grown as they had slept one and a half feet apart.

'I got you a change of clothes, a new jacket. A razor, shaving foam, hat, glasses. Toothbrush. I've ordered breakfast, should be up in fifteen minutes. I would like to leave after that.'

He nodded, looked down at the bags she'd placed on the bed.

'Thank you,' he said, his first words of appreciation since they had met the previous afternoon.

'That's all right.'

She stood for a second, and then walked to the desk beside the television, took a laptop from a small briefcase and set it up.

He watched her for a short while and then slowly eased himself out the side of the bed.

When he emerged limping from the bathroom, a short while later, he had shaved his head and shaved his five day old beard into an insubstantial goatee. Along with the plain-lens, black, chunky-rimmed glasses which she'd bought, he looked sufficiently different from the man in the photographs in all that day's newspapers.

'Your breakfast,' she said. 'I didn't order cooked. I guessed since you are British that you would take tea.'

He walked slowly over to where the trolley had been placed by the window. Pain killers and spray, a quick bath. He felt surprisingly better than he had the previous day.

She continued to type, her fingers a blur across the keyboard.

'You got the size right,' he said.

'I checked your pants.'

'Not sure about the jacket,' he said, smiling. Too late, deciding that maybe there was a place for some warmth in their conversation. He was fussy about jackets.

She stopped typing but didn't turn round. Her shoulders rose and fell, deep breath. Started typing again.

'I'm sorry,' he found himself saying, 'the jacket's fine.'

Finally she turned and looked at him. Her face looked strained for the first time since she had picked him up the day before.

'What?' he said. Suddenly uncomfortable.

She hesitated another second. Pursed lips.

'In the description that the police gave to the newspapers about you, they mentioned the jacket. You need to dispose of your jacket.'

Silence enveloped them. A long gaze into each other's eyes, then she looked away. To the window, where the cold raindrops had started hitting the glass. He looked at the breakfast which sat on the small table in front of him.

Two croissants, three rolls, butter, margarine, honey, strawberry jam, marmalade, glass of orange juice, pot of tea, sugar, small jug of milk.

He poured himself a cup of tea. It was already stewed and had lost the edge from the heat. A little milk. Lifted one of the croissants.

'It's not true,' he said.

This was it for him, for the first time confronted by someone who had read the allegations. Even as he said the words, they didn't sound convincing. Not even to him, the only person who really knew the truth.

'Someone's out to get me. Made up a story.'

He lowered his eyes, bit into the croissant. Crumbs on his lips.

'Who?' she asked.

Stopped himself before he said the words *the government*. What was he going to sound like? And in that instant had a great, all-encompassing moment of realisation. Nothing insightful, nothing that wouldn't have occurred to him if this case had been about someone else. But now, finally confronted with having to explain himself to someone, it was obvious to him.

He was a sex offender. It was in the newspapers, it was now the popular belief of most of the country. Lake Weston, sex offender. It didn't matter that he had never, in his life, committed such an offence, it didn't matter that he had never had the thought, had never gone near or even suggested anything improper to any child.

It was the government. They framed me. Who was going to believe that? The government knew it. They could say anything, get anything out there, use whatever underground sources they felt like using, and he was completely screwed.

To all intents and purposes, as far as everyone knew, just plain downright damned for all time, Lake Weston molested children.

'Was there anything about *Axis of Evil*?'

'What?'

'*Axis of Evil*,' he said sharply. Sudden urgency in his voice. She heard the fear. 'It's a book that came out a couple of days ago.'

She looked unsure, shook her head.

'One of them had the headline *Axis of Evil*, included a picture of your Prime Minister and a couple of others I did not recognise. But I think the story was to do with the banking crisis. That's what most of the papers led with. One of the bigger papers had a picture of you on the cover, but not the headline story.'

He took a long drink of tea. Here he was, not long before nine o'clock in the morning, and he needed something stronger. Two mouthfuls of food and he no longer felt like eating. That was breakfast.

'Tell me what it said.'

'I do not want to.'

'Look,' he said sharply, then took a deep breath, controlling his annoyance. 'I know you have no reason to believe me, but I doubt any of it will be true. I just need to know what it said.'

'There had been a complaint of sexual abuse made against you by a twelve year-old girl. Since that claim had been made public, some others had come out with the same claim. The police say that when they came to your house to question you, you assaulted three officers in the process. Two of them are still in hospital, one seriously ill.'

He looked up at her, mouth open, stomach in his chest.

'Holy crap,' he said.

He rubbed his forehead. Despite the fact that he knew the first part of the story to be untrue, he still automatically believed that there was a police officer seriously ill in hospital because of him.

'I didn't mean to hit them that hard,' he said.

'So why did you?'

'I... I needed to run.'

'Why? If it's not true?'

'I just.....I believe someone is trying to set me up. Whoever that is, I don't want to get taken into custody. I need to be out here.'

'Where you can hide in a stranger's hotel room?'

'I need to get to London.'

'Last night I was helping a guy, a cute guy, who seemed a bit lost. Today I'm helping a sex offender on the run.'

'I'm not a sex offender...'

'Then why did you run?'

He leant back. That was the question he was going to run into for the rest of his life. Why had he run?

'Did it mention the book, *Axis of Evil*, did it mention that it in the report?'

'I said no,' she said, shaking her head.

'Crap. I need to make a phone call. Can I use your phone?'

She smiled ruefully, looked away.

'Why not? You are fucking me over in no end of other ways.'

'I'm not...' He let the sentence drift off. He looked lost, desperate. She tossed her phone to him.

'Thank you.'

He flipped the cover, quickly dialled the number of Strachan's office. Would he believe him, or would he already be distancing himself from his most successful writer? Would he already have made that quote to the newspapers? *I barely have any contact with Lake Weston. Although I am his editor, he keeps himself to himself and we never meet...*

Joanne answered the phone. Voice sounded strained. Weston winced. He didn't have a plan for the eventuality that it wasn't Strachan who answered. Usually it was the man himself or his voicemail. He hadn't even had a plan for the voicemail.

'I'm looking for Eldon Strachan,' he said, broadening his Scottish accent. The accent he once had before he'd moved away from Glasgow, before he'd changed his name from Malcolm to Lake.

'Mr Strachan's not in the office today,' replied Joanne.

'Will he be in tomorrow?'

'We're not sure. Can I take a message?'

We're not sure... Weston's mind raced. What did that mean? Strachan was always available, always took calls. He lived on his phone.

'Why isn't he in the office?' he asked.

'Can I ask who's calling, please?'

Another hesitation. Having to think too many things through at once.

'It's me, Joanne,' he said eventually, softening his voice. 'Lake. Please don't hang up. Or anything.'

'Mr Weston? Where are you?' Sounded shocked.

Joanne had been in publishing a long, long time. Long past retirement age, but Strachan persuaded her every year to keep going. She liked to talk about the time she'd met Ian Fleming.

'I'm in London. I just need to speak to Eldon. Is he around?'

He heard a noise down the phone. She was trying to control herself and not succeeding.

'It's all lies, Joanne,' he said, wrongly assuming that she was upset about him. 'The stuff in the papers, none of it's true. Someone's...'

'It's Eldon,' she said, voice breaking. 'He's missing... His wife was found dead yesterday morning...'

Her voice cracked and broke. Lake Weston's mouth hung open. He lowered the phone.

33

Twenty minutes later he was ready to go. Bag packed with the clothes he'd worn for the past two days, a final check in the mirror. Thick-rimmed glasses, fledgling goatee, hat pulled down over his ears. Just a guy in a hat, two hundred pounds in his pocket.

He stepped out of the bathroom. She was at the window, ready to go.

'Thanks for your help,' he said.

She turned slowly. She looked bitter and annoyed rather than upset, which made him feel easier. He had hung on the phone for almost five minutes while Joanne cried.

'What was the phone call?'

He let out a long breath, squeezed the top of his stick.

'My editor,' he said. 'He's missing. His wife's dead.' The fear that had gripped him at various stages the previous day had come swooping back, grabbing his stomach, tightening, wrenching.

Nothing to say, she lifted her bag, tossed her small bag over her shoulder and walked to the door.

Along the corridor, down the stairs to reception. Without a word. Weston hobbling, all his weight on the stick. She stood at the counter, completing the transaction. Wondered how closely the receipt would be studied by accounts at her office.

He stood at the fireplace and looked at a picture of a herd of deer in a glen. Wondered if every single hotel in the Highlands had such a picture. Dark and brooding sky, dark green hills, deer huddled in a group, the occasional stag set apart. Dry stone walls in need of repair.

She came and stood beside him, but she wasn't looking at the picture.

'I believe you,' she said. 'But with all these stories in the media, you are screwed, you must realise this.'

He lowered his gaze, stared at the hearth. A hearth in need of warmth.

'I can give you a lift to the train station.'

'I'll be all right,' he said, 'it's not far.'

'Do not be stupid,' she said. 'You can still barely walk. I will take you.'

He nodded, moved off behind her as she walked to the door. Outside the day was cold and grey. The rain had stopped, the ground still wet.

There was a police car in the carpark, three officers sitting inside. They both hesitated when they saw it, then Weston started moving more quickly towards her car. Felt instant sharp pains in his ankle.

Maybe if they'd just walked normally they would have been fine. The police weren't looking for a guy with thick glasses. But they were looking for someone with a limp who panicked at the sight of the police.

Words were exchanged in the police car. Weston looked round. There was another car across the road, thirty yards from the hotel.

'Fuck,' he muttered. He looked sharply at her.

'I did not say anything,' she said.

'Just get in the car,' he said. 'Drive away slowly.'

The door to the police car opened.

'Oh, shit,' she said.

She blipped the lock, opened the door and threw her bags into the back.

'Excuse me, Madam,' said the policeman.

Weston opened the front passenger door, sat down quickly, bag at his feet. She hurriedly got in. The policeman approached. She glanced at Weston as she started the engine.

'Do it,' he said. The tone sounded like someone else.

She instantly gunned the car into second and screeched away through the car park, rubber and smoke, the policeman jumping out of the way.

'Fucking crap,' he muttered. He jumped back into the car, started the engine and was soon in tandem with the other car, in pursuit of the white Audi heading south on the A835.

◉

She drove expertly, but once out of town it is a long, mostly straight road, the bends fast and sweeping, and the police car had little trouble keeping up. Weston sat beside her, head in his hands. Worrying about Strachan, worrying strangely about what he was now going to do when he got to London. As if he was likely to ever get to London. Morbidly curious about his accomplice and her motivation.

They didn't talk. Sped past other vehicles. The road was quiet, other cars few and easily overtaken. Only twice did she have to pass on a blind corner. The police weren't trying anything fancy, knew that there was nowhere for her to go.

Weston had started thinking about road blocks. The police weren't just going to keep driving after them at one hundred and twenty miles an hour until they got to Dover. They needed to get off the main road, disappear somewhere. But they weren't in a 4x4, and even if they had been, the hills were still covered in white, their path would have been obvious for miles around.

She drove hunched over the steering wheel. He leant forward, head down, trying not to watch. The speed scared him.

'Look,' she said.

He glanced up. A police helicopter, hovering low in the sky, maybe half a mile away. She didn't slow. He didn't think.

'We need to get off this road,' she said.

He shook his head, then lowered it again. Couldn't look at the road. There was nowhere to go, no route that would be substantial and drivable and would give them a chance to escape.

Why was the helicopter hovering at that precise point?

He looked up. They were approaching a bend, braking hard. Still coming too fast. The trailing police car had dropped back a little further.

'Road block!' he shouted.

'Where?'

She turned the corner. The helicopter was right in front of them, above the road. There were three police cars strung across the road, barriers in front of the cars. Trees on one side, a building on the other. No space either side. A fourth police car behind, widening the barrier.

She didn't brake.

'What the fuck!' he shouted.

She had nothing to say. Adrenaline rush.

'Brake! Jesus! There's nowhere to go!'

She picked her gap in the trees, suddenly jerked off the road. Not thinking on any level. Going with the flow of the chase. Experiencing life beyond hotels and travelling and claim forms and promiscuous sex.

They cracked over a small silver birch, the car jolted, slowed. He let out another cry. The car bumbled heavily through the snow, over thick roots. She kept her foot down, dropped a gear, accelerated through a small gap.

The police hadn't followed her in. They knew these woods. So did Weston.

The clearing closed quickly. A dramatic swerve, she clipped a tree as she aimed for a small opening. The car spun up on two wheels then suddenly it had shot up vertically.

Weston closed his eyes, heart in mouth, buried his head in his knees. She had a look of horror on her face. They crashed into a tree. The

windscreen shattered, the car stopped dead. Airbags exploded, the car toppled to the side. Fell forwards onto the jagged stump of an old pine.
The stump burst the airbag and, with no windscreen to get in the way, wedged itself in the neck of Karin Asterman. Blood spurted from three different wounds, oesophagus crushed, neck snapped. Her head toppled forward, eyes still open, chin slumping on her chest.
Weston groaned.

The PM had been short with the Dutch Prime Minister for most of the meeting. The Dutch Prime Minister had been a little surprised but it had only confirmed his worst thoughts about the British and their rudeness. The PM had at least said all the right things with regards to European integration, the war on terror and the need to guard against overly liberal freedoms of human rights in these troubled and dangerous times.
He had switched the ill-humour off and the attempted charm on for the ten minute press conference.
They parted on brusque terms, neither of them looking forward to meeting again for dinner later that evening. The Dutch Prime Minister went off with his ambassador to a meeting with the head of ING in London, a meeting which everyone knew was of much greater importance to him. The PM quickly and quietly walked across Downing Street, surprised a couple of security guards, and entered the Foreign Office, muttering darkly, needing to find Bleacher.
He usually got the news from Bleacher. Even the world news, the American news, the sports news. Suited him, and most definitely suited Bleacher. Late that morning, for no particular reason, he had decided to take one of his sporadic dips into the one minute radio news headlines.
The top story had been the banking crisis and the threat to the British economy, political pundits guessing that the Chancellor would be gone in a matter of days, with the possibility of the PM following soon after. Second story, the book that was sweeping the country. *Axis of Evil* and a lengthening list of commentators willing to support its claims and its moral authority. And now the first three MP's had spoken up on its behalf, one of them from his own party. Third item on the news, the arrest of celebrity children's author and wanted paedophile, Lake Weston, now being held in custody in the Highlands.
A junior clerk walked past him carrying a brown envelope. Seemed surprised to see the PM walking the corridors of the ministry on his own. But the PM was looking for blood and didn't want company until he found his prey. He brushed past the clerk and swept angrily up the stairs,

two steps at a time. First floor, straight to the great wooden door, pushed it open.

He stomped angrily into the office, not closing the door behind him. The six people looked up at him as he entered. Anger, then surprise. The PM scowled. In his day the Foreign Secretary had only had four members of staff.

'Bleacher?' he snapped, not breaking his stride.

Three of them answered in the affirmative.

'Prime Minister?' said the Foreign Secretary's PPS, who had been standing up, checking the following week's diary. The PM ignored him, pushed the door open, marched into the office and slammed the door shut behind him.

Bleacher and the Foreign Secretary were drinking tea. The light was still bright from outside, but there were two table lamps on.

'Prime Minister!' said the Foreign Secretary, surprised.

They both looked guilty, which did not improve the PM's mood.

'Give me the latest,' he snapped.

From Day One the PM, like all his predecessors, had been looking over his shoulder. In jealous moments he could easily imagine Bleacher and the Foreign Secretary discussing the latter's ascension to the top job.

Bleacher looked at his watch as he stood up.

'You're due with the Home Secretary in thirty-two minutes, Prime Minister, to discuss the latest phone-tapping proposals.'

'That's not what I meant,' he snarled.

He looked at the Foreign Secretary. Maybe it was time for a reshuffle in the direction of incompetence, in the best Thatcher tradition.

'Right,' he said to Bleacher, 'you're finished here. Walk with me.'

Bleacher moved quickly, glancing back at the Foreign Secretary.

They marched back through the front office, out into the main corridor. Great murals of Empire stared down at them from the walls and ceiling.

'Three fucking MPs are supporting the moral authority of this book? Tell me their names.'

'It's seven now. There's a bit of momentum gathering. It doesn't look good. Two of ours so far, most of the others are Lib Dems.'

The PM stopped and stared at him briefly, then continued on his way.

'Jenkiss and Waterstone,' said Bleacher.

'Big fucking surprise. Has the Chief Whip been to see them yet?'

'He's waiting to talk to you. It's scheduled after the Home Secretary.'

'Well get on the phone and reschedule it. I want to see him now. I want this stopped. In fact, get me the other two leaders. We can't let this go any further. If these fucking MPs start making statements of their own accord, it's practically the breakdown of parliamentary democracy.'

Bleacher flipped open his phone. He had learned to just hear the instructions and not the absurd tangential commentary.

The PM crashed through a couple of doors, into the stairwell, started jogging down two at a time.

'And who the fuck arrested the writer? What is that all about?'

He stopped at the foot of the stairs.

'Seriously,' he said, 'who did that? He's not supposed to be in custody.'

'We couldn't tell every single police force that we were framing the man and didn't want him arrested yet. We hoped he would run, he did. Just turns out he was useless at it. He's a writer, not SIS.'

'Well get one of our people up there and bring him down to London.'

Bleacher nodded. The PM walked quickly along the short corridor.

'And we need to get the bank off the front pages,' he said. 'Where's the Chancellor?'

'Meeting the Chairman of the Bank of England,' said Bleacher.

The PM snorted.

'He's also scheduled to go to a queue outside a bank to try and talk to customers. Thought it would be good PR.'

The PM stared at the cold, stone floor. Felt almost uncontrollable rage. 'Holy fuck!' he exclaimed. 'What do you have to do in this town to get some competency?'

34

His name was Mr Higgins. Sitting at the table he betrayed many signs. Three pencils lined up beside the A4 notebook, which itself was aligned at precise angles to the corners of the small desk. The pencils were all new and unused, the ends perfectly sharp. HB.

He took an expensive cell phone from his pocket and placed it neatly beside the book. Took a second to make sure it was in exactly the correct position.

'This interview will be recorded,' he said, his voice a monotone. He was staring down at the blank page of the notebook.

'What by?' asked Weston nervously, looking at the phone.

Higgins glanced up, caught Weston staring, then automatically adjusted the position of the phone by a millimetre.

'You're here because of allegations made by a series of young children regarding your behaviour towards them.'

The nerves crept back into Weston's stomach. He had been held in a cell in Inverness for a number of hours. Had lost track of time. He had asked to call a lawyer, but had been refused. When he had demanded to call a lawyer, he had been quoted the Criminal Justice and Police Act 2001. He could be held for seven days before being allowed to call anyone. This had been news to him, as it was to most people held under those circumstances. The police could pluck you out of bed, lock you up, and they didn't have to tell anyone about it for seven days. As he had sat in his cell, he wondered what would happen if he was reported missing to the police. Would they start looking for him? Would they hold a press conference?

At some point he had been taken out of his cell, blindfolded, put in a van and taken to the airport. Put on a plane, which flew for about an hour and a half. He had assumed he was in London.

The frustrations had come and gone, risen fearfully in his stomach and disappeared in rare moments of resigned calm. He had cried at one point.

'No, I'm not,' he said eventually, decisively.

'Why do you think you're here?' said Higgins. Impassive face.

Weston held his gaze for a moment before Higgins broke it and stared down at the blank sheet of paper. Weston looked round at the man standing in the corner. Hands behind his back, legs slightly parted, straight shoulders, dead eyes, expressionless face.

'Because I wrote *Axis of Evil*,' said Weston quickly.

Higgins moved one of the pencils the merest fraction of a centimetre, and then had to adjust the other two pencils until they were in line.

'It says here you're a children's author,' he said, indicating the notebook.

Weston stared at the blank piece of paper, the perfectly neat book which had never been written in.

'I wrote *Axis of Evil* after the government banned one of my children's books. I was annoyed.'

As the words tripped off his tongue it did not even occur to him how soft an interrogation target he was. If they had him in here to extract a confession, they had it in under two minutes.

Higgins stared at the empty page.

'There's been nothing to indicate that you're capable of such a book as *Axis of Evil*. While it is obviously an illegal work, contravening myriad articles of anti-terror legislation, it is also a work of some quality. Clearly it was not written by you.'

'I wrote the damned book,' barked Weston.

'Why?'

Another short glance up from the notebook, a dead look into the back of Weston's head. Dropped his gaze. This time he lifted one of the pencils, the one on the right, and held it in his fingers, poised, as if he was going to write down everything Weston was about to say.

Weston was allowing him to push the buttons. Getting annoyed, worried, tense, all on cue.

'Because you can't write a children's book without the government sticking their nose in. Because you can't protest outside parliament. Because anyone, just about anywhere, can get access to your phone records and your bank account details. Because you can be held for seven days without making a phone call.'

Higgins drew a straight line, then another perpendicular along the bottom. Weston watched the movement of the pencil.

'You think we should sit back and give the terrorists free reign?'

The pencil moved along the top, completing the gallows. He fleshed out the blocks of wood, drew in a noose, the hoops in the rope intricately drawn. He shaded areas around the scene, started to draw in a platform.

Everything he did unnerved Weston.

'You think we should sit back and give the terrorists free reign?' Higgins repeated.

'No,' said Weston. 'But the government takes actions in the Middle East specifically designed to increase the enmity of these people, you make them hate us, and then you say, see, told you there were terrorists. Then you exaggerate the threat, so you can put in all this Soviet-style legislation. Where were these laws twenty years ago with the IRA? Why now? Why all this legislation that infringes civil liberty, when you didn't do it when we had an actual, credible, active terror threat on the British mainland for nearly thirty years?'

Higgins stared at him, a longer, withering gaze. Weston had said his piece, but his conviction had failed as he'd talked. It had been Morrison or Gilroy talking. He had written a book he thought worth writing, he had made a point he felt needed to be made, but he hadn't wanted his life turned upside down for it. He didn't want to die for it.

'Writers are supposed to be intelligent observers of life.'

Higgins had scribbled in the executioner, the rope dangled in the breeze.

'Only missing one thing,' he added.

'What are you getting at?' said Weston. 'You just said yourself that *Axis of Evil* was a work of quality.'

'However misguided,' replied Higgins in a morbid drone. 'The prose itself may have been well written, the author displays a confident ear for dialogue, but the subtext...'

He stared at Weston, the sentence hung.

'What?'

'The subtext,' continued Higgins, holding his gaze, 'is a piece of fucking crap. The work of a delinquent. The work of a twelve year-old on the cusp of becoming a communist for a few well-meaning years.'

'No!'

'Mr Weston, we live in an age of political correctness, an age where, thanks to the good civil liberties people, the criminals have more rights than their victims, an age where every act by the police and security services is scrutinised. It is the age of human rights and of the human rights lawyer. It is the age of television adverts promising money to the weak, if only they can think of some way in which the poor souls have been abused by authority.'

'What does that have to do with it?'

'All these powers that the police and security services now have, all these anti-civil liberty acts which they can now carry out, you really think they didn't used to do them? They have been doing this stuff for fifty years, a hundred years, just the same as they're doing it now. Thirty years ago, however, they were doing it illegally and it didn't matter, they still got their men, they still got the convictions. Now, there'd be a lawyer on the ten o'clock news before you can issue a warrant. All the work of the police has to be legalised, so that now when they catch a terrorist, the terrorist isn't going to get off on some legal loophole. That's why the laws are there when they didn't used to be.'

Weston stared across the desk. Once more out of his depth. He needed Morrison, sitting there beside him, talking for him. Morrison would have had an answer for that, as he had for everything.

'Your argument is that the police have been acting illegally for decades?' he said weakly. Desperate to find some certainty in his voice.

'The police have been protecting us for decades, by whatever means is required.'

Another dead stare across the table, then Higgins looked down and started to draw the figure in the gallows. Started with the feet, twitching through the trapdoor.

'Anyway,' he said, 'that's not why we're here. I don't believe that you wrote *Axis of Evil*, and neither will anyone else. We're here because of allegations made by young children that you're a paedophile. Would you like to have a conversation about that?'

The pencil moved slowly across the paper, drawing in the legs, the waist, the torso, the arms. The flailing arms.

35

Paddington Station was no busier than normal, but on that day there were still an average of one thousand three hundred and seventeen people in the station at any given time.

At the moment when the suicide bomber pulled the chord to the seventy pounds of explosive attached to his vest the number was slightly higher, due to the recent arrival of the 10:59 from Bristol Temple Meads and the late departure of the 12:26 to Swindon.

He picked his spot, just outside the barriers to Platform 1, as the rush of passengers swarmed through. Most of the passengers decanted from the 10:59 from Bristol Temple Meads noticed the man who stood in their way. Shaking, nervous, looking very hot and uncomfortable on a cold winter's day. They stepped out of his way, staring at the ground, trying not to look him in the eye. Assumed he was drunk.

When he put his hand inside his coat in order to pull the chord, three people noticed the movement, three people caught the glimpse of what was strapped to his chest. The one closest was frozen by uncertainty. Not quite able to believe she was seeing what she was seeing, unable to cry out or reach out. She slowed, a man bumped her from behind. Her mouth opened in shock. Someone else pushed desperately past her, reaching for the man in the coat, his fingers on a small piece of chord.

The bomb tore through the crowd. People, limbs, blood, body parts flew. Two nearby kiosks vanished, the adjacent café was destroyed. Two men emerging from the toilet were thrown back. Porters, passengers, security guards...

Fifty-seven people died. One hundred and fourteen injured.

The bomb went off with a deep, reverberating explosion, heard by much of London. In these times, no one had to wonder anymore. No one thought gas explosion. No one was in any confusion as to what might have happened. When the slightest incident could be interpreted as a terror attack, a massive explosion at one of London's major rail stations left no doubt as to what had happened.

Lake Weston heard the explosion from inside the back of a van. The van slowed for a moment and then speeded up again, making a quick left turn. Blindfolded and disoriented, he had been travelling for about half an hour.

Being deprived of all senses, of time and place, is part of the training of all intelligence officers. They say that when the trainee is first kidnapped and placed in confinement, they know it to be a test. However, consumed by darkness and the unknown, the mind starts to play tricks, it starts to tempt the person with fear and uncertainty. In the end the test is not about whether the agent will crack. They all crack. It's how long they last that determines their suitability for the job.

As Bleacher had noted, Lake Weston was no secret agent. Weston was expertly trained in extending publisher's deadlines and in drinking three bottles of wine in one night without throwing up. He was not trained in keeping his senses, in keeping his perspective of place and time.

The van slowed, parked, the engine turned off. The nerves that had faded over the course of the short journey, started up again. His stomach felt hellish. No food since his two mouthfuls of croissant the previous morning, nothing to drink, stress and nerves. Heartburn.

More than anything he yearned to get his music back. He wanted to wallow in Dylan. He wanted mid-60's, rocking out Dylan, he wanted to surround himself with no stimuli but *Leopard-Skin Pill Box Hat* or *Maggie's Farm*. But at that moment, he would have settled for anything. *Self Portrait... Down In The Groove...* The addict needed his fix.

The doors at the rear of the van opened. Heard movement, no voices. A hand on his shoulder, keys in the lock, he was pulled up and he staggered, bent double, out of the van. Solid ground. Handcuffs undone, the black bag was pulled off his head. The day was dull grey, but the brightness still made him squint uncomfortably.

'All your things were lost.'

Weston looked at the man who had let him out. He hadn't seen him before. Shaved head, a scar at the very top of his forehead. Hard look. The look of the man you don't want your daughter to marry.

'If you want to come by tomorrow you can fill out a form.'

The man laughed then turned, walked quickly, got into the passenger seat of the van, and then the van moved slowly off down the small side street and took an immediate left.

Weston watched the empty space where the van had been. Still numb. Started walking in the direction of the van. He was in a small street, three and four story buildings on either side. Neither new nor derelict, just lived in and drab. Not much sign of life. Impossible to tell where the sun was.

He came to the junction where the van had turned and looked along the street. Slightly wider, a few pedestrians now, a lot more cars parked. Could see the busy road, running perpendicular, about a hundred yards along the street. Traffic at a standstill.

'Hey?' he said quietly to a guy walking past.

The guy barely slowed, looking annoyed at being spoken to.

'Am I in London?' he asked. Felt stupid as the words came out.

'Fuck's sake,' he heard, as the bloke walked on, quickening his stride.

A few cars came along, refugees from the queue at the end of the street. Another pedestrian walked past, but Weston wasn't about to talk to anyone else.

He reached the end of the street. He looked along in both directions. Cars were blocked solid heading in one direction, the line moving slowly in the opposite. Despite the heavy queuing traffic, the van which had dropped him was gone. A grey day, impossible to tell what the time was. In the distance he could see the Post Office Tower.

Despite the confirmation that he was in London, he still felt utterly lost and very, very small. Total isolation. Confusion and hunger. As if to add to his discomfort, his ankle suddenly shot a sharp warning pain up his leg to remind him of his two day old injury. He winced, and for a moment he felt the most overwhelming notion of despair.

He remembered a story that EmmyLou Harris told about being given a bracelet with the initials WWDD inscribed on it. When she had inquired about the abbreviation, she had been told that it was short for *What Would Dylan Do*?

He asked himself the question again, as he had done a couple of days earlier. What would Dylan do? As if Dylan was some superhero, a masked and caped adventurer, capable of anything.

His head dropped, he turned slowly and started walking in the direction of the even bigger traffic jam he could see at the end of the road.

👁

The official government line would be that there was no CCTV footage of the Paddington Station bomber. The public was sceptical, given the amount of cameras that exist in Britain, and the fact that virtually every incident on the news is accompanied by CCTV footage. However, such was the shock at the level of carnage, the lack of CCTV evidence would become just one small part of the story. There were so many victims, so many heroes, so many political implications, that there was plenty for the media to be getting on with.

The CCTV footage which did exist of the actual event showed a man in his early forties. A rough beard, bobble hat, a grey jacket. It showed him reaching inside the grey jacket, it was even clear enough to show him pull the chord. For a fraction of a second it showed the bomb explode and rip through the crowd, before the camera itself was blown out.

The footage was seen by four members of staff at Thames House before the only copy was wiped. Two of those agents had known what was coming. One of the others hadn't, but was on board with the need to take care of business and to keep secrets secret.

The other agent had kept her own counsel, but had felt her stomach crawl as she'd watched the footage. And her stomach had not crawled because of the high body count or because of the woman's arm which could be clearly seen spiralling quickly through the air just before the camera was blanked out.

36

Weston stood at the door to his apartment block, built in an old terrace in a small street just off Mayfair. Coded entrance. He stared at it for a second, unwilling to try. Assuming the code would have been changed, not wanting to have his fears confirmed. Deep breath, he finally pressed the number. Seven. Eight. Zero. Zero. Zero. Five.

Turned the handle, the door clicked open.

'Holy fuck,' he muttered.

Stupidly he allowed himself luxuriously warm thoughts of dinner and a hot bath, cold wine and putting his feet up, Dylan on the hi-fi. Money in the drawers, a long sleep in a comfortable bed, a chance to regroup. He still had to get in the front door, but he wasn't going to let one inch of wood stand between him and *Desire* and a glass of Pouilly-Fuissé.

He walked up the stairs, the pain in his ankle subsiding for the first time in half an hour. As he had walked to his apartment, he had realised the explosion had been at Paddington. The angry, sick feeling in his stomach had worsened, the weight of the last few days had become heavier. Now he foolishly allowed himself the chink of light.

He reached the second floor. Stopped, listened for a second. Curious, rather than worried. Then the hair rose slowly on the back of his neck. He had never before come to this point on the stairs and heard a television playing.

There were only two apartments on each floor. Janice, the cat owner – it was how he defined her – didn't own a television. Which meant she had got one in the few weeks since he'd last been here, or else...

He approached his front door, put his ear up. The noise was coming from inside his house. Nothing loud, nothing intrusive. Just the news. Everyone in London was watching the news.

He stood for a second. Stepped back, looked at his front door, turned and looked over his shoulder. Everything was as it should be. Except there was a television playing in his apartment.

He stepped forward and tried the door handle, then quickly knocked. A few seconds, footsteps on a wooden floor. He had carpet. He was aware of the peculiarity of the sound, although not the reason for it.

The door opened, a young woman, early twenties. She winced slightly at the sight of Weston. Shaven head, insignificant goatee, unshaven, dirty, dishevelled, the lines of pain etched on his face.

'Hi,' she said, forcing the good humour.

He stared at her. Didn't know what to say. Glanced behind her. The corridor was completely different. Walls of magnolia, a mirror, a large Mucha. An ornate lampshade over a simple lamp. Wooden floor, two small, thin rugs. He could hear someone else in the house. She glanced over her shoulder, then back at Weston.

'You live in the block?' she asked. How else would he have got in?

'Yeah, I, eh, I'm from upstairs.'

'Oh. I thought that was Mr Woodcock.'

How the hell do you know that, he thought.

'Yeah, I'm a friend, I'm staying with him for a few weeks.'

'OK. Cool. Is everything OK?'

He stared at her. Hazel eyes. A woman walked past the end of the hall, glancing curiously out. He caught her eye, looked back to the woman at the door.

'I was wondering how long you'd been here?'

She looked slightly surprised, then shrugged.

'Six months maybe.'

He glanced past her again. He wanted to burst in, he wanted to expose the front. He wanted to charge past the exterior to find that the rest of the rooms were exactly as he had left them. He wanted to open the cupboards to find all his stuff crammed into them. He wanted to burst through to the bedroom to find the MI5 listening station.

Footsteps behind her and a small girl came up behind the woman, her blonde curls appearing at her mother's legs. She peered up at Weston.

'Who's that, Mummy?' she asked.

'Just a friend of Mr Woodcock's,' she replied.

Weston looked deep into the eyes of the young girl.

Penny's block was a shorter walk than Travis's, so he chose there first. By the time he arrived it was completely dark. Had taken him two painful hours, ankle getting stiffer and more resentful by the minute.

There would be one of three guards on duty.
He hoped it would be Alex, the old Glaswegian. They had a rapport, a natural understanding of what it was like to have been married to someone like Penny. There was a new guard, a Sri Lankan whose name Weston had yet to master. Then there was Miller, who Weston presumed was attracted to Penny, and who resented her continuing dependence on her ex-husband. He hoped it wouldn't be Miller.
He limped into the reception area of the building. Derek Miller looked at him suspiciously from under a raised eyebrow, leaned over and turned off the small television set, then stood up and folded his arms.
'Hi, Derek,' said Weston. 'Is Penny at home?'
As he spoke he realised that Miller hadn't recognised him at first.
'I think she's busy,' said Miller gruffly, losing the air of the polite and subservient concierge.
'I need to talk to her,' said Weston. 'Can you call her please?'
Miller sniffed, controlled a slight facial spasm. He reached down, lifted the phone. Stared at Weston throughout, as if expecting him to suddenly pull out a gun. Weston was too tired, too sore, too hungry to care.
'Mrs Weston,' said Miller, 'your ex-husband is in the lobby. Yes…yes… Very well, ma'm.'
He hung up, lowered himself back into his seat.
'She'll be down in a couple of minutes.'
Weston nodded and limped over to the armchairs which were arranged beside the large window adjacent to the revolving entrance. By the time she arrived, Weston was almost asleep. The tiredness had engulfed him the second he'd lowered himself into the chair.
He stood at the click of her shoes on the floor. She stood before him, Miller a couple of yards behind, watching. Guarding. Weston glanced at him, hoping she would turn and dismiss him. He suddenly wondered if they had discussed the possibility of him turning up and she had asked Miller to stay close. Just in case.
'I thought you were in prison,' she said. Her voice sounded strange. He was so used to her either being normal or annoyed. The strained quality that her voice had now was new to him.
'They let me out. Listen, I need...'
'You can't contact the boys,' she blurted.
'What?'
'I've had a restraining order issued. You can't see the boys, or contact them in any way. Not until I've spoken to them and established if you've harmed them.'
Behind her, Miller narrowed his eyes.

'When are you going to see them?'
'In a couple of weeks.'
'What? Jesus, Penny.'
'That's just how it is, Lake. I'm busy. And you have to live with the consequences of your actions.'
'None of it's true. I've never done anything to the boys, any child.'
'It said you had in the paper.'
'Come on...'
Shoulders straightened. She wasn't about to argue the merits of the media versus verisimilitude with the accused.
'I just need your help for tonight,' he said. 'Please...'
'No,' she said, staring at the ground. 'I can't. Maurice says I should keep you at arm's length until this is all sorted out.'
'Maurice?'
'I have a restraining order against you as well. You can't come here.'
His mouth dropped slightly open.
'You've leant on me for seven years,' he said, instantly regretting the words as they left his mouth.
'What?' she barked. 'You left me, remember! With two boys and barely enough money. And God knows what you were doing to those boys. Maybe that's why you left, because you couldn't live with the guilt of what you were doing every night.'
'Holy crap,' he said. 'Come on, Penny. That's absurd. I left because you were a pain in the fucking neck...'
Words out, too late to reel them in.
She held him in a death stare. He blinked the words away, but this was no moment of hurting truth. She took it as an insult and nothing else.
'Get out of here, Lake,' she said. 'I don't care where you go or what problems you've got yourself into. Just leave.'
She turned, walked quickly past Miller, so that he was immediately between them. He stepped across her back, arms folded.
'Penny, can you just help me out. Give me some money or something.'
More words to regret as soon as they were out his mouth. She pressed the button and stepped into the elevator. As the door closed over, Miller took a step forward.
'That was pathetic,' he said. 'Now you heard the good lady. Fuck off.'
'I don't think those were her exact words,' said Weston.
Another angry look, and then he turned and walked slowly out of the building. As he stepped outside into the cold, he shivered and felt the chill wind to his bones.

The Prime Minister gravely surveyed the scene, Bleacher, as always, at his armpit. Paddington Station was in bloody chaos, the explosion massive and devastating. The PM had been advised not to come. Partly because of security, but mostly because the last thing the emergency services needed at this stage of the recovery/rescue/investigation, was the Prime Minister, with everything that entails, pitching up to take a look.

They were approaching the Chief Constable of the Metropolitan Police.

'You can see where the expression *looks like a bomb hit it* came from,' muttered the PM to Bleacher.

Bleacher nodded gravely, as if the PM had just said something sombre and important. The PM stepped over rubble and debris. Bricks. A handbag, clasp broken, the contents spilled. A shoe, the foot still inside.

'Prime Minister,' said the Chief Constable, 'we all appreciate you coming down,' he added.

'It's important,' replied the PM. He shook the Chief's hand, then stood and surveyed the scene of horror. In his way, although his eyes were open, he saw none of it. He saw opportunity and he saw dark forces. He saw no corpses, he saw no blast site, he saw no wreckage.

'This,' he began, aware that the television cameras were rolling, 'is why we need to keep fighting. We cannot be defeated by the terrorist, and we *will not* be defeated by the terrorist....'

The Chief Constable looked over his shoulder. Bleacher closed his eyes and re-lived the split second of devastation.

37

Weston turned away from the door to Travis's apartment block and looked up at the third floor window. The lights were out and he presumed that she was genuinely not at home. Inexplicably bizarre behaviour from Penny was one thing. Travis would believe him. At least, she would give him some time. And food.

He looked up and down the short road. All was quiet. Few people were out that night. Everyone was huddled up in front of their televisions, scared and desperate, consumed by fears of war with an invisible enemy. The death toll had risen by another seven as the day had progressed.

Britain was under siege. No one was talking about Lake Weston.

He was out of ex-wives. He had been walking around for nearly four hours. So many parts of his body were aching he could no longer pinpoint exact areas of pain. He felt sick, his stomach had curled into an angry, uncomfortable knot. He was getting colder, his shivering uncontrollable. He was exhausted. It had only been three days on the run, and one of them he had spent in a four star hotel, with wine, food and sex; but he had lost track of time, his tiredness seemed of all the ages.

When he had approached his own flat, when he had approached Penny's, when he had come looking for Travis, each time his hopes had grown, each time he'd imagined going inside, flopping down; warmth and comfort and food.

Penniless, hopeless. Bobless.

An idea had grown as he had walked here, as he had passed hotels and restaurants along the way. It wasn't something he wanted to do, and given the state of him, not something he was sure he would be allowed to, but he had been thinking of taking a seat in a restaurant, eating the dinner, facing the consequences when he couldn't pay.

Maybe he could dine and dash, and he smiled grimly at the thought of being able to dash anywhere. If he ended up in a police cell for the night, then that might not be so bad. He was confused about the fact that he was obviously wanted, but had been let go. Confused enough that he knew there was no point in trying to second guess anyone. He just needed to sit down somewhere warm and eat. The rest of the evening could take care of itself.

He selected a Garfunkels. Didn't think they would turn him away because he looked too unkempt. A few customers, he sat alone. No one recognised him, no one spoke to him except the waitress. There was a subdued atmosphere.

He lingered over every course, letting his stomach recover slowly. A lot of food, but took his time. Garlic mushrooms, fish and chips, lemon drizzle cake. Half a bottle of Australian chardonnay, two bottles of still water. Cup of coffee. A second cup of coffee.

Gradually he was infused with life and warmth. It was an hour in before he started to wonder what was going to happen when he couldn't pay the bill. He sat for a full extra hour, enjoying the calm, having not taken so much pleasure in food and silence in a long, long time. The three days felt like three weeks. Three months. Timeless. He wondered about people who went through real hell. This didn't qualify. Not yet. Maybe this was just the beginning.

The waitress was Polish, late twenties, there had been no spark between them. The customers were thinning out, the day winding down. He was only ten or fifteen minutes off having to go outside and face the night. The relaxed feeling that two hours' respite had given him was wearing off, the fingers of the night were encroaching on his tiny oasis of idyll.

Time to face the next part of his day. The part where he owned up to being unable to pay his bill. Wondered if it was too late to make a friend of the waitress, to use her the way he had used the German girl the day before. Humour too shredded to care about his thoughtlessness.

She approached, looking slightly less stressed than earlier, but now tired and disinterested, wanting to go home for the night.

'Czy mogę prosić o rachunek?' he said.

She stopped, smiled, looked surprised. 'Mówi pan po polsku?'

He nodded. Life was full of opportunity. If his waitress had been any other nationality, the conversation would have been entirely in English and he would have been struggling.

'Trochę…'

She smiled. He returned the smile. There had been an old Polish girlfriend who he hadn't thought about in years. His Polish wasn't going to get him too far. But maybe he didn't want to go very far.

'Mieszkał pan w Polsce?' she asked.

'Z przerwami. Spędziłem jakiś czas we Wrocławiu.'

'Był pan w górach? Pochodzę stamtąd.'

'W górach, na wybrzeżu, Szlakiem Śmierci Drugiej Wojny Światowej.'

He smiled again. His last remark had been flippant, but he was gauging his audience and she smiled with him. Yet his heart wasn't in it, wasn't in the mood for some light chat, the possibility of mutual attraction.

'I can't pay the bill,' he said suddenly. 'Sorry, I'm sitting here engaging you in conversation and I have no money.'

Her face fell, the light went out. Just another *frajer*.

She glanced over her shoulder. He stared at the table.

'I'll need to get the manager,' she said, her voice bereft of the life it had had ten seconds earlier.

She turned, stopped, looked back at him.

'Please don't run out,' she said. 'I will have to pay.'

'I'm done running,' he said.

She walked quickly through to the kitchen.

The police were a long time coming. They had better things to do than book a bill dodger on this day of brutal terrorism. When they had arrived they hadn't been interested. The manager had been close to hysterical, as if associating the crimes of Weston the bill dodger with the man who had put his hand inside his coat and pulled a short chord. In the end the police had taken Weston away and put him in a cell, as much as anything to keep the hysterical Simon Harris happy.

The cells were empty. The bombing of Paddington had had the same effect as a bout of terrible weather. The criminals had stayed inside. No one felt like drinking, no one felt like getting too happy about anything. No alcohol, crime was reduced by eighty-seven percent.

Weston was placed in a cell and forgotten about. It was dry, he was alone, he had a toilet.

A woman's footsteps stirred him from an uncomfortable sleep. A vague dream about his former Polish girlfriend, transplanted to the ski resorts in the south of the country. Standing in amongst the trees, his bald head transferred to her.

He snapped awake as the key turned in the lock. A moment's confusion, the former girlfriend had become Travis. He sat up. Mouth dry. Had been

sleeping with his mouth open. The dream was gone, Travis was standing in the doorway to the cell. Sharp grey suit, red shirt. Hair up, her fringe down over her forehead. She looked tired, stressed.
'Travis,' he said.
She pulled the small wooden seat towards her and sat down. He raised himself so that he was sitting, leaning forward, forearms on his knees.
'Tell me everything,' she said.
'What?' Still groggy.
'Tell me everything.'
'What do you mean?'
Wondered if she knew what had been going on. The Home Office. Made some sort of sense.
'This evening you ate dinner in Garfunkels *and* didn't pay for it. Both of those statements are off the scale. If it wasn't for your old nemesis Harry Potter, you would be the richest author in Britain. Tell me every single thing that led to this evening. Everything, including the haircut.'
He didn't recognise her. This was the working Travis, the Travis he never had to deal with, the Travis he had never seen at home.
'The Home Office gets involved in every case of fish 'n chips non-payment?' he said flippantly.
'I'm not in the Home Office.'
If there had been one person in his life, the old romantic notion of a *one*, it had been Travis. Starting with the cancellation of the publication of *Fenton Bargus Takes On The Prime Minister*, he told her everything.

'Where did all that come from?' The first thing she said to end the five minute silence which had followed the completion of Weston's story. It had taken him forty-five minutes. He hadn't heard a sound from the rest of the police station in all that time.
'You think I'm making it up?' he said.
'No, I don't. I'm just wondering why now. You had this great life, and now you've completely fucked it up. Why?'
'I...,' he began. His words, whatever they were going to be, drifted off.
She leaned forward, so that she was sitting in the same position as he was. Three feet between them. They recognised the strain in the other.
'Dylan?' she said.
He smiled ruefully and nodded.
'I've done the drugs, I've done the women and the alcohol. I've done the amphetamine-fuelled best three works in a year, I am most definitely in my fallow, can't think what to write next period.'
'Thought it was about time you did the protest thing?'

He didn't answer. Eventually he nodded.

'You know why Dylan stopped protesting?'

'You're going to say it was because he was scared he'd go the same way as JFK...'

She nodded.

'I think there was more to it than that.'

'Whatever. Here's the thing. The establishment, the people out there who don't want you protesting, they're a lot more sophisticated than they were in 1963.'

'What do you mean?'

'You already know, Lake. They're not making a martyr out of anyone. If someone's going to criticize them, they're not going to put a bullet in them from a grassy knoll.'

'They're going to discredit them.'

'Yes. They have things now that they only dreamed of in 1963. And I'm sure they did dream of them.'

He lowered his head. Let out a long breath. Travis stared at the bald head, the first signs of hair beginning to creep through the scalp.

'What did you mean when you said you're not Home Office?' he said, looking up. 'Who did you transfer to?'

'Lake, I've never been Home Office,' she said.

'What do you mean?'

She shook her head. 'How did you ever have the wit to write one book, never mind a series that people actually wanted to read?'

'What?'

38

She opened the door to her apartment. Simple, small, quietly decorated, nothing fancy, nothing cluttered. He liked coming here. She had never asked for any of his money, had lived a modest life of her own.

When she had entered his police cell, she hadn't been sure that this was where they would end up. However, as soon as he had started talking, she had known.

'Can I get you a cup of tea?' she asked, hanging her coat on the hook just inside the door. He limped in behind her.

'Wine, I think,' he said.

'No alcohol,' she said shortly. 'Tea or coffee?'

He gave her a hurt expression, but her look wiped it from his face.

'Tea,' he said. 'Thanks.'

She walked briskly into the kitchen, he hobbled into the sitting room. Slumped down into a seat, let his head fall back.

The painful thoughts of what he would have been doing now, if he hadn't started along this insane road, were getting more frequent. Failed to see that those thoughts were of a time that was deeply unsatisfactory for him. Maybe his eyes had been closed when he'd walked into this, but some part of him had known he'd needed the change.

She placed the cup of tea on the table beside him. He smiled weakly. She always boiled the water in a kettle on the stove, made the tea in a pot, poured it into a cup, put the cup on a saucer. Noticed that her fingers were trembling slightly as she set it down.

She walked over to the DVD player, put a disc in, stood back and lifted the handset, turned on the television.

'I work for MI5,' she said, without turning.

'No fucking way,' he said forcefully to her back.

'Oh, for God's sake, Lake. How can you have been so naïve? What did you think I did? Why did you think I never talked about work? Why did you think I used to go to the office at 2am?'

He stared at her back. He suddenly felt very stupid. He had just thought her job had been boring compared to his cool, rock 'n roll, famous author lifestyle.

Felt small, selfish, stupid.

'What I'm about to show you is classified beyond words...'

'What is it?'

'I'm telling you! Jesus.'

She took a deep breath. He sat forward, had a sip of tea.

'This is footage of Paddington.'

'Heard some guys talking about that. Thought there wasn't any.'

'This is Britain,' she said curtly. 'There's footage of everything.'

She clicked the handset and the black and white footage started up. Paddington Station. The morning rush hour dance, hundreds and thousands on the move. They watched for a minute or so. She paused the film, pointed to a man on the screen.

'Recognise him?' she said.

Weston got up and walked towards the television. Had a strange sense of turmoil in his gut. Peered at the screen, the grey blur.

'No,' he said.

She continued the film. The man approached the exit to Platform 1. They clearly saw his hand reach inside his jacket. His face turned a little so that it was more obvious to the camera. She stopped the film.

'Holy fuck!' The words spat out of Weston's mouth. Stomach crumpled, could almost feel a physical blow to the chest.

She played the film, although it only had another five seconds to run. They watched Eldon Strachan lift the chord, hesitate for barely a second, pull hard, the briefest scene of explosive, bloody carnage, bodies and debris flying, then the film went dead.

She clicked the off button, removed the DVD from the player, snapped it in half over the end of the table. He stared at her in horror, looked back to the television, as if expecting it to still be showing his editor. His former editor.

'That's not true,' he said, slumping back into his seat. He glanced at the tea, but he really did need something stronger.

'That's one way of looking at it,' she said.

She looked down at him, arms folded. She also looked nervous, slightly scared, but he recognised that he was completely out of his depth while she was doing what it was that she did.

'The suicide bomber at Paddington yesterday morning was Eldon Strachan. However, no one, at least none of the British people, as our Prime Ministers like to call them, will get to see Eldon Strachan as the suicide bomber. He was used, he's dead, and now he'll be forgotten. When the list of the identified dead goes up, he'll be on it and everyone can just think that he was another poor sap who chose the wrong time to walk by Platform One.'
'Why? But why?'
'Jesus, Lake. He knew about *Axis Of Evil*. You told me the story, you laid it out. There were three of you who knew.'
'But he didn't write it, he didn't publish it, he just...he just read it.'
'Of the three of you, he was the most anonymous, and so he's had the most anonymous demise. Just a guy who died in a terrorist attack.'
'What d'you mean, the most anonymous demise? I'm not dead. Is Morrison dead?'
'You're not dead? Hallelujah for you, Lake Weston. Go out there and try and find a book shop that still has one of your books on the shelf. If we were in the mid-West people would be burning them. As it is, this is Britain, and people are just quietly taking the books out of their children's bedrooms and putting them in the bin. You are finished, your career is finished. Even if you could get every kid who ever met you to testify on your behalf, no one would believe them. You're tarred, Lake, you're done. You don't think that's a demise? Your money's gone, your houses are gone. You can't go home, your name is ruined, you have no friends, no one will ever trust you again. You have a better word than demise, and being the big celebrity author maybe you have, then on you go. I'm all ears.'
He sat back. The brutal truth, rammed down his throat. Nothing he hadn't already realised. But he hadn't faced the facts yet. He was still waiting for everything to bottom out, so that he could see where he was, reassess the situation, and then start to work out how he was going to get back up. Hadn't considered the fact that the well might be bottomless.
'A deafening silence,' she said caustically.
'Morrison?'
'Only got himself to blame. You piss off that many people, you get screwed. He had it coming, this just speeded things up a little.'
'He's dead?'
'The Americans have him.'
'Fuck,' he said. He pushed himself down a little further in the seat, head back, staring at the ceiling. She didn't sit down. Stood with her arms folded, staring at him. She had only found out the previous day that he

was the writer of *Axis of Evil*, and then a few of the right questions asked in the right places had told her what was happening.

She had been proud of him, if aghast at his bloody-minded stupidity, his lack of realisation of what he would come up against and the futility of someone in his position so obviously raging against the machine. The successful ones were the ones who acted by stealth. The campaign of posters in shop windows all over the country may have gained them publicity, but it had also been guaranteed to get them noticed, and for action to be taken against them by the people they were trying to attack.

'You need to leave,' she said.

'What do you mean?'

'You need to leave the country. Tonight.'

'How can I do that?'

She glanced over to the door and nodded. There was a small backpack resting against the wall.

'I accessed your accounts. You won't have much time. There's just over a hundred grand in there. A passport in the name of Tom Paine.'

He smiled. She didn't.

'You're going to leave here, go to Victoria, get on a train, head to the south coast, get on a ferry, never come back. Your life in Britain is over. You need to find somewhere to go, and then stay there.'

He didn't know what to say, didn't know if he was ready to leave Britain behind. Didn't know if he had any choice.

'Can't I go to the press? Isn't someone going to be interested?'

'Too late. You're a non-person, no one is going to go sticking their neck out for you, no one is going to believe that you wrote *Axis of Evil*. And if they did, if it looked like someone was going to come to your cause, the screw would be turned. It just wouldn't happen.'

'So why did they let me go? Why not keep me in prison? Why not charge me with all this anti-terror stuff?'

'They're ruining you, making you pay. And I suspect, although I don't know this, that at some point, when your reputation as a child molester is well and truly established, they will let it be known that it was you who wrote *Axis*, and then they will pin some terrorist outrage on you and you will be brought into custody and very publicly charged, tried and convicted. And, you never know, you might even be earmarked to be the first person killed under the reinstated death penalty.'

'No fucking way,' he said slowly.

She stared at him, then pointed slowly at the television screen.

'You need to disappear. Your life here is over. It's up to you if you want to take the chance to start a new one, or whether you want to sit around and see what happens.'

Had thought that he would have longer sitting in Travis's lounge. Had imagined that he might even get to go to bed for the rest of the night.

'Now,' she said.

He nodded. Closed eyes. Hating every minute of the run, the chase, the desperation.

'I need music,' he said suddenly. 'I need it,' he added.

She sighed heavily, aware of his addiction, walked quickly out into the hall, came back into the room, tossed an MP3 at him.

'What's it got?' he asked.

'*Highway 61*, *Knocked Out Loaded*, that's it,' she said, knowing what he'd meant by the question. He wasn't interested in the KT Tunstall and the Jack Johnson and the Maroon 5. 'You can live with it. You should get going.'

Knocked Out Loaded. One of Dylan's nadirs. No one listened to *Knocked Out Loaded*. Except he himself had been into it when he'd first met Travis, and she'd been forced to listen to it endlessly. It reminded her of those days, the first short weekend in France.

He smiled, recognising the moment. She shook her head.

'Don't get all sentimental on me, it's not like I ever listen to the stupid album,' she said. 'You need to go. Now.'

He stood up, turning the MP3 over in his hands, looking at it, keen to get the earphones on.

'What about you?' he said, looking up. At last, an unselfish thought. Had been so consumed by his own concerns that he hadn't been thinking of her own part in his flight. 'Giving me the money, the passport. Isn't someone going to notice?'

'I'll be fine, I covered my back,' she said.

The words were convincing, but he didn't believe it. However, he wanted it to be true, and so couldn't allow himself to see what he was doing.

Strachan was dead, Strachan's wife was dead, Morrison was in prison, the German girl was dead. Now Travis had put herself at risk for him, and all because he had thrown his teddy in the corner over the rejection of a Fenton Bargus book.

The thoughts flitted through his mind, fleeting glimpses of arguments that he hoped he would have time for later. It wasn't him who had killed three people, he had just been exercising his democratic right to publish. The arguments swirled on, but his continuing flight had been so

relentless, his mind a kick-started, on-going adrenaline rush, that he was incapable of reasonable, logical thought.
'Stop looking at me like I'm dying of cancer,' she snapped. 'I'll be fine. Now get a move on.'
He smiled, stood up, walked quickly out into the hall. A life on the move. Hadn't he always wondered about that, even before he'd fallen into the trap of the Z-list celebrity?
He picked up the backpack. It felt lighter than he was expecting. Wondered what kind of notes were crammed inside. Without worrying what she would think of him checking, he pulled the cord on the top and looked inside.
'Don't trust me?' she said sharply from behind. 'You're such a prick sometimes, Lake. Pick up the fucking bag and let's go.'
He turned. She stopped at the look on his face.
'There's no money in here. Paper, it's all just paper.'
She felt the instantaneous stop of the heart, then she automatically pressed herself back against the wall. Eyes closed. Thinking.
'What?' said Weston.
'Oh, fuck,' she said. The words whispered from her mouth. They knew. She hadn't seen it coming, thought she had covered herself, but they knew. She'd been clumsy. Because it had been Weston, she had allowed herself to make stupid mistakes. The kind of mistakes that led to masked men standing outside your front door.
'What?' he said. 'You're scaring me.'
She put her finger to her lips. Masked men standing outside her door. She wasn't being dramatic, she knew how it worked. And if they were there, it wouldn't be for Weston. They had let him go. They just didn't want him leaving the country.
She let out a long breath, leaned forwards, hands on knees. Her hair fell around her face. Weston looked at the door, as if he could see through it. Pointed towards it, eyebrows raised. She shrugged, indicated *maybe* with her face. Weston didn't really understand, was still thinking of himself, wondered who was after him now.
'Butch and Sundance?' he said quietly.
She smiled, shook her head. Finally she straightened herself up.
'Come on,' she said, voice normal. 'If we're being dramatic, there'll be no one there. If there is, I'm just going to get my balls rapped, and presumably they'll let you go again. Come on.'
Still not thinking straight, despite the obvious warnings.
Weston lifted the bag. She looked at him curiously, shook her head.
'Sorry,' he mumbled, dropped it.

She put her hand to the door, nerves calmer than they had been a minute earlier.

'At least I've got Dylan back,' he said.

'Well that'll get you far,' she said, opening the door.

She had been wrong about one thing. The agent waiting outside wasn't wearing a mask.

She didn't recognise him, but then she hardly knew any of the field agents, and none of the ones who were sent out with a gun.

Standing behind her, Weston only saw a blur of movement. The lifting of an arm sheathed in black. Travis let out a small gasp, the bullet punctured her forehead from seven feet, wasn't designed to come out the other side. She toppled to the ground, blood oozed from the clean wound.

Weston looked into the eyes of her killer. They were empty. He braced himself for the shot, did not even think of a sudden dash for freedom. A reprise of the leap through the window.

The killer lowered the gun and then tossed it casually at Weston. Weston dramatically lifted his hands out the way, took the knock from the gun just above the waist. The killer turned and jogged easily down the stairs, banging on doors as he went. Letting others know, making sure the police were called, making sure that Weston couldn't drag the body inside and then make himself comfortable for the night.

The Prime Minister was in the bath. Bleacher, to his general discomfort, was sitting on the toilet seat, trying not to look. He was used to coming when he was called, but usually the PM wasn't naked.

Bleacher stared at the floor. The man hadn't even had the decency to fill the bath with bubbles.

A new crisis, to accompany all the other on-going crises. This one was a more basic and fundamental ministerial sex scandal, but the timing wasn't great. Not with the public agitated about the imminent collapse of the economy and the latest terrorist attack on the capital. The news was unremittingly bad. The PM did not need one of his senior ministers to have been photographed in bed with two other men. For the moment the man's wife was standing by him, albeit only so she could stay close enough to insert the stiletto when the time was right.

'You can't,' said Bleacher. 'You need to cut him loose. Tonight.'

'We all know he does this stuff, who cares? Does it impact on his ability to do the job? No. And if we give him the bullet this quickly, it just looks like we're pandering.'

'Well pander then. If you don't, you look like Thatcher.'

'Fine woman.'

'You look obstinate, uncaring, you look like you have different rules for you. The electorate still haven't got the hang of the whole gay thing. Fine, if some politician owns up to it, the British people can bury their heads in the sand and forget about it. But a nominally happily married man with three kids, caught in the sack with two men? Forget it.'

'Doesn't feel right,' said the PM obstinately.

'Sir, we don't give a shit about the man, and we don't give a shit about his Ministry. It's not about him or them. It's about you. It's about how you look at this time. You're being screwed from all quarters, you have to take care of yourself. Get out the bath. I've written the speech, get down there and talk to the press and send this sick bastard firmly out into the political wilderness where he belongs. He's already fucked enough men without you being the next in line.'

The PM looked up, his eyebrows raised. That had clinched it.

39

The temporary redemption of Lake Weston started on a small side road off the bottom of Tottenham Court Road, not far from Oxford Street Tube Station at 11.23 in the morning.

He had spent the rest of the night cold, sleeping up against a wall. The day had dawned the mild, dull grey of a British winter. Weston had dawned cold and hungry. Had slept poorly, short bouts of restlessness. Had turned to the MP3 constantly, listening to the same Dylan songs over and over. Mostly *Like A Rolling A Stone*. Seemed so apposite. He started hating the song. Couldn't turn it off.

The MP3 finally ran out of power at 9:14 a.m. He bowed his head and cried. Finally he felt desperately crushed. He had been running on adrenaline, he had been fire-fighting. Now there was nothing left. No one to run from, no one looking for him, nowhere to go. No money, no house, no Bob. There was no one else to turn to, and even if there had been, how could he ask anyone for help now, having witnessed what happened to those who tried?

He wept. Someone threw fifty pence at him.

He sat, curled up against a wall, weeping for just over an hour. Arose at a little after ten and wandered off down the street. Ventured into a newsagents to see what he could buy with fifty pence. Ended up with a bar of chocolate.

He wondered how he could get the MP3 charged, wondered if he should just park himself in a nice spot where he would be passed by a lot of people, and stick a cup out. If he could find a cup.

Wandered. Cold. The taste of chocolate turned bitter. He saw it at not long after eleven, down a side street. Hadn't realised that pawn shops still existed in the e-Bay era. Walked on, although the thought immediately struck him. He had one thing left that he could pawn, but it would mean parting with Bob. And even though he couldn't listen to it at that point, there was still the promise of Bob, somewhere, somehow.

Fifteen minutes later he had turned back and was standing in front of the pawn shop. In the window there was an old acoustic guitar. £25. Nothing but a simple twist of fate.

Robert was on full broadcast mode. An endless stream of unconnected questions and observations. There's no particular reason why it should be so tiring, thought Ben Hammond, but it was.

He'd thought Burger King might slow him down, but he had talked through it, ignoring the constant exhortations to not talk with his mouth full. They had walked on, up Tottenham Court Road, going to meet a small publisher about a small publishing idea.

'Dad, why are there so many women's breasts in advertising?'

He put his hand on his son's shoulder.

'That's how it works, Chief,' he said. 'Men like women's breasts, so advertisers try to associate different things with them.'

'Even cars?'

He nodded. Smiled. Noticed the guy on the other side of the road singing. A car passed, he couldn't hear him. Didn't like buskers.

'Even cars,' he said.

'Why?'

'Don't know,' said Hammond for the thirty-seventh time that afternoon. No one was counting, although his son might have been.

'Why do women have breasts?'

Hammond stopped. Could hear *From A Buick 6* from across the road. He hated it when he heard a Dylan song murdered by a busker. If ever he was walking through the Underground and he heard someone warbling *Blowin' In The Wind*, it made him want to bend down and lift the coins out of the guy's hat. *From A Buick 6*, however. No busker he'd ever heard had sung *From a Buick 6*. He stopped, looked over. The guy was doing a passable Dylan. No murder there.

The boy looked at his dad, then followed his gaze across to the busker.

'Is that a Bob Dylan song?' said the boy, knowing that it was.

'Yeah,' said his dad. 'From *Highway 61*.'

'That's the *do you Mr Jones* cd?'

Hammond looked down at his son.

'Yeah,' he said. 'Come on, let's go, I don't want to be late.'

He walked on. The boy stood looking across the road at the busker for another few seconds and then followed his dad.

'Stop,' said Hammond. 'Car coming.'

'That man looked like Lake Weston.'

Hammond looked along the road, waiting to see if the next car would stop. Glanced down at his son, the statement registering a few seconds later.

'What man?'

'The man singing the Bob Dylan song. He looked like Lake Weston.'

'He was bald, wasn't he?'

'He looked like Lake Weston without hair.'

Hammond pulled his son back from the edge of the road and looked across at the busker. He watched for a few seconds, listened to the tones of the man's voice.

'Holy fuck,' he said quietly.

'Dad!'

'Yeah, yeah, sorry. Come on.'

He looked both ways and then started to walk across the road.

Weston saw him coming. The friend he hadn't seen in twelve years with a son he didn't even know he had. Instant recognition. The day before he would have loved to have bumped into him. Not now.

They stood in front of Weston for a moment, watching.

'Lake?'

Weston sang on. Finally the selfishness had left him. People were dying because they tried to help him. He had no idea if he was being watched, if anyone who stopped to talk to him would be followed and chased. But he had to stop taking chances with other people's lives.

He abruptly stopped playing *From A Buick 6*, started on *Restless Farewell*. It had been their old code. They had played guitar together so often. Pubs, clubs, street corners. It was their code for when one of them wanted to leave. More of a joke. *Restless Farewell*.

Hammond stared curiously at him for a second, quickly tossed a coin down in front of him and then took his son's hand. 'Come on, we're wrong.'

'It looks like him, Dad.'

'It's not.'

They walked away, Weston stopped himself watching them go, his insides curled and hurting. The woman sitting in the small café across the road watched the man and his son come towards her. She made a quick mental picture of them, then looked away as she casually lifted her phone. Hesitated a further second. Watched their backs.

They were pushed this afternoon, the day after the latest London bomb. She couldn't go calling in a tail for everyone who stopped to listen to Weston for a few seconds.

A movement across the street distracted her, an old man who was standing in front of Weston, staring at him intently. She closed the phone. Ben Hammond and his son were forgotten.

An hour and a half later, the surveillance had moved on. Cuts everywhere, not enough manpower, especially not on the day after a terrorist attack. People were needed everywhere, albeit almost all of them were being used to hunt down a non-existent terror cell. And while someone somewhere had made the decision not to watch Lake Weston for a while, Weston had no passport, no money and had had a small chip inserted under his right thumbnail during his short period of incarceration. He wasn't going anywhere that the security services would not know about.

40

Weston was in the middle of *The Times They Are A-Changin'* when Hammond abruptly arrived, guitar in hand, and sat down beside him. Had changed his clothes, left his son at home, hat pulled down low.

'That's a bit more like it,' he muttered. '*From A Buick 6* for fuck's sake. No one plays *From A Buick 6.*' Started strumming his guitar.

Weston stopped singing and glanced sideways at him.

'Think I'm being watched,' he muttered.

Felt a wave of gratitude to the man for coming back, for bringing his guitar, for sitting down beside him. Also had a strange wave of hope, as if this man, this old friend, might be his deliverance.

'Nice to see you too, Lake.'

Weston started on the last verse. Hammond left it a line or two, then started singing, their voices perfectly pitched for each other, as they always had been.

They felt the rush of the past.

The song finished. Weston didn't look at him. Kept strumming.

'I'm scared here, Ben. Fucking scared. Travis got killed last night.'

'The woman you left Penny for?'

'Yeah. This is too freaky.'

'Tell me.'

Weston strummed on in G. Started singing *I Pity The Poor Immigrant*. Hammond joined in, expecting that Weston's story would gradually unfold.

An hour later they hadn't moved. They also hadn't been moved along, shot at or chased. As the time had passed, Weston had gradually become more comfortable, had talked more between songs. The full story of *Axis of Evil* and the Framing of Lake Weston. Hammond had asked no questions, had allowed Weston to talk when he wanted to, and had sung along with him when required.

It might have been twelve years since Weston had seen Hammond, but the affection and trust he felt for him wasn't just borne out of desperation and a friendly face in amongst the mire of hopelessness.

Weston finished *Things Have Changed*, a song too new for them to have sung together before, but they had both known it from start to finish.

'So that's all?' said Hammond. 'They're not accusing you of melting the Arctic, kidnapping Madeline or crucifying Jesus?'

Weston ruefully shook his head.

'As the Lord said, the cup of accusation already runneth over.'

'You are so fucked, man.'

'I know.'

'All that stuff about you doing things to children. I mean, my two aren't quite old enough to understand it, but they're just adamant that you couldn't do anything wrong. Not Lake Weston.'

Weston started strumming idly, no particular song in mind. At the end of every song, the break was getting longer, the chat more involved.

'Jesus, this sucks,' said Hammond. 'Man, what happened to you?'

Weston shrugged. 'It's just this book, you know, until then...'

'No, I mean, twelve years ago. What happened? We were, you know...'

'Ah. Penny, it was Penny. She just fucked me over in as many different ways as she could manage. I'm sorry.'

'Women,' said Hammond, joining in the casual strum. A basic 12-bar in E.

'Some of them are bearable,' said Weston. He thought of Travis. The taste of the words turned bitter. A brief explosion of grief in his stomach.

'And you think I might be compromising myself just by sitting here?'

Weston stared at the passers-by in the dark, cold evening.

'Looks like it. I'm sorry.'

'I'm here by choice, man, so don't sweat it. Listen, you must be hungry, let me get you a sandwich, something to drink.'

'Take the money from the hat,' said Weston. There wouldn't have been enough for the drink.

'I'm good,' said Hammond.

He propped his guitar against the wall next to Weston and walked quickly down the road. This is where he gets stabbed in the side by a guy passing by in the street and I never see him again, thought Weston.

He laid his head back against the wall. No tune in mind, but Bob all the same, an early 60's picking. The sounds of the street swept around him.

He was stiff and cold, didn't feel like moving. Was intending to drift off to a pub at some point, for a few hours' warmth at least.
Weston snapped awake. Had fallen asleep for less than a minute. Hammond sitting down beside him, a bag full of food and drink. Felt like he had been asleep for hours.
'Have some food. If we're being watched, we're already blown.'
Sandwiches, crisps, wine, two cups of hot coffee.
'Really, thanks, this is fucking brilliant.'
Hammond lifted his guitar into his lap but then started eating a sandwich at the same time. Not about to play.
'So,' he said, 'I've just been wondering what I can do to help you.'
'You don't have to do anything,' said Weston quickly.
'I know,' he said. 'But maybe I want to and maybe I can.'
A car drove past, music blaring. Guns 'N Roses, *Knocking on Heaven's Door.* The music disappeared into the night.
'You're a journalist?' said Weston.
'Spammer.'
'A what?'
'I run a spamming company.'
'There are spamming companies?'
'Of course there are spamming companies. Where the hell do you think you get all those annoying e-mails from?'
Weston looked at him as if Hammond was the one being accused of heinous crimes.
'You send out spam e-mails?'
'Yes.'
'You're Franklin T. Wildebeest and Confuscious Z. Spudsucker? How are you going to help me? Get me a fifty percent bigger dick in ten days?'
Hammond smiled. 'Actually it's one of the guys who works for me who's Franklin T Wildebeest.'
'Holy crap. Jesus. I mean, someone actually does that job?'
'What did you think happened?'
'I don't know. I thought it was a computer or something.'
'Computers still more or less do what they're told, you know. Someone has to input the information, manipulate the process, all that kind of stuff. There are seventeen of us.'
'Is it legal?'
Hammond waved his hand from side to side. 'Mostly.'
'Mostly... How does it work? I mean, how do you know that I even exist?'

'The computer just sends spam to a gazillion e-mail addresses every day. Names and addresses at random, but on a huge scale. So you don't know that there actually is a JohnMacWank@yahoo.com but what are the chances? Pretty fucking high, man. It works like that. It makes names up, pumps them out at a colossal rate.'

'And if anyone is stupid enough to open their personal e-mail from Cupid H Furtwurter then you've got them?'

'Exactamundo.'

'Jesus. How many active e-mail addresses do you have in Britain?'

'About twelve and a half million.'

Weston stopped, sandwich halfway to mouth. He wasn't sure what answer he'd been expecting to that question.

'Holy crap. That's a lot of e-mail addresses.'

'It is.'

He looked at his old friend, for the first time in ages not feeling the cold or the pain or the discomfort. Here was a way to fight back. Unexpected, out of the blue, a way that they might not see coming.

'What would you do?' asked Weston.

For the first time in days, for the first time since he had walked over the hill above his home and looked down at the house, he felt hope rather than just a temporary relief.

'I can put something out. A title that people are actually going to want to read, a source e-mail address that implies authenticity. I mean, man, that's totally frowned upon in the business. No one approves of that shit. Sending spam that actually looks like proper mail. Jesus, it's not done. Well, obviously, there are guys who do it, but the rogue element. But this, maybe this is worth breaking a few codes for.'

'Twelve and a half million e-mail addresses?'

Hammond nodded.

'Holy crap,' said Weston, still getting used to that number. 'How many people are likely to open it?'

Hammond shrugged.

'Impossible to say. It's not usually done like this. We'd never spam that many people at once with the same thing. And, you know, when the title of your spam is *Free Meds For Erectile Dysfunction*, the uptake is never great. So, we'd use the name of a phoney press agency, I don't know, London Media something like that, title the e-mail *The Truth About Axis of Evil*. A lot of people are still going to see it as spam. But at the same time, there'll be a damn sight more opening it than if it was about the size of your knob. Even if it's ten percent, and I reckon we can hope for more than that, that's still 1.2 million. Even taking off large chunks for people who open but don't read, and people who read but don't believe, that's still reaching a hell of a lot of people. You want me to write it?'

'I don't know,' said Weston. Trying to keep the smile from his face. He shouldn't be smiling. People had died. His life was in tatters. And the merest glimmer of hope that this was giving him was not going to bring back Travis or Strachan or all the people who had died at Paddington. But the insane pleasure of the moment, at finally being presented with a way to fight back, was spreading across his face. He laughed to get rid of the smile, shook his head.

'Let's do it together,' he said.

'OK. But we need to do it now, sitting here. In our heads, I'll write it out when I get home. Can't take you there, I'm sorry.'

'I know, I know.'

'We need to keep it snappy. Bullet points. And, at this stage, we need to leave the more incredible things out of it. We cannot, *we cannot* mention Paddington. Just don't, not yet. We need some things up our sleeve, we can't be too outrageous or people just aren't going to believe it.'

Weston nodded. The heady moment of pleasure and expectation had gone. They had work to do, the future was still bleak, the break in the clouds merely a change in the shade of grey, not the promise of blue skies.

Weston took a bite out of a sandwich and turned the screw top of the quarter bottle of Semillon. Hammond took a bite from a ploughman's sandwich, then laid it on his knee and started strumming the first few chords of *Only A Pawn In Their Game*.

41

Weston spent a comfortable night in the Travel Inn at Euston Station. Plenty of rooms available. A lot of people had cancelled their travel plans to London. He had paid cash at the desk, although they had regarded him suspiciously. The pickings from over seven hours of Dylan had been slim, but Hammond had given him a couple of hundred pounds in cash as he'd left.

He'd eaten well at the restaurant, had left his clothes to be laundered, had bought shaving equipment. A long bath, finally settled down into bed at just before ten-thirty to watch Newsnight.

The credits made their dramatic roll, the picture turned to the scenes of devastation at Paddington, and Paxman grumbled over the top of it all, 'A few nights ago we were talking about *Axis of Evil*, the book that told of a government which ruled by fear and created a self-fulfilling prophecy of terror in our streets. As the dust settles on one of the deadliest terrorist strike ever seen in British history, are we seeing the pages of *Axis of Evil* come to life, as the government contemplates Draconian measures to increase police powers and extend the already far reaching anti-terror laws...'

◉

The Prime Minister hurled the empty glass of whisky at the television screen. Missed by an inch, the glass smashed into the wall.

'Jesus fucking cunt!' he yelled, the words barely understandable, the voice distorted by apocalyptic rage. 'What in the name of Christ is that?' He stood up and marched towards the television, swung a boot at it, intentionally missed. He looked round at Bleacher who was rubbing his forehead. Bleacher had made a few calls, having wondered how Newsnight was going to play it.

The day before it had been about the news, now it was time for British introspection. What was to be done about it, how could they stop this kind of thing happening again? Most of the media had been on their side, but politically there were really only a few outlets that mattered. Despite everything that successive governments had tried to achieve, the BBC was still one of them. He had known this was coming, hadn't said anything to the PM. Thought he might as well wait it out, see how bad it was.

The show started, Paxman started, the PM waited until about halfway through his first sentence.

'Don't they know anything about the fucker who wrote that book? Now they're using it to undermine my government!' He looked round at Bleacher. 'Don't they know that this bastard is a child-molesting, left-wing Islamist propagator of terror?'

Bleacher stared back at the PM.

'Sir, he is not an actual propagator of terror. There's nothing to imply that he's left wing, just because he's to the left of us. He has no connection with any form of Islam, and we invented the allegations about child molestation.'

The PM gave him the look of the mentally deranged.

'Yes, but they don't know that! What the fuck are they doing giving any credence to a man like that?'

'They don't even know who wrote it,' said Bleacher.

'Where is he?' snapped the PM, looking back at the TV and turning the volume up so that he could hear Paxman above the sound of himself.

'In a hotel at Euston.'

The PM turned back, savagery on his face.

'What the fuck?'

'We ruined his reputation, took away his money, moved people into his homes, removed his associates from the field, left him destitute and in disgrace. When the time is right, we will bring him in and publicly hang him.'

'You just said he was in a hotel?' shouted the PM. 'That's pretty fucking destitute, isn't it? The poor bastard, he must be freezing. If he's got the fucking windows open!'

'He managed to get hold of a guitar...'

'Where in the name of fuck did he find that?'

'He pawned an MP3 player. Took the guitar, busked for seven hours.'

'Holy Christ! Whose genius idea was it that we let this guy out onto the street?'

Yours, thought Bleacher.

'If he was in custody the entire time it would give him an alibi for any other crimes that we decided to pin on him. We need him desperate and on the streets.'

'Well he's not on the streets, is he? He managed to make enough money from busking to get a hotel room for the night. What the fuck is that? The bastard can make more than me strumming a fucking guitar.'

'Presumably that was how he made the money,' said Bleacher, ignoring the absurdity of the PM's previous remark. 'We don't know because the surveillance had to break off midway through the day.'

'Holy mother of crap! Why, in the name of fuck, would that be?'

'Because it was all hands to the pumps trying to find the perpetrators of yesterday's terror attack in Paddington.'

The PM felt the next explosion die on his lips. He cursed silently, looked daggers at Bleacher as if everything was his fault, and then turned back to the television.

'Jesus, this is a fucking shambles.'

He slumped down into his seat. The Home Secretary was sitting across from Paxman, her face thin.

'She's not showing enough cleavage,' grumbled the PM.

He looked round at Bleacher.

'You know what we need? We need a month, five months, when absolutely nothing happens. Nothing. Steady growth, no terrorism, no scandals, no bank collapses, no lost documents, no downturn in the housing market. Nothing.'

Bleacher stared at the PM and then looked back at the television.

42

From: info@londonmedia.co.uk
To: albutler41@yahoo.com (more…)
Subject: The Truth About *Axis Of Evil*
Date: Thurs, 5th February 01:00:39

- *Axis Of Evil* was written by children's author, Lake Weston.
- As a result, the Government has attempted to frame Lake Weston. NOTHING you have read about Lake Weston in the past three days is true.
- Once his reputation is shattered, they will acknowledge that he wrote the book, their intent being that the book's reputation will similarly suffer.
- Not one child has made an allegation against Lake Weston. The charges are ALL FALSE.
- Lake Weston wrote a book entitled *Fenton Bargus Takes On The Prime Minister*. This book was banned by the government under Part 1, Section 2, Paragraph 4b of the Terrorism Act 2006. The Terrorism Act 2006 was supposedly introduced to combat terrorists, not children's authors. As a result, Weston wrote *Axis of Evil*. The government is now fraudulently attempting to oppress this legitimate use of freedom of speech, using laws brought in to fight terror suspects.
- Weston's publisher has disappeared, his editor is missing and his editor's wife was mysteriously killed in an accident at her home.
- The government does not want people reading this book. The government is banning this book under sections of Terrorism legislation meant for terrorists, not for literature. This is an extraordinary suppression of civil liberties.

- BIG BROTHER IS NOT JUST A TELEVISION PROGRAMME. It is a system of government and one which has been introduced by stealth in the United Kingdom. The British people need to wake up to this before it is too late.
- *Axis of Evil* is the wake up call.
- State Terror is at hand!

Ben Hammond reread the e-mail for the fiftieth time. Knew it wasn't right. This was a one shot chance and he had to nail it. But he hadn't. Struggling with every word. It was clumsy, it had conspiracy theory written all over it. It was the kind of thing that can be found on five zillion pages on the internet. The CIA killed Kennedy. America faked the moon landing. The White House planned 9/11. Lake Weston wrote *Axis of Evil* and the government are trying to set him up.

Why would anyone believe this any more than they believed any of the other monstrous stories? Maybe some of them were true, and maybe some people believed them. But they needed this to be something which entered mass consciousness. Everyone in the media needed to believe it, the public needed to believe it.

He pressed send, and the great machinery of the on-line mass spammer whirred into action. Aiming at all the addresses they knew to exist, and as many again in hope of existence rather than expectation, twenty-five million e-mails went out at once, on the press of a button.

Hammond looked over his shoulder. In the basement of his house in Croydon. As he had all night, he expected to see the police standing there, waiting to put a bullet in the back of his head. If they had done it now, it would have been too late. As it was, all he saw were the usual cabinets piled high with disks, the poster of Dylan on the wall, the post-it notes stuck to the back of the door.

Ben Hammond was right. It wasn't enough. On its own it was never going to get very far. Fortunately for Ben Hammond, and very fortunately for Lake Weston, the e-mail did not have to act on its own for very long.

It was a desperate night at the Press Association. Everyone stretched, the organisation's under-manning hopelessly exaggerated by the news crisis in the wake of the London terror attack. The hardened hacks trawling the wires and the streets and the other newsrooms; a few trainee journalists scratching around for angles.

It was one of the trainees who received the e-mail. Thought he could make a small story out of it. Had been told to put out five stories on his evening shift. He did some quick research on Weston – five minutes on Wikipedia – then cobbled together a story for the wires. Put it out before anyone higher up the chain could have conniptions about the possible government reaction.

All the media outlets which were in a similar position to the Press Association – understaffed and under-financed – picked up the story and ran with it. Late editions, if they still had the time, or websites. Radio news. A small item at first, because no one was quite sure how big a story it was, whether or not it should be taken at face value.

But great stock is put in the Press Association, and so many accepted it as fact. It was entirely coincidental, that on this occasion, the facts that the media happened to pick up on, actually happened to be true.

The ball was rolling. The mountain was steep.

43

Weston didn't know that he'd had a chip inserted under a thumbnail. He presumed rather that he had been followed, which, as of halfway through the previous day, had no longer been the case. Hammond had given him enough for two nights at the Travel Inn and told him to lie low, something which Weston was quite happy to do after the previous week. Two days in a hotel room, sore ankles resting, watching television, sleeping and eating. As with Hammond, sitting alone in his basement in the middle of the night, Weston constantly expected his hotel door to suddenly come battering in. However, as the hours passed and he slept, and morning came and still he remained unfound or unharassed, he began to wonder if perhaps he had managed to lose them.

He slept well, not waking until the knock at the door which heralded his breakfast. He tipped the waiter, turned on the television and settled down to his bacon, three eggs, toast, coffee, orange juice. He hadn't got as far as the first mouthful before seeing a picture of himself on the television. He cursed, expecting the worse, more allegations against Weston the paedophile. Didn't know that Hammond had already put out the e-mail. Didn't know that after a slow start, once the story had been picked up and had started to spread, the e-mail had shot around cyberspace with terrific velocity, so that take-up of the e-mail had already reached seventy-nine percent. Didn't know that the e-mail had been forwarded to more than eighty-one percent of addresses in Britain by nine in the morning. Didn't know that every single news channel in Britain was running with the story and the extraordinary allegations. From nowhere, Hammond had produced the kind of thing that conspiracy theorists dream of. Instant belief.

Weston turned the television up so that he could hear it properly. The bacon turned sweet in his mouth.

The PM watched the Home Secretary on breakfast television. Could see his whole premiership unravelling. All because of Lake Weston and Fenton Bargus. He flicked channels. The Justice Minister on one, the Chancellor let loose on another, the Foreign Secretary, the Environment Minister. On every channel they were there, the cabinet out in force, protecting the record of the government, denying all knowledge of Lake Weston. Just because *Axis of Evil* was a work of literature, did not mean that it was exempt from anti-terror laws voted in by the democratically elected parliament; the government had no knowledge of who wrote the book, although they were keen to find out; the allegations against the paedophile Lake Weston were a matter for the police.

Bleacher was by his side, as ever. Sancho Panza. With a howitzer. The PM had slept for a few hours, Bleacher had hardly slept in seven days. The PM had lost his anger and fervour of the night before. He was tired, hopeless. Could see the end.

'Why does anyone believe this crap?' said the PM darkly. His voice tinged with sadness. 'I mean, why do they believe some absurd conspiracy theory rather than the government? And why are they even reading the fucking book? No one reads books anymore. They watch *Britain's Got Talent*, they look at the pictures in Heat and FHM. Who reads books?'

He looked round at Bleacher as the Justice Minister allowed himself to get annoyed. Bleacher held the PM's gaze for a few seconds.

'I feel like Nixon,' said the PM turning away.

'Don't,' said Bleacher bluntly.

The PM's eyes dropped to the floor. His fingers automatically found the remote and he turned off the television. He had to stop watching. Constantly searching for affirmation for himself and his government, when there was never any to be had.

'We know that Weston is still in his hotel?'

Bleacher nodded.

'We can't let the media get him, not now. It's too late to pull strings, and I don't want to owe anyone that much. Get there, bring him into custody, don't tell anyone. We can stick him in a cell and decide what to do with him later. Weston disappears, we ride this out.'

Bleacher got to his feet. Nothing else to say. He walked quickly to the door and stepped out into the maelstrom.

In less than fifteen seconds he had been told about the first three backbenchers demanding that the Prime Minister step down.

The maid knocked. Weston's heart leapt, as it had for room service, and when his clothes had been returned half an hour earlier. He sat up, put weight onto his feet. Winced. Sharp pain, less severe than it had been but still a sharp crack with a cane whipped up his legs. Hesitated. The key was inserted into the lock, the door opened.

A young woman, blonde, a mass of dark roots. She smiled.

'Sorry, you didn't answer. Can I come in? Only be five minutes.'

Weston let out a long breath. For all that he was on edge and expecting the worst, it did not even occur to him that she might be other than she seemed. The wolf in maid's clothing.

As it was, she was no wolf. The wolves were at that moment, however, coming up in the elevator.

'Sure,' he said.

He took a pace towards the door, let out a small groan.

'It's all right,' she said, as she pushed open the door further and brought in her trolley of goods, 'I can work round you.'

'I'm just going to stretch my legs,' he muttered.

He lifted the key from beside the television and eased past her. She smiled, he winced in return. Four times in his life of travel as an international best-selling children's author, Lake Weston had in such circumstances, nailed the maid.

He reached the corridor, she didn't watch him go. He started towards the lifts, changed his mind, turned and walked along the corridor to the window at the far end. A restricted view of a small part of London.

Closed his eyes, tried to ignore the pain. Walked slowly, hand close to the wall, trying not to lean. A little further along another bedroom door was open. Cleaning Staff At Work. Weston moved towards it, the door that would prove his salvation. Awkward on his feet.

Behind him, around the corner, the elevator door opened with a ping. Heavy footfalls stepped out. The hairs stood up on the back of Weston's neck. He stopped at the open door. Inside the room the large backside of a man, white shirt, black trousers, bent over, tucking sheets into the bed.

Weston didn't look over his shoulder. Felt the approach of malevolence as sure as he would have felt a hand clasped to his shoulder. He stepped into the room, silent footfalls, into the bathroom. Tucked himself in behind the door, sat on the toilet. Light off. In the dim light from the main room he could see that the bathroom had already been cleaned.

Out in the corridor, footfalls banged along the floor. They stopped at his room, the door was pushed open with a foot. Shouts.

He closed his eyes.

Fifteen minutes later the fire alarm went off in the hotel. Weston hadn't moved, the door to the room had been closed. He wondered how long he would have to stay there, but reasoned that if you're going to be stuck anywhere, a bathroom is as good a place as you could get.

Someone had stuck their nose into the room on seeing the door open, but after a couple of barked questions, had moved on. They had stopped short of knocking on or kicking in every door, settling instead for guarding all the exits from the hotel and then sounding the fire alarm to clear the building.

Weston listened to the alarm. Leaning forwards, head in his hands. They would be going room to room. He was only minutes, seconds, away from discovery. The door to the room was about to be opened. There was nowhere to hide that would not be checked.

He looked at the ceiling. Wondered if there was a panel in the roof he could push up. The ceiling was divided. Along the corridor he heard a door bang. He stood on the toilet seat, raising himself gingerly. His ankles cried. He reached up and pushed. Didn't budge. He hit it harder.

Another door banged. He tried another panel. Pushed, unbalancing, both hands. Nothing. Stepped even more cautiously into the sink. Bent his knees, tried the panel directly above. Footsteps in the hall.

This is how it feels, he heard himself say.

He pushed more firmly at the panel, a small break in the rim. Heart in mouth. He hit it harder, the panel cracked up and backwards. Along the corridor the evil moved closer. He felt up around the gap for something solid. Felt concrete. No time to think. Hands up on either side of the gap. Key in the lock of the bedroom door. Face screwed in torture as he tried to lift himself up. A tight gap, not enough space to get proper leverage. A panted breath. Footsteps into the bedroom. All his weight on his ankles, he screamed silently at the dark and pushed himself up from the sink. His fingers were ripped on a nail. He hauled himself up into the dark. The wardrobe door slammed shut. He moved to the side, hard against the wall, unsure of where he could put his weight. Swung the panel roughly back into place. The bathroom door opened, light switch.

Lake Weston held his breath.

The PM was due to give a press conference on the latest London attack and the steps the government would be taking to combat terror. Unlimited detention was at the top of the list. It had been there for some time, they had been waiting for their moment. The speech was ready, the list of demands of parliament and the British people had been set.

Massive police powers, deportation of all asylum seekers and all foreign nationals suspected of illegal activity, the ID card system expanded, every person over the age of twelve to be put on the DNA database, border controls increased, an extra layer of security at airports and train stations, CCTV cameras on every street corner. Closer ties with American intelligence and a greater presence for their security agencies in the UK, the new front line of the war.

Fortress Britain.

The speech had been planned and written for some time. They had tinkered with it overnight, stopped short of invoking Churchill, but had made it quite clear to the British people that they were at war. If they wanted to keep their gadgets, if they wanted to keep their Sky TV and their MP3s, their iPhones and their Macs, their Premiership and their Ashes tours, their Sunday lunches and their twenty-four hour Tescos on every corner, their cooking shows and their pre-packaged chopped up fruit, if they wanted to keep Ant & Dec and Dawn French and the Sun and garden centres and unlimited credit cards and no win-no fee lawyers, if they wanted the life they had come to expect, then they were going to have to make sacrifices. They would have to accept a new kind of democracy. One where they could choose to eat Sunday lunch in the pub or spend £120 to watch Chelsea, but where they could not choose to complain about government action, where they could not walk down the street holding a protest banner, where they had to accept that every now and again someone might be wrongly suspected. Every now and again.

The PM, dressed in a dark suit and red tie, was looking in the mirror. Silently mouthing his speech. The look of sincerity. The demeanour of the honest, bold leader. Shoulders back. Solemn. He was announcing measures that he desperately did not want to have to take. But the British people needed to understand the peril they were in.

'Should we use peril?' he said. 'It seems very Robert Louis Stevenson.'

'We need to go, Prime Minister,' said Bleacher. 'The speech is fine.'

The PM looked around. Noticed, for the first time, just how awful Bleacher looked. The penance for no sleep, the pills which had kept him going, the stress which was killing him.

'You look like crap, Bleacher. Don't get caught on camera.'

Fuck you, Prime Minister.

Bleacher nodded.

'What was it Bob Dylan wrote?' said the PM, giving the knot in his tie a final tweak. 'The times are changing, something like that?' He turned and glanced at Bleacher again, his eyebrows raised. 'This country is about to change.'

Fuck you, Prime Minister...

It took less than three minutes for the PM to regret his decision not to call in any favours from the media. The pack was in full voice. Suddenly they scented victory. The tide had turned in an instant, and it wasn't even about Lake Weston and *Axis of Evil*. Already the book had done its job. Weston had wanted to create debate, and with the help of a piece of state-sponsored terrorism and some low budget PR, he had managed it.

The questions weren't about what the government could do to combat terrorism, but about the fact that everything they did, every step they took, increased the risk of terror. They were knowingly fanning the flames of violent dissent as the police state grew. This wasn't about the terrorists, it was about the government.

He never got to finish his speech. The questions started as he walked to the podium. The pack were quietened down, he began to talk. However, one minute in and a freelancer, there for the Times and with not long to go until his retirement, had the balls to shout out a question over the PM.

The pertinence of the question – how long have you been waiting to deliver this speech – took the PM aback, and he hesitated before continuing. He coughed, started again, but that moment's hesitation, the obvious disquiet, the pack scented it, and their own hesitation was brief.

They pounced. They were the wolves. The Prime Minister wasn't a lamb to the slaughter, he was just a politician for whom no one in the room had any respect. They attacked, and the PM did not leave the room until his flesh had been ripped apart, his bones licked clean.

44

'Holy mother of fuck,' said the Counter Terrorism Command detective in charge of the search site, Edgerrin McKenzie. After complaints from the hotel management, aided by the presence among the guest list of a senior FBI official on holiday in London, the police had been forced to concede that they could not find any trace of Lake Weston in the hotel, and had allowed the cold and bitter guests back inside.

'Room 403,' said the sergeant, ignoring the senior official's anger.

'Thank you,' said McKenzie, bitterly. He walked away, barking, 'Find me whoever the fuck checked that room in the first place.'

It had taken one hour and thirteen minutes to locate the department of MI5 which was tracking the movement of Lake Weston by means of the device in his thumbnail, the department that had pointed them in the direction of the Travel Inn at Euston in the first place. This was partly because the computer system linking the two bodies which would have aided inter-departmental cooperation was running three years behind schedule, £17billion over budget, and was still some six months short of limping miserably into service. Not that a correctly placed phone call wouldn't also have done the job much more quickly.

The hotel manager was waiting in the lobby, having been expecting police re-entry at any moment. He had already made it clear to the police that he was personal friends with Lord Cornbury.

He looked expectantly at McKenzie, thinking that he didn't even have to express his disapproval.

'We have information that the suspect is in 403,' said McKenzie.

The manager nodded. He turned and walked over to reception.

'Has anyone been checked into 403 yet today, Agnieszka?' he asked.

The receptionist's fingers had already whizzed across her keyboard.

'No, sir,' she said. 'They're not due until 4pm this afternoon.'

McKenzie turned and nodded at his subordinate, who turned and waved at the troop of police officers who had remained outside. Seventeen armed officers rolled quickly into the building. The manager of the hotel squeezed his fists together.

They swarmed up the stairs, they moved up the lifts. A large group of men and women formed at the door of Room 403. Three officers waited outside on the ground beneath the fourth floor window. There would be no escape for Lake Weston.

The officer at the door glanced at his superior, who nodded.

Boot up, thudded into the lock, the door burst open, smashing into the wardrobe behind. All they'd had to do was ask the manager for the key.

The armed men and women of the Metropolitan Police Force CTC swarmed into the room, filling it with their brawn and their testosterone. The room was empty. Under the beds, behind the television, in the wardrobe. One of them even checked the mini bar. Weston had not squeezed in beside the gin and the Coke.

The bathroom door was pushed in with a smash. The room was bare, the bright white emptiness of it stared back at them. In amongst the stark brilliance of an untouched hotel bathroom, one bright shard of colour. In the sink, a spot of blood. Three men stared at it. Their eyes drifted to the ceiling. Blood etched around the corner of the panel above the sink.

Police Sergeant McGuire did not hesitate. He leapt up onto the sink, a big man, tall, legs like trees, had to bend. Pushed the panel up, whisked a torch from his belt, shone it along the vent in both directions.

No one. The vent, too, was bare. On the edge of the panel he saw a larger spot of blood, a piece of human fingernail encrusted. The spot where Weston had ripped his thumb as he'd clambered desperately to safety. The spot where he had unwittingly, to his very good fortune, deposited the small chip through which MI5 had been tracking his movements.

Weston walked out the front door, casually reading that morning's Independent. So rightly paranoid that he didn't want to be seen reading anything about himself or the government or *Axis of Evil* or the terror that had been visited upon London, he was reading the sports pages. Chelsea thinking of making a £15m bid for Alan Hutton. They didn't need a full back, they just wanted to annoy Spurs.

The police were congregated at Room 403. The two officers left standing at the main door of the hotel were still armed with photographs of Weston with a full head of hair. Not the man with the skinhead and the face ravaged by five days of pain and stress, the man who had aged fifteen years. That they had not closed off the hotel once again was due to the renewed interference of the FBI official who had thought it an outrage that his holiday had been interrupted in such a fashion.

O the irony!

Weston still had seventy-three pounds in his pocket. He walked across the road to Euston Station and in through the front door. The station was slightly quieter than usual, but really not so different. A few tourists were absent, but generally people were getting on with their lives. No one thought there would be another terrorist atrocity so soon after Paddington. Great British pluck, the politicians called it. Really it was just Great British it-won't-happen-to-me. Neither brave nor indifferent.

He stood in the midst of the crowd. Clothes dirty from the underbelly of the hotel, unshaven, skinhead. No one looked at him. He looked at the departure board. There was a train leaving for Inverness in ten minutes.

It was time to get out of London.

Lake Weston turned and walked in the direction of the ticket office. Realised that he felt a little bit hungry.

45

The Prime Minister felt shredded. This is what it's like, he thought, as he walked back into the pits of Number 10. Too battered to be angry, too flattened to have any fight left in him. He needed a couple of hours, the meeting with the Chilean ambassador, which he'd wanted to cancel, but which Bleacher had insisted he left on the schedule. He was glad now. Half an hour talking about Chilean wine imports to the UK was what he needed. Normalcy. Regular government. A hand shake, idle chat, a few guarded promises. Diplomatic governance. Why he was here.

Before that he had to make a call.

He closed the door behind himself, walked slowly over to the drinks cabinet. Didn't even look at the clock. Didn't care what the time was.

'How long before the ambassador?' he asked, his voice a strange croak.

'Twenty-one minutes,' said Bleacher, wondering if the PM was about to start crying.

'OK. You know who we need to call.'

Bleacher nodded. The media magnate was the last person anyone in their business wanted to have to phone. You didn't call him when everything was well, because you didn't have to. You called him when you needed his help, when the shit was hitting the fan, when you needed damage control. The bigger the problem, the more you needed to offer in return. Had the PM called him an hour earlier, it would have been bad. Now the PM was going into contract negotiations on the back of having just played the worst game of his life. His position could not have been poorer, he was open to being utterly screwed.

Five minutes later, Bleacher walked back into the office. He looked pale. Paler. He'd had the pallid hue of the vampire for several days. The PM hit the mute button on the television. In five minutes he had heard the word resignation seventeen times. Always in reference to his government, to his own position. People were actually being serious when they used the word.

'Is the call coming through?'

Bleacher stared solemnly at the PM. Slowly he shook his head.

'He can't take your call.'

The words crept across the room in slow motion. A dreadful silence.

'Holy fuck,' muttered the PM. 'Holy, crapping, fuck.'

The media magnate always took your call. Apart from when he didn't need to. The awful likelihood of the truth hit the PM as quickly as it had hit Bleacher. If the man didn't need to take the PM's call, it was because he had already spoken to someone else and had already made a deal with someone else.

They had a mole in the office of the leader of the opposition, absurdly named Firebrand. The PM did not even get to formulate the thought before Bleacher spoke.

'I've already spoken to Firebrand,' he said.

The PM raised his stunned eyes from the carpet. His throat was dry. His heart crashed.

'They spoke this morning.'

'How long?' asked the PM. The last time he'd been on to the magnate the man had given him little over five minutes.

'They had a conference call for an hour and a half.'

The blade slammed into the PM's back. He felt it, the physical act of being fucked, as surely as he would have done had there been a real sword.

'Jesus...,' he said, the word dribbling pathetically from his mouth.

'The dogs are unleashed,' said Bleacher, unnecessarily. The PM had been at the press conference. He already knew that the dogs had been unleashed. Now he knew the reason why.

'Your premiership is unravelling, sir,' said Bleacher. 'I don't know how to stop it.'

The PM leaned back against the desk, the fat on his buttocks flattening out, pushing the material of his suit. He hadn't touched it, but the knot in his tie had loosened slightly, now appeared untidy. He would have to straighten it before meeting the ambassador from Chile.

A car drove noisily past the end of Downing Street. On the television, pundit after pundit spoke silently of the deepening crisis within government. He couldn't read their lips, but he didn't need to. The words were tattooed on their furrowed brows. He had lost the trust of the benches. The cabinet were in disarray. There wasn't one person in the country who felt secure. Opinion polls taken since the bombing showed that people were now blaming the government because of their heavy-handed policy in the Middle East and Afghanistan. The swell of public opinion now said that the British men who were choosing to bomb their own country, would not have done so had Britain been...... Switzerland. Troops out, stop treating your own people like suspects, came the cry.

The pundits spoke, there wasn't a government minister to be seen. The PM watched in silent and impotent horror.

None of the journalists and professors and commentators spoke the real truth however. A PR meeting somewhere had chosen this new line, and there was nothing the government could do. The new agenda had been decided. The multinational media barons were behind it, the multinational media barons were behind the leader of the opposition, the people were buying into it. The opinions of the masses had been formed in small rooms, behind closed doors, in video conferences which spanned the globe. The British government, as it had been for fifty years, was just a very small pawn.

That evening, Lake Weston sat in the front room of the small B&B on the outskirts of Inverness, watching the television. Watching the government unravel, watching the British media lay the guilt of terrorism at the door of a ruthless government attempting to install a police state by stealth.

He was tired, his nerves were shot. It didn't cheer him as he watched and as he came down from the high. He thought of Eldon Strachan and he thought of Travis. He knew that the time was coming when he would be able to walk back in from the cold, but the life he was going back to was going to be empty of the two people who had had the greatest impact upon it.

He was empty. And as the Prime Minister appeared live on TV, bullishly confident about his own position, before an enthusiastic and over-excited Andrew Marr, Weston drifted off to sleep.

Epilogue

'Have you written any books other than Fenton Bargus?'

Lake Weston smiled ruefully. He looked at the seven year-old boy and nodded before glancing round at the class teacher. She smiled back, he thought there was genuine understanding between them, thought that perhaps she would be with him later to fill the ever empty other half of the bed. The teacher, like the boy, had no idea that Lake Weston had written *Axis of Evil*.

Axis of Evil had had its moment in the sun, but it had been a stalking horse. It had made its point, it had started the debate, rocked the boulder on the top of the mountain. But it had been other forces and other incidents which had set the boulder on its hasty and devastating descent down the hill, and *Axis of Evil* was soon forgotten. Having been built up so quickly, the critics were keen to turn on it. Especially when it was discovered that it had been written by a children's author. What seemed on the surface to have had some merit – they all wrote – on closer inspection was shown to be empty and vacuous and worthy of little further consideration.

By the time Weston had spoken publicly about how he had chosen to write the book after the government had banned *Fenton Bargus Meets The Prime Minister*, the Prime Minister in question was already gone, and the British people were no longer interested. Weston had just sounded churlish and petulant for having written *Axis of Evil*, rather than brave and provocative and defiant.

The book had quickly been dropped by all who were once its advocates, and within a few weeks, Lake Weston, serious literary author and commentator, had been returned to his rightful position as Lake Weston, children's author. The allegations of sexual misconduct with minors had been dropped, because there hadn't been any in the first place. No one was writing about Lake Weston, child molester anymore. The old rules no longer applied. Life moved on. People, the media, forgot much more quickly than they had in the past, because Lake Weston wasn't enough of a celebrity. No one cared.

It was just eight months later, and Lake Weston was sitting in front of a classroom of seven year-old children answering the same questions he had been answering for ten years.

'A few,' he said, smiling, 'but Fenton Bargus is what I do best.'

How could he argue with that statement himself, especially with the new title in the series, *Fenton Bargus Takes On Tesco* already an early favourite for Children's Book Of The Year?

The teacher pointed at another enthusiastic kid in the front row.

'Jamie?'

Jamie beamed.

'How much money do you get paid to write Fenton Bargus books?'

Lake Weston smiled.

He had lunch in the club. The club where once he would have dined with Eldon Strachan. Nowadays he always ate alone. No one had filled the gap. His relationship with Millhouse's new editor had yet to, and likely never would, transcend business.

And there was no new Travis, although he lived in hope. If the episode of *Axis of Evil* had had any positive effect on his life, it was the wedge it had driven between him and Penny. She had eventually allowed herself to believe in her ex-husband's innocence. Weston, on the other hand, had taken the opportunity to not forgive her for siding against him. Penny had been successfully kept at arm's length.

He ate bayonne ham with celeriac remoulade followed by grilled cod on pommes sarladaise. Drank a single glass of Sauvignon and a bottle of water. He was running at a bottle and a half of wine a day, but he had another school engagement that afternoon, and didn't want to breathe wine over them all. He would be able to catch up afterwards. Perhaps he would have better luck with one of the teachers.

'Would you like to see the dessert menu, Mr Weston?'

Weston looked up from the paper. He had been absorbed. The new government had arrived on its white horse a few months earlier, proclaiming freedom and a return to the great British democracy. Distance from the European Union, tough on crime but large on the freedom of the individual. No more unnecessary overseas interventions. No more sucking up to the Americans. Or the French. Or the Germans.

No more talk of ID cards. Positive engagement with minorities. Had ticked all the boxes.

Six months in and the troops were still in Afghanistan and Iraq, although the Prime Minister talked regularly of their imminent withdrawal. There had been a couple of scandals, another bank had collapsed, but they had easily been able to pin that on the previous administration, the British people understood that. With the crisis in the financial and housing markets, the on-going wars, the continued terror alert, no one had really noticed that the government had repealed not one of the previous government's laws. Everything that had been in place was still there.

You still couldn't wear an anti-war t-shirt near Westminster, you still couldn't choose to walk down the street waving a placard. You still had to answer fifty-three questions before travelling abroad. Over two hundred railway stations had introduced airport style security. You could no longer drop someone off outside a shopping mall.

The British people understood, it was just how it had to be. And they had responded with total acquiescence as they had snuggled down further beneath the blanket of the state.

No one seemed particularly to mind. The media had moved on. There were other things to get upset about. The new series of Pop Idol, the football, the cricket, the price of petrol.

When the new government had introduced unlimited detention, it had eased it through with its massive majority, the day the winner of the latest Celebrity Big Brother was to be announced. The media had other things to talk about. The journalists who tried to bring attention to the detention story had been pushed deep into the inside pages. If they had made any page at all.

The new government had followed the path of the old government, but the media were not interested in portraying the story in quite those terms, and so public perception was very different.

Lake Weston, along with a few others, had noticed.

'You have the crème brûlée today?' he asked.

'Certainly, Mr Weston,' said the waiter. 'Would you like another glass of wine.'

'Have to speak to schoolchildren.'

The waiter smiled, lifted the empty glass and turned away from the table. Weston watched him go, watching but seeing nothing, then looked back at the paper.

The other thing the new government hadn't done was actively work for the release of Richard Morrison from the secure detention facility at Guantanamo Bay. There was at least now an official acknowledgement that he was there, and Weston had been paying a lot of money to a few lawyers to try to do something about it. So far they hadn't even been able to let him know that he was being represented.

Weston's championing of Morrison's case had at least had one positive effect; albeit, not that the results for Weston were going to prove so positive. While *Axis of Evil* had dropped off the public radar, relegated to the netherworld of the brief and soon forgotten media flurry, and the public saw Lake Weston as just another children's author on the children's book shelves, the government were aware that he was still out there.

They were aware that he had written a very damaging book, they were aware that by continuing to champion the cause of a suspected terrorist, that he was still active in the cause. He was a supporter of terror, he was anti-government. He had helped bring down one government, there was every possibility that he might well attempt to bring down the next one.

There were people in the security services who still held a grudge against Lake Weston. There were those who didn't hold a grudge, yet still thought he was a menace to the public and that something ought to be done about him. There was no one in the security services who did not at least acknowledge that Weston was something of a problem. This meant that he had no one on his side. When the case of Lake Weston was discussed behind closed doors, there was no one pleading his cause.

Lake Weston was going to have to be dealt with.

He finished off his crème brûlée, took the time to drink two cups of coffee. The second was unnecessary and rushed, too hot and scolded his tongue. He stepped out of the club into an unusually warm afternoon. Checked his watch. Going to be late. His sense of time remained hopeless. He'd had plenty of time to spare, had dallied over lunch too long.

Deep breath, turned and walked at a measured pace towards the tube station. Lake Weston wasn't going to hurry. The school would still be there, the kids would still be sitting in a semi-circle waiting for him, poised to ask him how much money he had made and how many books he had written and had he ever written anything other than Fenton Bargus and was Fenton based on himself.

He would go along there, he would pick one of the young female teachers to hit on, he would leave with her or not, and then he was going to drink at least two bottles of wine in an attempt to forget that his life which had been empty a year ago, was now even emptier.

The car which had been sitting untouched in a no parking zone across the road from Weston's club, moved off slowly. The man who had been sitting in the café just across the road, folded his paper and mumbled something incoherent seemingly to no one in particular. Further up the road two more men turned and began to walk with purpose back towards Weston.

Lake Weston looked up at the sky. It was a muggy day, cloudier than it had been previously. Heavy rain forecast. He sighed heavily, his head twitched at the thought of the rest of the afternoon, he speeded up slightly. For all his cool, he would feel bad if he was too far behind the primary school curve.

He reached into his pocket, pulled out the earphones and turned on his life's relief. Bob was still there, as ever present as Chablis. *Another Side of Bob Dylan. My Back Pages*. A song, like so many of the others, which he could never hear too often.

He glanced over his shoulder and looked across the road.

All around him the security services closed in. And this time, Lake Weston did not see them coming.